**"I need you to help me and that will keep my secret."**

Her eyes fixed on the warrior.

Storm swallowed and looked at his face. Handsome, hopeful. There was a crease between his dark brows and his full mouth pursed as he stood for her scrutiny.

He looked like many warriors, but somehow he was different because of the way she felt when she looked at him. And there was something else—an important difference between this man and all other men. He knew she was the daughter of Heyokha and a medicine woman and still he wanted her. Not for herself but for what she might do.

Night Storm did not see her as dangerous. Or if he did he was willing to take the risk.

## Author Note

What a joy it has been to create two sequential historical romances that include Native American heroes and heroines from the Sioux and Crow people. Thank you to all who reviewed my last story, *Running Wolf*, and who wrote to tell me how much you enjoyed hearing the story of my warrior woman.

This tale is of a woman who wants to be a great healer, like her grandmother, and a man who wants only to regain what he has lost: his ability to fight for his people. For, as anyone who has ever suffered a life-altering injury or accident knows, it is sometimes impossible to return to the life one led before. This is the story of a warrior's struggle to become what he once was and the healer who believes he can be so much more. As you've already suspected, the ride will be rough, the stakes high and the outcome uncertain.

In this story I have blended real medical conditions with the mysticism of the Plains Indian tribes in the 1800s. I hope readers will indulge my blending of science and spirituality and enjoy the adventure of Night Storm and Skylark.

To help you keep time with the Crow people I have added a moon calendar at the back of the story. Each tribe called the moons by different names. This is my interpretation of the appropriate names for the moons in each season.

Happy reading and, as always, enjoy the adventure!

# THE WARRIOR'S CAPTIVE BRIDE

Jenna Kernan

MILLS & BOON

Published in Great Britain 2016
by Mills & Boon, an imprint of HarperCollins*Publishers*
1 London Bridge Street, London, SE1 9GF

ISBN: 978-0-263-91725-3

Our policy is to use papers that are natural, renewable and
recyclable products and made from wood grown in sustainable
forests. The logging and manufacturing processes conform to the
legal environmental regulations of the country of origin.

Printed and bound in Spain
by CPI, Barcelona

Award-winning author **Jenna Kernan** writes fast-paced Western and paranormal romantic adventures. She has penned over two dozen novels, has received two RITA® nominations, and in 2010 won the Book Buyers' Best Award for her debut paranormal romance. Jenna loves an adventure. Her hobbies include recreational gold-prospecting, scuba diving and gem-hunting. Follow Jenna on Twitter @jennakernan, on Facebook or at jennakernan.com.

For Jim, always.

# *Prologue*

*Many Flowers Moon*
*Northern Yellowstone River Valley,*
*Crow Territory*
*1859*

Night Storm stared down at the young woman standing before his horse and felt his throat go dry.

It was her.

His heart beat as fast as running feet and accelerated again when her eyes met his and she realized she'd been discovered. A glance would tell her that he was not enemy Sioux but one of the Crow people.

She grasped her collecting bag and straightened, her hand going to her skinning knife. What a picture she made, outwardly plain, her clothing drab as the feathers of a female pheasant. But it was not her clothing that appealed. Not even her elaborate moccasins and the ornately quilled sheath for her knife that fell between her full breasts. His little quail's beauty was more subtle. She did not need feathers and beads. Her dress was not dyed a bright yellow or green or red like so many women he could name. Neither did she sew coins or elks' teeth to the yoke of her dress. Her hair was long and braided, but she did not dress the braids with fur or trade cloth. In fact she seemed to have secured the ends with green grass. He chuckled at her complete lack of guile.

This one needed none of those adornments to shine. Her beauty came from her face and figure, her grace and poise, and also from her skills.

He knew of no other woman who would ever consider straying on her own so far from her tribe. But when she stood to face him, he did not see fear, just a kind of watchfulness.

"Why are you out here all alone?" he asked.

"I am not alone."

"No?" He glanced about for some rival. Had she come to this place to meet someone? His teeth locked together.

"I am with you."

His gaze snapped back to her to find her smiling. "And I am searching for someone else."

"A lover?"

She flushed. "A heyoka."

His dog, Frost, whined and then gave a single bark. It had been that bark that had given him away when he had discovered her here alone in the forest. He quieted his dog, who thumped to his seat. He should have left the mutt at camp, but since his accident Frost had been a near constant companion, and in truth he was good company.

"The heyoka. He is your father."

She did not deny it but her eyes rounded. Was she surprised to discover that he knew this about her? She shouldn't be. She was the most desirable woman of either the Wind Basin or Low River tribes. But none had offered for her because of her father's power. It frightened most of the warriors. But he was not like the others. He had a secret he had kept since his vision quest. And his survival in the last battle proved he had powerful magic. Dangerous magic. His injury should have sent him to the spirit road. Why had he lived?

"How do you know my father?"

"I have seen him at the gatherings. And I have seen you."

He knew she lived with her aunt, uncle and occasionally her father.

A heyoka was a difficult thing to be. And to choose this path was to choose a holy journey. Her father was a wise fool, a contrarian, revealing the people's follies by demonstrating their foibles. He suspected that her father's spiritual powers shone in his daughter. That power and wisdom, he needed it to understand his path.

"I could help you look."

She stared up at this warrior of the Black Lodges people. His hair was black and braided at each temple. The rest fell down his shoulders and back like the mane of his horse. His forelock was cut and his bangs stood stiffly up in the fashion of all Crow warriors. He displayed the record of his accomplishments tied with leather cording in his loose hair, each eagle feather signifying honor earned in battle, in raids and in counting coup against his enemies. About his neck hung his medicine bundle, a string of white glass beads and a copper coin on a leather cord. She looked at the clean line of his collarbone and the smooth brown skin she could see through the opening in his hunting shirt, and felt the urge to touch him.

She had seen him at the gathering of tribes in the Winter Camp Moon. He had caught her eye immediately. But she was not alone in her interest. Many of the unmarried women had made complete fools of themselves as they vied for his attention. But she would not. Though now his steady stare made her skin itch and she resisted the urge to cast him a look of invitation.

She even knew his name. Night Storm. His name had power in it.

His gray dog came forward, bushy tail wagging, and sniffed her offered hand before trotting back to his master.

"We have not been introduced," he said.

She lifted her chin and wondered if he found her as appealing as she found him.

"I am the daughter of Gathers Quills and Falling Otter. My name is Skylark."

"I am Night Storm of the Black Lodges people."

"I know."

His brow quirked and his smile widened. Her breath caught at the transformation. This steady stare and the curling of his generous mouth made her twitch.

"You do?"

"I saw you at the gathering, as well. It is my honor to meet you, Night Storm."

"Will you ride with me?"

She knew what he asked. It was not unheard-of. A woman met a man from another tribe. They rendezvoused in secret and one day he took her from her parent's lodge. When the tribes gathered in the fall, she would return to her people with a new husband from another tribe. But she did not know this man.

Oh, she could see his accomplishments and his strength. But who was he on the inside?

"I do not know you well enough to ride with you."

"Riding with me is a good way to get to know me better." His smile coaxed and the glint in his eye enticed. She wanted to accept his offer, but that was not all she wanted. The tingling in her belly told her that. She also wanted a man of her own.

But she shook her head.

"Or, I could help you look for your father."

She must find her father and get him back to camp, and she could use his help. He had a horse, after all.

"Come," he coaxed.

He extended his hand and Skylark stared at the broad palm and long, elegant fingers. She was so tempted, but she remained where she was. Once on his horse there was no guarantee that he would help her search. He might just take her to his tribe. And while he was handsome and finely formed, she resisted her longing. She could not deny her desire, but caution still ruled. She ground her teeth together as she considered what to do.

She shook her head.

"I could just take you," he said.

She weighed her options. None of the warriors

of other tribes had offered for her. Her aunt, Winter Moon, said it was because they did not wish a wife who had more power than they did. Yet the man before her was handsome and willing. And he did not seem afraid.

The chance she took was small and mighty all at once. He was strong. She found his face appealing with a blade of a nose and thick arching brows set above deep brown eyes that watched her every move. She admired the clean line of his jaw and how the corners of his mouth lifted under her gaze in an expression of confidence and interest…in her. It was the sort of face she would never grow tired of seeing. Her heart ached just at the sight of him. Was this the longing her aunt had described, the kind she had never felt until she looked upon this man?

But who was he really? Did he have a good heart?

"I am a medicine woman. I do not cook or tan or sew. I would make you a bad wife."

"You do not need to cook or tan or sew."

Skylark's eyes narrowed. What man would wish a woman who did not perform her duties? And then it struck her.

Her mother's warning came to her as if whispered in her ear. Skylark straightened. He already had someone to do these things.

"You already have a wife?"

His smile flickered and the pause was a little too long. "I have not yet wed."

*Not yet.* She narrowed her eyes feeling the half-truth crawling over her skin like a spider. "But you have offered for one?"

"You are too clever for a woman, Skylark. Why do you not come with me? You can meet Beautiful Meadow. You two could be as sisters. She will cook and you will make strong medicines."

Skylark backed away. She would *never* be a second wife. Her mother had often told her that a second wife was little better than an enemy slave. She might fare better in the hands of the Sioux than in the lodge of a woman who did not want her there.

"I will never be a second wife."

"Then be my first wife. I will marry you first."

"You do not even know me."

His eyes swept over her. "My eyes tell me all I need know."

"Then know this, I will not share a husband with another. Go back to the Black Lodges and marry your Beautiful Meadow, for I will not go with you."

His brow lifted as if seeing her rejection as a challenge. His eyes fixed upon her and she knew in that moment what it was to be hunted. She dropped her gathering bag and ran, darting in and out of the tree trunks and leaping over fallen logs. He gave her a head start. It was several moments before she heard the horse's hooves pounding on the soft ground.

One moment she ran and the next her feet left the ground. His strong arm gripped her, pulling her up and over his lap. Now, tipped over his muscular thigh with her head down, she watched the terrain below her flash by until she grew dizzy. Skylark clung to his leg to keep from falling headlong from the saddle. He rested a hand on her backside and laughed.

Finally he slowed his horse. She struggled and succeeded only in rising to a seated position before him. His arms looped about her waist, pressing her hip to his middle.

Now that she was in his arms she felt the rush of excitement.

"Tell me that you do not wish me to touch you and I will set you down."

He stroked her cheek and then his fingers glided over the bare skin at her neck. The sensation was delicious and she gasped. He blew in her ear and she had to catch her lower lip between her teeth to keep from groaning aloud.

His breath was sweet as he whispered, "I have

an empty lodge. I have horses. I have led many successful raids and will be war chief one day."

Night Storm knew he wanted this woman. He should have spoken to her at the gathering. He had not for two reasons. First, he'd let his friend fill his head with stories about her mother, the one who left her husband and his first wife to live with the heyoka of the Low River tribe. Skylark's mother had remained with the heyoka even after she had received offers from many, including the medicine man, himself. Her mother had survived unaided by trading her quillwork for all they needed and kept her lodge for only her daughter and the man touched by the spirit of chaos until her death. The second reason he hesitated was that he did not know if he wanted a wife who spent half her time chasing after her heyoka father and the other half digging roots alone in the forest.

"Come with me willingly," he said, whispering into her ear and thrilling as she trembled and fell against him. "I will provide for you. I will bring you the softest furs. You will never go hungry and I will keep you warm every night."

Beautiful Meadow had made it clear that when she was his first wife she would like him to marry again as soon as possible. He had promised her a second wife. He had not promised to take either of the women Beautiful Meadow had suggested.

She said she would miss her sisters, but she had not asked him to choose one of her sisters. His mother, Red Corn Woman, said it was because she was lazy. The women she wanted were hard-working, but one was doughy as a grub and the other had a face that resembled a stone hatchet.

This woman in his lap was not the sort of woman Beautiful Meadow had in mind. Beautiful, skilled and wild as a puma. And this medicine woman had a reputation for healing that had reached the Black Lodges.

But Skylark did not wish to share him. That made him even more tempted. But it was a problem because he had made a promise, given furs and horses for Beautiful Meadow. To withdraw his proposal would be a great dishonor. A woman could break a marriage. A man could not. Besides, he would need a woman to provide meals and keep his lodges repaired and to make the clothing. This woman in his arms was not that woman.

"You don't want me," she said.

"I want you very much. Too much."

Truthfully he wanted this woman because of the challenge. None had taken her. None dared. But he dared. And he would make her his own. Gentle this wild mustang until she fed from his hand like the horse beneath them.

He enfolded her in his arms and brushed his

mouth across her cheek. Her skin was softer than the velvet of a deer's antlers. He took her lower lip between his teeth and sucked. She shuddered and pressed closer to him.

"I have watched you at the gatherings. You have power. Great power. You are respectful and loving to your aunt. But all say you do not stay put."

"That will not change. I wander. It is my nature."

"Wander as you will as long as you do not wander into another man's arms."

He wondered if he had found the one in his vision. The woman who stepped from the flash of lightning to join him in the forest? His desire for her was strong as a lightning strike.

"I have had a vision of a woman. I think you are she."

She turned to him, lifting her chin to stare up at him. He lowered his lips to hers. She made a sound on an exhalation and then gave a hum of pleasure as he explored her mouth with his tongue. She tasted of mint. Finally he cradled her head against his chest and found her the perfect fit.

Her words were low, intimate, though she spoke not love words but words of warning. "Let me go before it is too late."

He stroked her hair.

"Too late for what?" he asked.

Other men thought she was dangerous. But it was that danger that appealed. She was perfect for him. She simply needed convincing and he knew just how to do that. He glanced to the bed of thick, spongy moss and his body ached, pulsing with need.

Night Storm pressed Skylark tighter. He had been attracted by her face and figure. Intrigued by her skills as a healer. Now he wondered just how powerful she was.

He winced as the dull headache that had plagued him all morning changed to an expanding pain that now made his stomach churn. He sucked in a breath as the pain grew worse.

He looked to the heavens for some answer and saw instead the bright spring leaves of the birch trees above them, flashing like swimming fish against the blue sky. They swam and swam, coming closer.

His dog began barking again. But, unlike earlier, this was that high, frantic bark that he used when he was frightened. Night Storm told him to be quiet but Frost only barked louder.

"Night Storm? What is happening?" Her words seemed to come from far away, even though he held her in his arms.

He heard the humming that went on and on. He

swayed as he smelled burning flesh. Night Storm slid from his horse. He could not see the woman in his arms because his vision dimmed and his hands began a tremor that rolled throughout his body like thunder.

# *Chapter One*

❧❦❧

*Three Moons Later*

Skylark's father often hid in the trees, so she searched the branches overhead for any sign of movement. Earlier in the day she could hear him laughing at her from a thick canopy of pines and, after that, from a grove of brambles. But now the woods had gone silent except for the jays warning the other creatures that one of the people walked in their midst.

"Father. I know you can hear me. Come out now." She waited in the silence, broken only by a rustling that turned out to be a ground squirrel. Skylark flapped her hands in frustration. "They are striking the tepees! We are moving today. Auntie says you must come with us."

She wondered if she tried ignoring him, rather than searching, whether he might come out. Skylark crossed her arms. Such games might have been amusing when she was a girl. But she had seen twenty winters and spent much of each summer chasing after her father. What had begun as a game had become a burden.

Her father was a trickster. She longed for a father who did not throw mud at her when she had just bathed in the river or who sat in the snow when everyone else huddled in their lodges close to the fire. His contrary ways were sometimes wonderful, but mostly they were just trouble.

"I'm leaving without you." Skylark waited, tapping her foot with impatience. "Fine," she muttered, and began walking back the way she had come. With each step, she listened carefully for the thump of her father dropping down behind her or the creak of branches that might reveal him as he moved from tree to tree like a possum.

This was the time of the Hunting Moon and the leaves above made good cover. Too good. She might pass directly underneath him and never know. Back at the river, the camp was struck. Some of the families were already moving and they would not wait for her. So of course, when the tribe was in a hurry, her father dawdled.

Skylark sat on a downed log.

Some said she was already a heyoka, because of her powers to heal. They came to her for care and treatment. But no man ever played his flute for her or asked her to stand wrapped in a buffalo robe before her aunt's lodge. Only one man had dared touch her and look what had happened to him.

Was it true? Did the young men avoid her because they feared her father's power or because they feared having to take care of a man who was as unpredictable as the rain in the Fast Water Moon. If it was hot, her father shivered. If there was ice on the water, he went swimming. By doing everything the wrong way, he taught the people the correct way of doing things. When the people were sad, he could make them laugh. When they were happy and behaving foolishly, he wept, cautioning them against their folly.

Or was the reason men avoided her, as her uncle said, because a man chose a wife who could make his clothing and keep their cooking pot full. That was something she would never do. She hated the stink of tanning hides.

Her aunt said that if she stopped wandering in the woods she would not seem so odd. But the truth was she did not want to be like other women. Perhaps she was more like her father than she cared to admit.

She missed her mother. Gathers Quills did not think Sky's wandering was odd. But her mother had left this world for the Spirit World in the Freezing Moon of Sky's seventieth winter.

Winter Moon was the sister of her father and she said it was not seemly for a single woman to live alone with only the occasional company of her heyoka father. So Sky had moved in with her aunt and uncle, Wood Duck. Would Winter Moon have been so insistent that Sky live in her lodge if she had known that after the move there would still be no warriors to offer a bride's dowry for Sky?

Familiar laughter reached her. She did not pursue. Instead, she rested her head in her hands.

Her father called himself Falling Otter, choosing that name because otters never fall. And because otters are playful.

Once her father had been perfect in her eyes. Important. More important even than the chief because only he could question the chief and even sometimes mock the medicine man, something no one else was brave enough to do. He made the people think of things they had not before and that made him a powerful teacher. Didn't it?

Skylark indulged in tears and immediately heard laughter. She lifted her head to see Falling Otter dancing off with his loincloth on his head. This was exactly the sort of behavior that she found embarrassing, and then she felt guilty for her reaction.

"Wait. Papa. We have to go."

"Daughter. Stay, stay. Stay all day," he sang, and vanished into the thick shrubs.

She hurried after him and decided that when she saw him again she would insist that they stay, stay, stay all day. Maybe that would get him moving back to camp. He was so thin now. Her aunt tried to feed him, but he insisted he was too full. Then he would beg food from someone else. Where had he left his horse?

The ground changed from thick ferns and dried leaves to a stretch of exposed rock. She paused, glancing about the clearing, and a chill climbed up her neck. This was the very spot where she had met her warrior.

He wasn't hers, of course. But he had tried to make her so. She wondered what would have happened if she had let herself be taken.

"Papa. I'm going to stay here. You should stay, too! No reason to go back and eat breakfast with Auntie. Your sister said to stay away. She doesn't want you there."

She noticed the sunlight streaming down in golden beams through the tall trees, illuminating the small clearing. She spotted something of interest and paused to gather goosegrass. The roots made a nice red dye, but she collected the entire plant because it could also make the bowels move and cool a fevered body. She stuffed several handfuls of the spindly plants into her pouch noticing the tiny white flowers that bloomed all the way to the War Moon.

She glanced about the clearing, recalling the man, his horse, his gray dog. Then it had happened. The sun had streamed down upon them, the light flashing off the new green leaves, shimmering like water from a lake. His dog had started to whine and then bark, his pointed ears up and alert. The warrior's smile had dropped away, his eyes had rolled white and he had fallen as if shot. They had tumbled together from his horse, rolling on the soft mossy ground. But his body had gone limp and she feared he had died. His dog had been near frantic, but the animal had let her tend him. She'd had time to check him for wounds before the tremors began, shaking his entire body. She had seen it before. It was not the palsy of the old or a simple hand trembling, but full-out witchcraft frenzy. He was cursed by a witch or perhaps an enemy. At least, that was what she had learned from Spirit Bear, their shaman. That the ghosts of the fallen might haunt the living. Despite what some of her tribe said, she could not lift a curse or rescue the haunted. Only a shaman could do that.

But her grandmother, Smiling One, had said that plants could heal any ills if only we knew which one to use. Was it true? Could all curses and maladies be healed?

It was that possibility that sent her searching for the plant that could cure her mother. Her first and greatest failure. There had been others since, ones she could not save. She could heal many things, but not all things and not the malady that sent her warrior into fits.

She had kept him from choking on the blood from his lacerated tongue, set him on his side and waited at a distance until he woke. His dog had not left his master's side and had watched her go, giving a whine as she slipped away.

Now she wondered if she should have stayed.

Her father broke her musings by dashing across the clearing waving his loincloth in one hand and a thick stick in the other. He ran in the direction of their village.

"Can't be late, daughter. Everyone must take a nap at midday."

Skylark turned to follow him. Of course, everyone would not nap at midday. They would be doing the complete opposite of resting, which was exactly why her father had said this. By midday the entire village would be struck and moving to their next hunting site. The Hunting Moon was a busy time with the buffalo hunts and preparation of meat and hides. All would be working hard except, of course, her father.

* * *

Night Storm led his horses through the dense undergrowth with his dog at his heels. He didn't know if lightning would strike twice, but he was growing desperate. This was very near the place he had met her, during the Many Flowers Moon. Only three moons ago and his life had changed completely. The time of first meeting her had also been the last time he had ridden his horse. She had looked like an ordinary woman, but now he knew better. What they said was true. She had unnatural powers. Her exceptional beauty was just a lure. A trap. He recalled her thick ropes of hair and wide eyes that sloped upward at the edges. That was what he remembered most, her eyes and her smiling mouth. But her form had also been perfect, full and lush as the ripe berries she gathered. Perfect, too perfect, he now realized.

He had been so taken with her that he had tried to carry her off. And she had warned him. Told him to let her go before it was too late. He had thought the warning odd. But he had not recognized then that she had cursed him.

Now he understood why she had not shown the least bit of fear at his approach. Because, like the puma, she was beautiful, powerful and deadly.

How had she cast a spell without his notice?

He was uncertain. What he did know was that

he must find her, capture her and then, somehow, he must make her remove the spell.

But what if she was not even a witch? What if she was a spirit? Anog Ite, Double-Faced woman, or Kanka, the greatest of all witches? Night Storm knew that it did not matter. If he found this woman, he would succeed in getting her to restore him before someone found out. Even his father had asked him why he did not ride. Any day now those of his tribe might discover he was cursed. And then he would be outcast.

At the very least he would lose his status as hunter and warrior and that was a fate worse than death. His malady even kept him from fulfilling his promise to wed Beautiful Meadow, the niece of Thunder Horse, who was their shaman. Her uncle was very strict. Men unfit to hunt or raid were stripped of their duties. If Beautiful Meadow discovered his affliction, would she help him or tell her uncle?

It was his doubts that kept him from speaking the words that would make her his wife. But she was growing impatient.

He must find Skylark and make her reverse her magic. Then he would kill her so she could never do this to another man.

An unfamiliar sound drew his attention. Something large was crashing through the forest in his direction. Frost whined but he ordered him to heel and the dog sat, his ears alert.

Night Storm slipped his bow from his shoulder and notched an arrow. From the sound it was an elk, though soon he realized that it made too much noise. He sighted down the long shaft. Perhaps he would bring home meat for his mother and father after all. If it was an elk, there would be more than enough to share with many families. His mother would be so happy to have the fine white teeth to decorate his sister's dresses.

But the creature thrashing his way now howled like a wolf and then quacked like a duck. Night Storm lowered his bow and watched as a naked man leaped over a rock and headed straight for him. The man waved his arms and shouted.

Falling Otter, he realized. Skylark's father. He glanced about. Was she here?

"Napping at noon. Everyone nap. Feasting, napping and then games!"

The man spotted Night Storm and slowed. He grinned and came forward at a trot, holding out a stick.

Night Storm returned the arrow to its quiver and slung the bow across his shoulder.

"For your new home, unless you think to live with your mother forever."

He didn't live with his mother. "Here." The

man extended the loincloth. "Put this over your eyes for a napping. It will block out the light. Have to go. She is after me again."

She? Night Storm looked back the way the man had come. Skylark was here. He knew it.

The man did a little circle dance, a dance reserved for women and then continued on.

"Tell her she'll be late for staying put. Hurry, hurry. I'm so full."

He lifted a new stick and used it to hit each tree trunk he passed. The knocking sound continued long after he was out of sight.

Night Storm turned in the direction the man had appeared. He had a certainty growing within him that he would find her soon. He had first found her here on a day when the new green leaves were so bright with sunlight that they hurt his eyes. He dropped the stick and tucked the scrap of buckskin in his pouch. Then he moved as quietly as he could, but still the jays called out from the treetops warning all creatures of his approach.

He saw her then, moving with a delicate tread in his direction. He ducked behind a thick tree trunk and drew out one arrow, gripping his bow. He pressed his naked back against the rough surface of the tree's solid trunk.

He peered around the tree to watch her approach. She was just as lovely. The fringe of her simple dress swayed with her graceful stride. If he killed her would it break the curse?

He didn't know.

Could he force her to remove it? If he captured her, would she trade his freedom for hers?

He could only try. Night Storm lifted his eyes to the heavens and offered a prayer to the Great Spirit asking for his help. Then he stepped from behind the tree and drew back the bowstring far enough to send an arrow cleanly through her heart.

Her step faltered and she stopped, staring with widening, mysterious eyes. Her mouth dropped open next as she gasped.

"You," she said.

"Me," he answered, and sighted the arrow.

## Chapter Two

Night Storm held his bow poised. Beside him, his dog whined and crept forward, gray eyes fixed on the woman as he wagged his narrow tail. He ordered his dog to stay and Frost dropped to the ground.

Skylark's eyes went wide as he held her in his sights. Had she now realized that he had not mistaken her for game but was intentionally targeting her?

She lifted her hands and waved them before her.

"You know me. I am Crow!" Her voice rose in volume and pitch on her last word.

"I know you." He held the bow steady.

She shook her head, her expression bewildered.

"Witch. Remove the curse," he said.

"What?"

"Witch! You cursed me."

Her head shook from side to side. "I am not a witch."

"It is what a witch would say. Remove the curse or I will shoot."

Her eyes narrowed, sparkling bright as she fixed them upon him, and for just a moment he feared she would bring on another spell. But his vision remained clear and he heard no ringing in his ears.

"Even if that were true, killing a witch would not end a curse."

That made him hesitate. He had not expected the witch to do anything but what he asked. Why did she not fall to her knees and weep like an ordinary woman? Instead, she met his gaze with an unwavering one.

His grip tightened on the bow, but his conviction faltered.

"The spell you had here in the forest. You think I caused that?"

"And the ones that have followed."

"Why would I do that?" she asked.

"Witches need no reason to curse a man."

"Of course they do."

"You knew that I would take you with me, so you stopped me." Doubts filled him. Was this just another trick?

She scowled as if his words angered her. "You

say I did this thing. Now, I will tell you what I did do. When you fell, I went to you and put you on your side so you would not choke on your blood. I put your bag under your head, to protect you from striking the ground.'

He stared, not knowing what to believe. Although the tension in the flexed bow urged him to release his arrow, he pointed it at the ground.

"Did you find your horse tied to a tree?"

He had.

Astonishment filled him. All she said was so. He had awakened on the ground beside his dog with his bag under his head like a pillow. The buffalo skin he used as a saddle blanket covered his body and his horse had waited patiently for him, saddle hanging over a branch by his side.

She lifted her chin as if he had answered her.

He released the tension of his bow, easing it back to rest but keeping the arrow notched.

"If I meant you harm, why did your dog not attack me then or now? I have not cursed you. I have saved you."

"You are not a witch?"

"I am a medicine woman and the daughter of a heyoka. I heal with bark, roots and growing things. I help people as I helped you. I do not curse them."

His skin turned to gooseflesh again. He slung

his bow over his shoulder and returned the arrow to the quiver on his back. If he needed a weapon, his ax and his knife were close at hand and he could throw both with deadly accuracy. Neither, however, could defend against magic.

"Have you asked your medicine man to help you?" asked Skylark.

He had not. Because to do so was to admit to all that he was no longer a man.

"I do not need medicine. I need only find the one who has cursed me."

"You could come with me to my home and consult with our medicine man. Spirit Bear is very powerful."

He would not be seeing her shaman, either. Word would travel from her village to his at the winter gathering, and he would lose his place as a warrior of the Black Lodges. That was his deepest fear. He must keep this secret and find a cure.

His gaze fixed on this medicine woman.

Could she help him?

She paused and glanced in the direction of her village. Then she bit her bottom lip. The act sent a growling need through him that took him by surprise. When she cast her gaze back to him, his skin felt hot and prickly. He recognized that now she wove a different kind of spell. He knew it instantly, though he had not felt it with any other woman. But he had experienced it once before, the first time he had spoken to her, alone, in the forest digging roots. It was elk madness, the love sickness which was the cause of much foolishness by many great men. This was why a man, a serious man, with many coups and a reputation of profound honor, could follow after a pretty woman, playing his flute for her at night and pursuing her like an elk in rut. This power was just as strong as bewitchment and he did not want it. Not with this woman.

She stooped over to pet his dog, her elegant fingers gliding over Frost's short coat. He could see the outline of her full breasts and the curve of her flank. She was perfect in his eyes, which brought him back to his original worry. What if she was Double-Faced Woman?

"How do I know you are not a spirit?" he asked her.

She glanced up from his dog and laughed. "What?"

But her smile dropped away and her hand left the dog's head as she looked at him. Did his expression reveal the real seriousness of his question? Skylark drew out her skinning knife from the elaborately quilled sheath she wore about her neck. She lifted the knife and her left hand, and nicked the round flesh at the base of her thumb. Immediately she bled.

She extended her hand to show him.

His shoulders sagged with relief. Spirits did not bleed. He rested a hand on the bone grip of his iron knife.

She glanced at her bleeding hand and returned her knife to the sheath. Then she searched in her bag and retrieved only a sprig of leaves, which she crushed, rolled into a ball and pressed to her wound. Making a fist, she held the poultice in place.

He reached out and captured one of her wrists. With a little tug he brought her tight against him, her soft curves contacting his chest. The sensation was like diving into cold water. His body felt charged and alive. She did not struggle. In an instant he had her hands gathered in one of his own and pinned behind her back.

"Can you remove the curse?"

She lifted her chin. "What kind of curse? Were you cursed by an enemy in battle? Or are you haunted by a ghost? Or perhaps you have had unclean relations with someone? All these could bring you to this place."

He did not know. "I have not had unclean relations. But I have killed enemies. Many."

He wanted to leave her here. But more than

that he wanted to press their hips together, fall upon the green grass and taste the sweetness of her body. His heart galloped as the musky scent of her rose all about him in a different kind of spell.

This attraction that he had felt for her on first sight was even stronger now. He stared at her beautiful flushed face and the full, parted lips where her breath came in erratic little pants. Was that her reaction to him or the fear? And then she shifted, moving their hips closer and pressing herself to him. He should have known. This one did not show fear. But her desire was clear. He did not trust her. Those things they said about her, that she was odd and dangerous and could heal or kill, he now thought they might be true.

Night Storm thrust her away. The poultice had fallen off, but already the bleeding had stopped.

"How do you know about ghosts and taboos?"

"I am learning about such things. I have learned all I can from the wisest women in our tribe. I wish there were someone who knew more than I do, so I could…find cures for the incurables."

Was he an incurable? He longed to ask but feared she would hear the desperation in his voice.

"Did you really do those things? Tie my horse? Cover me?"

"Who else?"

It was an excellent question. He had been alone.

His first ride since his head injury. He had seen her. Remembered her. Wanted her.

"If you are a healer…" How did one ask a favor of a woman he had just threatened to kill?

"Yes?"

"Do you know what causes me to fall?"

She considered him. He felt small and vulnerable and he hated it. This was why none must know of his weakness.

"There are many things that will still tremors and quiet the winds that blow through the mind. But I know some medicines and charms that can send away trembling and shaking and even falling. Does your mind disappear?"

That was what it felt like exactly. "Yes."

The knowledge she had might save him, keep him whole, give him back his life or end it.

What would she do if he asked? Laugh? Give him medicine that was actually poison? Or, worse, reveal his secret?

They stared in silence for a moment and then he performed the bravest act of his life, braver than riding into battle against his enemies or placing his lance in the hump of a charging buffalo. He asked for her help.

Skylark's mouth dropped open in surprise. Her warrior had asked for her help. Hers.

She took a step closer and then paused, glancing in the direction she had come. Would her father be all right without her?

He had his sister. Her auntie fed him and clothed him and let him sleep by her fire during the cold moons. She just did not have the time to follow him about, talking him down from trees and coaxing him to eat.

Night Storm took her hand and she looked into his dark eyes. A yearning pulsed within her and she did not resist as he drew her closer. He was a full head taller than her and his shoulders were broad.

"I need a healer. One who can help me and one who will keep my secret."

Her eyes fixed on her warrior.

He swallowed and she looked at his face. Handsome, hopeful. There was a crease between his dark brows and his full mouth pursed as he stood for her scrutiny.

He looked like many warriors, but somehow he was different because of how she felt when she looked at him. And there was something else, an important difference between this man and all other men. He knew she was the daughter of heyoka and a medicine woman and still he wanted her, not for herself but for what she might do.

Night Storm did not see her as dangerous. Or if he did, he was willing to take the risk.

He looked at her with hope. She did not need any man. Her healing talents could more than provide for her. She did not need this man. But somehow she did.

He wanted her because she knew his secret and would not tell.

He thought she could help him.

But what if she could not? After all, she had failed to save her mother.

"I have responsibilities in my tribe," she said.

His mouth went grim and his grip on her hand tightened. "Have you taken a husband?"

She blinked in surprise. To have him think she was married, that she would be desired by a man enough for him to overlook her flaws, made her throat close and ache. She shook her head.

"I still live with my aunt and uncle."

"They can do without you."

It was true and that hurt her. The only one who needed her was Falling Otter. "We are moving."

"I can return you to them, wherever they go."

The look he gave her was full of hope and longing. She tingled with awareness at the way he stared at her. Was that the need of a man for a woman or of a desperate man for a cure? She didn't know, but, oh, how she wanted to be the object of that desire again. Everything about him called to her except that he had a falling sickness. She hedged.

He laid aside his bow and then removed the beautiful strand of white beads from about his neck. He held them before her in both hands, presenting them for her inspection and then draping them over her head. They settled warm upon her skin. Gently he pulled her braids from beneath the necklace. The way he slipped his hand down her braided hair made her stomach quiver and her skin tingle.

"One so beautiful needs no such adornments, but I would give you this. It has value."

She pressed a hand over the beads and felt her heart pounding in her chest. "I know of roots and plants that are known to stop hand trembling, shaking and some that quiet the mind. I know several that ease dizziness," Skylark said. "But I will not promise I can stop this falling sickness."

"But you will try?"

"I cannot change those who are possessed. I cannot lift a curse or chase away evil ghosts."

"Am I cursed?" he asked, and rubbed his thumb on the back of her hand.

The motion was just the simple brush of skin on skin, but the sensation that rippled through her made her gasp.

"I do not know. But this thing that has happened to you, it is sudden. So perhaps it is an ailment of the body."

He took her other hand, forming a sacred circle between them, and somehow this felt holy.

She stood before him, thinking she was not up to the task. She had confidence in her plants, roots, barks and minerals. But she had never tried to cure a man who fell. She had seen his sort of sickness. It was a fearsome thing.

He waited, his eyes glittering with hope as he set his mouth tight to receive bad news.

"I will try."

Winter Moon heard her brother's arrival before she saw him because he was clapping his hands to the beat of an imaginary horse. His arrival was well-timed, as many of the people had already begun their journey. She had tied the household belongings on one travois and two packhorses. She smiled her welcome.

In search of Skylark, Winter Moon glanced the way her brother had come but did not find her. Her smile faded.

"I must see to my horse," said Falling Otter.

"Where is Skylark?"

"She is coming right along."

Winter Moon frowned. Her brother's words meant Skylark was not coming.

"Is she hurt?"

"Yes. Very badly." He held both hands over his heart.

She breathed a sigh of relief.

"Can she come?"

"She cannot."

Winter Moon flapped her arms. "Can you not just tell me?"

"Yes."

She sighed and began again. "Is she alone?"

"Yes."

"Is she with someone from this tribe?"

"Yes."

A flash of fear danced through her. "Oh, Great Spirit. She's been taken by the Sioux." She called to Wood Duck. "Husband, come quick. I think something has happened to Skylark."

Her husband was much more patient with the questions than she ever was. She relayed what she knew.

Wood Duck took over and interrogated Falling Otter and then turned to his wife. "She is with a man, not of our clan but of our tribe. It may be that she has finally found a suitor."

"Did he take her?" asked Winter Moon, now gripping her brother's arm.

"Yes," said Falling Otter.

Winter Moon sagged in relief.

"So she has gone," said Wood Duck. "It is good."

"How is this good?" asked Winter Moon.

"She has chosen a man, and we will see her at the gathering. Perhaps she will even be a married woman."

## Chapter Three

Skylark attempted to lower Night Storm's expectations. "I do not know exactly which medicine will work. So we will try them one by one."

"How long will that take?"

She grimaced. "It might take several moons."

"You will stay with me that long?"

"No. Two nights. Then I must return."

"Two. It is impossible," he said.

"You could come with me to my village. Then we would have more time."

He shook his head. "I am a chosen hunter for my tribe. If I do not return, two widows with children will have no meat."

This was the way in her tribe, as well. Young single men were designated to provide for the families of those who had died in battle, from disease or on hunts. She knew it was a great honor and marked him as a man of promise with a bright future.

And it gave him another good reason to hide his weakness.

"The longest I have ever been away from camp is two nights," she said.

"That will not be enough."

They faced each other. She felt pulled in two directions at once.

"Let us see what we can do in the two days. Then we will decide what to do next."

He stared for a long moment and then nodded his consent to this.

"Why does your aunt let you leave the village alone and stay away for days?"

"So I can gather plants for medicines."

"That is dangerous. You should not be alone. What if I had been a Lakota warrior instead of one of your own people?"

"Then I would be taken. I know the risks. Still I would not give up my freedom because of fear. It is like sunlight to a flower. I need this time to keep…"

He waited and when she did not speak he repeated her last word. "Keep?"

"Keep from going mad." Just like her father. She could see herself as a heyoka. Going out when others went in. Tanning roots instead of hides. Making medicines instead of food. Gathering Osha Root instead of the life-sustaining Bitterroot and Timpsula tubers.

"Other women live in camp and leave only in groups for safety. You could venture out with them."

"And you could learn to paint tepees or make weapons instead of hunting buffalo."

"That would kill me."

"Then you understand my need to wander. Even if it comes at a cost. It is who I am."

He met her gaze and then nodded. "I understand."

Night Storm's dog sat beside Skylark, leaning heavily against her leg.

"Ah. You two have not been formally introduced. This is Frost."

She stared down at the now-familiar dog. "We have met but I am glad to know his name."

The dog's head reached her hip. He was lean and lanky. The tips of his ears stood up like a wolf's and his tail was full and bushy as any fox. The rest of his coat was short and uniformly gray except for his white muzzle and the spots upon his chest that spread outward and did look very much like his hairs were frosted. His eyes were clear, alert and the color of a lead bullet.

Night Storm squatted and scratched the dog, who sat down, tail now thumping the ground.

"He has been with me since…" His hand traveled down the dog's spine and Skylark found her own spine arching at the sensual sight of his big, broad hand stroking over Frost's body.

It was her physical reaction that caused her to fail to notice immediately that he had stopped speaking in midsentence. She saw that he was now staring up at the treetops with unfocused eyes. Frost noticed his master's distraction, as well, and poked Night Storm's bare leg between his loincloth and the tops of his leggings with his cold wet nose. This brought Night Storm back to attention.

Night Storm petted his dog and Frost's tongue lolled as his eyes half closed.

"What was I saying?"

Skylark frowned. "You were telling me when you got your dog."

"Oh, yes. He came to me after my last battle. He kept coming into my mother's lodge. Finally my mother just let him stay. She thought he would be good company for me. And so he is." Night Storm straightened.

She offered the back of her hand to Frost. He licked it. Then she scratched his cheeks and petted his head. When she glanced up at Night Storm, it was to find him staring at her with an expression that reminded her of pain.

"Are you all right?" she asked.

"No. I don't think so."

Their gazes held fast and she felt the blood rising in her body. Was he having the same sensual reaction to watching her stroke his dog as she had felt watching him? The possibility filled her with a giddy longing mixed with terror.

They stood, hands at their sides, eyes dipping and returning to meet. She remained fixed to the earth, stubbornly refusing to yield to the calling of her body to touch his. At last he looked away.

"What should we do next?" asked Night Storm.

"I suppose I should find out all I can about you. Ask you many questions. I will need to know your signs before you fall and all about your falls. Have you had many?"

"Three."

"When was the first?"

He glared at her and she knew. Of course, it was when they met. That was why he thought she had cursed him. His eyes narrowed.

"I am not a witch. I cannot bring frenzy witchcraft or love magic. I cannot shape-shift, nor do I see visions."

His eyes widened and then his gaze darted away. Did *he* see visions, she wondered.

"But I know many cures. Some for falling." She folded her hands and squeezed one with the other.

"Start with those," he said.

The silence stretched and she cleared her throat. "Now about my questions."

"I will answer, but let me first see to my horses and make a camp."

A camp. Her stomach lurched. Of course, he would make a camp. She was staying here in the forest with him for two days. And two nights. Alone.

Fear and anticipation mingled.

She warned herself against his appealing mouth and the enticing line of his jaw. He retrieved his bow and she watched the muscles of his forearm cord. His body was strong and muscular. It appeared perfect, but, just like her, he had flaws. This was not the kind of man she should want. Still, some part of her did. Was it because he had been bold enough to approach her in the woods that day?

She recalled their first meeting and his offer to make her his second wife.

"You were promised to a woman. Have you taken her as a wife?"

He stilled and spoke to her over his broad shoulder. "No."

She nodded and he turned away from the direction where she could find her tribe.

No wife, she thought, watching him. He looked so strong. So perfect.

"Because of…" She wanted to ask if it was because of her but could not.

"I will not marry her until I am well."

Skylark absorbed this blow. He needed her help to return him to his path. But he did not want her in the way she wanted him.

*Heyoka*, she thought. Wanting a man who did not want her.

Sky stiffened her shoulders and her resolve. Certainly she had enough sense not to become involved with a man who loved another.

He glanced back at her. "Are you coming?"

"Yes." *But I will not share a buffalo robe with you. No matter how handsome you are.*

He led the way to his horses and Frost trotted along with them, occasionally darting off after a ground squirrel or some other alluring scent.

She was surprised to see two pack animals, a chestnut and a red roan. Neither wore a saddle.

Where was his mount? The men always rode. Women rode only on traveling days and only if there was room on the horses after they were packed with the household gear. Men needed to be free to protect their families and so their horses carried no gear and their hands held only the reins and their weapons.

He tied his quiver to the nearest pack saddle

and hooked his bow over a pommel. When he turned back, he found her studying him.

"I no longer ride," he said.

She realized why instantly. His falling made it too dangerous. Their eyes met and she saw the pride in the lifting of his chin as he waited for her to say something. This was why he did not wish his people to know, because of this feeling she had for him right now.

She forced a smile.

"Soon you will ride again."

His guarded expression switched to confusion as his brow furrowed.

"That is what I pray for every day, to be a warrior once more. I want to serve my people. But to be a burden…" He shook his head in dismay.

"I understand that. Everyone needs a purpose."

"And I have lost mine."

"We will find it again, together." She spoke with a confidence she did not feel, but still she held her smile and finally she saw his mouth quirk. The transformation was immediate and startling. He looked less severe and even more handsome. She could not keep from reaching out to stroke his cheek. Excitement buzzed through her, tickling her skin like bees on an open blossom. She leaned toward him. His hand captured hers, trapping it to his jaw for just an instant. Then he released her and stepped back.

She stood, bereft by his withdrawal. "Tonight we will talk," she said. "Tomorrow I will begin gathering plants."

"Yes. That is good."

"I have to know all about you. If I am to treat you, I mean." It was true, but she was grateful for the excuse to hear his voice.

When he spoke, the low rumble tickled her deep in the pit of her stomach. A warning prickled her neck. He had asked for her help. Nothing more. Yet he seemed to also feel the lure that tugged between them.

"Well, that may take some time."

He picked a place with a wall of rock beside a small, pretty lake. The open ground had tall green grass for the horses, and nearby a cold spring tumbled down the rocks, giving them drinking water. It was a good camp. The rocks behind them protected against the wind and the ground all around was scattered with much firewood. She set to work gathering timber and kindling as he unburdened his horses and hobbled them to keep them from wandering. When she returned, the horses were happily munching on grass, unconcerned that their front feet were tied with a leather binding.

Frost was sniffing about in the cattails, and trying and failing to catch frogs.

The sun was directly over them, so they sat in the shade beside the lake and shared a meal.

They drank cold water from the cascading stream and ate the pemmican they both carried. Hers was filled with wax currants mixed with tallow and his was filled with nuts and dried Saskatoon berries. Traveling food, portable, dense and delicious.

Frost appeared, his tail wagging, hopeful for some food. Night Storm fed him some of his pemmican and then waved him off. Frost left in good humor, returning to his futile attempts at hunting. The process involved a great deal of leaping into the water, swimming back to shore and shaking off only to leap in once more.

"He will chase away all the fish," said Night Storm.

As they ate, she began her questions with ones about his family, learning that his father, Many Coups, was one of the chief warriors of his tribe and the head of his medicine society. Every tribe had secret warrior societies and their business was never shared with women. Just as women had rites and ceremonies kept secret from the men. Red Corn Woman had born Many Coups three children. His brother, the oldest, had already taken a wife from the Wind Basin people who bore him a son. Night Storm also had two younger sisters, six years his junior at seventeen winters and another who was fourteen winters and already a woman.

Skylark realized that at twenty-three winters, Night Storm was three years her senior.

"Most of my friends and family call me Storm. You may do so, as well."

She nodded her acceptance of this. "My family calls me Sky."

"Sky? A pretty name. I understand that you have no brothers or sisters," said Night Storm.

"Yes. That is so."

"And you live with your father and aunt and uncle."

"Yes." Her mother was gone because Sky could not heal her. Sky was silent. Should she say that her mother had left her husband before the time of Sky's birth? Did he already know that Sky and her mother had lived alone for much of her childhood? Perhaps she should tell him that her mother's family had advised against her marriage but her mother had left her people to wed a man whose first wife was of the Low River Tribe and when she left this husband a few years later she was too proud to go home to her family. Thoughts of her mother saddened her and even after three winters since the passing of her mother, the pain was still heavy on her heart.

"Some say you are like your father."

"I have heard that said. Do you think so?"

"I have not decided yet."

"Why have you not married Beautiful Meadow?" she asked.

"You need to know this to cure me?"

"No. It is a woman's curiosity."

He made a face. "She is angry that I have not yet married her. Her father, Broken Saddle, was of the Shallow Water people, like my father, until he married. Now Broken Saddle is chief of the Wind River tribe and his brother, Thunder Horse, married one of our women and joined the Black Lodges. He is our shaman."

She raised her brows at the implications of this. No wonder he had not wed. A shaman's niece would quickly note his illness and seek her uncle's help. His condition would be raised at tribal council and then known by all.

"I see."

"And understand why I have not yet taken her to my lodge?"

She nodded.

He liked that he did not have to explain everything to her.

"Beyond that, I cannot hunt for her or protect

her." His eyes lingered on Skylark. "No woman wants a man who cannot ride."

Except perhaps a woman who did not sew? They were a strange pair, she thought. She almost said that aloud and then quickly reminded herself that he would not marry while he was ill and if she managed to cure him, he would marry Beautiful Meadow. She needed to cease her folly and get back to her people as soon as she could.

Storm growled and lifted a stick, preparing to throw it into the water. But his dog placed his mouth over it and Storm let go. Frost sank to the ground and began gnawing on the branch.

"Is that all?" he asked.

Her gaze shot to him. She had promised to try to help him and instead she had become consumed with her own wants, needs and burdens.

"No. Not all. If your falling sickness is from a ghost or curse, then your children would not be affected. If you are ill, we will find a cure."

"I hope so. Because becoming a burden, it would be worse than death."

The responsibility she had taken now weighed upon her. Why had she thought by leaving her tribe for a few days she would be free? Free from the burden of chasing after her father, free of the curious stares of the men and the pitying glances of the friends who had found good husbands. But this new burden was heavy, indeed.

"What other questions do you have?" he asked.

"Have you had visions?"

He scrubbed his face with his hands as if washing. Then he blew out a breath to the sky.

"How did you know this?"

She shrugged. "A feeling I had. And falling is like sleeping, dreaming. Many visions come with dreams."

"Yes, they do. I will tell you something else that I have shared with no one. During the time of my vision quest, I had strange dreams."

"That is not unusual, I think."

Much of the process of becoming a man was kept a very carefully guarded secret, just as the entry process of becoming a woman was held from the men. But she had heard this and that. She knew, for example, that when their mentors deemed them ready, a boy left the tribe with his mentor, went into the forest and stayed there. Many days later the boy would return, gaunt and changed in ways that frightened her. The candidate left as a boy and returned as a man. The tribes' celebration for these new members was jubilant, as was the welcoming for women who were of marriageable age.

She was well past her womanhood and still the

men of her tribe had done no more than steal a few kisses and bestow a few trinkets.

Skylark focused on Storm. "I know little of the vision quest."

He nodded his understanding of this. "And I can tell you little, except to say that my name must come from what I saw and I saw many things. Terrible things. I was told to choose my name from the visions or from the first creature I saw upon waking. I did not do as I was told. Do you think this could have brought this sickness?"

"Possibly. Why did you not do as you were instructed?"

He made a face.

"It *was* night when I became aware. But it was not storming. And the first creature I saw was the same one that came to me in my visions. They came again and again. They still come. Follow me in dreams and while awaking. I thought it called me to be fearless in battle and to take many enemy lives. Now I do not know what they want from me."

"But you should use this creature for your name. Is that right?"

His expression turned grim.

She cocked her head, the unease growing at his silence. She swallowed back her trepidation. What could possibly be so terrible?

"What animal?" she asked, the dread creeping into her with the evening chill.

"A white owl."

She could not contain the shout of fear as she threw her hands across her chest. Her skin went cold as she stared in shock at this man.

It was the worst of all possible omens.

Storm placed a hand over his forehead and kept it there as he spoke, the horror of his disclosure clear in his voice. "I saw many strange things, but the animal I saw again and again was the owl."

She could not find her voice and so spoke in a whisper. "Death. Your death or the death of those you love."

"Or the death of enemies in battle. I saw the owl in visions and dreams and upon waking. A white snowy owl in the summer time. A horned owl perching over my head and the sound of screech owls during the night."

"Perhaps…" Her mouth was so dry from the fear that she had to clear her throat before she could speak. "Owls are messengers. They bring word of impending death, that is true. But perhaps…" She was reaching for some glimmer of hope. "Perhaps… Perhaps they only foretold of this time. If this is spiritual, then you are called to interpret this message. A message from the world of the dead."

"Instead, I have hidden it from all but you."

She could understand why.

"I knew that they called me to something. I assumed they called me to battle my enemies. I rode into all battles expecting to send many ghosts to the spirit road."

Or to die, she thought. She shivered at the thought. Had it not occurred to him that the owls called him to his own death?

"My name should be chosen from my visions, but I knew that my tribe would be afraid, if I called myself White Owl or Shrieking Owl or Evening Owl. So I chose Night Storm, for the storm that finally quieted the owls."

"This is a terrible omen."

"Yes. I am linked to death. I just do not know how."

"Do you see the dead?"

"No."

"Do you think the owls were the spirits of the dead?"

"I do not know." He turned his head and looked at her, his brow furrowed. He seemed to be puzzling something out.

"What?" she asked.

"Why are you still here?"

Now she was the one who was confused. "You asked my help. Don't you remember?" Was his mind worse than she supposed?

"Of course, I remember. But most women would have run screaming in the other direction the minute I told them of my vision. Why didn't you?"

Why hadn't she? "Well, I suppose because you need help and because I think I might be able to help you."

"You are not like anyone I have ever met. You are either the bravest of all Crow women or the craziest."

"Don't call me that," she snapped, and immediately recognized what she had done. Her eyes widened. Women did not speak to warriors in such a way. It was within his right to chasten her.

He tucked his chin and stared through thick lashes at her. But he did not chastise or raise his voice, showing so clearly the kind of control a warrior must have over his emotions. He just watched her as her face grew hotter and hotter. She wished he'd say something. Finally he spoke.

"We'll speak of this later." He stood.

She followed him and stepped before him when he tried to move away. "Is it because of what I said?"

His mouth quirked. "No. It's just that my head is hurting again."

"Where?"

He gripped his forehead.

"Does that happen often?"

"Less often than at first."

*At first?* What did that mean?

"When did it begin?"

"In the Fast Water Moon."

That was the time when the old man of the north finally released his grip upon the land and the snows receded and the green shoots poked up through the ice. A time of great change in the land. Melting ice and rushing water. What had happened to him at that time?

She was about to ask, but he placed his broad hands on her shoulders and gave a little squeeze. "Enough talk for now. I would catch us fish or it is pemmican again for supper."

Frost returned, tail wagging, carrying an enormous bullfrog in his mouth. He laid it down before them and the frog leaped into the tall grass. Frost pounced like a fox on a mouse but missed, judging from the sound of the splash coming from the lake.

Storm collected his fishing line, bone hooks and the stone sinker. But he paused before leaving. "What will you do?"

Skylark stood and swept the folds from her dress. "I have plants to collect." She slung her carrying bag over her shoulder and then hesitated.

"What?" he asked.

"Will you be all right alone?"

His face reddened. "I am not an invalid, nor a child. Of course, I will be all right. Will you?"

She nodded and he stalked away.

This, she realized, was why he had not gone to his shaman. He did not wish to be watched and coddled. How could she blame him? She felt much the same. What was the point of living if she did not have the freedom to come and go? He was a man. And a man must have his pride and his dignity.

Skylark watched him walk to the lake and cast his fishing line into the water. Then he tied off the line and removed his fringed hunting shirt and leggings. Finally, he lifted his spear, wading into the blue lake up to his waist. He held the spear poised and ready.

She blinked at the picture he made, with the late-afternoon sunlight glinting on his muscular shoulders and chest. She had seen many men fishing, but none transfixed her the way this one did. She studied the curves and hollows, the play of tension in the cording muscles of his arms and shoulders, and found her breathing grow fast.

He must have sensed her study for he glanced to her, scowling.

She dropped her gaze and hurried away. Once out of his sight, Sky hesitated. They both knew that he might have a falling spell right there and drown before she could reach him. So she stayed close, listening for the splash that might indicate a fall.

Frost accompanied her, which surprised her. Perhaps Storm had sent the dog along to keep the animal from disturbing the fish or for her protection. She walked along the bank, digging cattails for their roots and cutting the reeds for the inner sweet stalky stems. The tops made excellent bedding material. She cut with her skinning knife and in only a few minutes she had carried enough back to their camp for their bedding. Then she returned to the shore and used an antler from her bag to dig several fat tubers before moving on.

She hunted for specific plants but also collected anything of use that fell into her path. Yarrow was first, what her grandmother called Nosebleed Plant and her aunt called Thousand-leaf. She knew this would help heal the small nick she'd cut to prove she was not supernatural. She chewed the leaf and then pressed it to her wound. The sting reassured her that the leaf worked to help keep away pus and to speed scabbing.

Skylark continued wandering as she pressed the sodden crushed leaf to her palm.

Jimsonweed was one she particularly wanted for she knew that, if eaten, it could cause visions and fanciful dreams. But it also could still tremors. She did not know if it could stop moth madness. This sickness was named after the moth that, crazed by the firelight, flew directly into the flame. Victims of moth madness also fell to the ground and twitched like a dying moth. Perhaps Jimsonweed might prevent a spell. But she found none. She did find Motherwort in the open area near the lake. This plant she knew stopped twitching, when in the correct amounts.

By the time she had circled the lake, her bag bulged with green plants, roots, cactus, pine needles, flowers and berries. Why, she even had enough to feed them if he did not take a fish or two.

She could no longer see Storm. But she had glimpsed him from time to time as she made her way around the small lake. She must be nearly back to him. She was humming a tune as she went. Frost had been good company, even helping her dig when she asked him. He was a very good digger and it made her think she might want to get such a dog.

The splash that sounded from a place just ahead

made her steps falter. She came to an abrupt stop and Frost cocked his head to listen. She strained for some other noise but heard nothing except the sound of the insects' steady buzz and the hammering of her own heart. And then it reached her, the low hoot of an owl. Skylark clamped her bag to her chest and ran toward Storm with Frost at her heels.

*Please let him be all right*, she thought as her feet tore over the open ground.

Skylark ran as fast as she could toward her warrior.

She dropped her bag on the shore and threw the knife, sheath and carrying cord over her head. Then she thrashed through the high cattails until she was waist deep in the lake, still wearing her ornate moccasins. The sight that greeted her stole away her breath. There was Storm, faceup, on his back, gliding through the water like a fish, his powerful legs kicking in a smooth rhythm. The picture he made seemed to fix her to the spot. He rolled and dove, disappearing for a moment, which gave her the moment she needed to recover her wits.

The sight of the man in motion was emblazoned in her mind as she backed toward cover. The wide plains of his working chest and ripped muscle of his stomach enthralled. And she had seen the root of him, nestled in the thatch of glistening black hair. His wet skin reminded her of a beaver, slick and glossy. The image made her body twitch and her stomach clench.

He resurfaced closer to her, popping up from the blue waters just two body lengths from where she stumbled back through the tall cattails.

"Aha. An enemy scout," he said, his grin playful.

And again she stopped, staring like a ground squirrel who, when confronted by a fox, finds herself too far from the safety of the trees. The smile transformed him from a seriously handsome man to one that made her blood rush and her body quake. What had she gotten herself into with her foolish promise? She would not be able to sleep a wink knowing what lay beside her in the dark.

He frowned now. "Why are you wearing your dress?"

Storm studied her now, treading water as smoothly as a duck. Did he see her flushed face and round, frightened eyes? Did he see her heavy breathing and clenched fists."

"Did you come to swim?" His words sounded like an accusation.

## Chapter Four

⌁⌁⌁⌁⌁

Skylark met the smoldering fury of his stare and realized that her assumption had injured his pride. She shook her head in answer to his question, *did she come to swim*? The truth, she wondered, or a lie. Truth, she decided. "I heard the splash and…"

"Naturally you thought I was drowning. Why should I be capable of taking care of myself?" He spun in the water and swam smoothly back to the rocky bank beside their camp. She watched him stride quickly from the water, trying and failing not to stare at his wide shoulders, narrow waist and muscular backside. Then she turned tail and threaded herself more carefully through the reeds, recovering her bag and knife. She sat on the bank to pour the water out of her moccasins and decided to carry them. He wanted her help. But she must find a way to do so without stealing away his dignity. Besides, she would be here only two nights. After that there would be no one to watch him but Frost.

As if thinking of the dog had conjured him, the dog charged out of the reeds and then shook away the water droplets clinging to his skin. Skylark squeaked and vainly tried to ward off the unwelcome shower with her hands. Frost sat, tongue lolling, eyes half-closed, as she stood and shouldered her bag. She slipped the cord holding her skinning knife over her head and then completed the circle, returning toward their camp. She paused at the fast-moving stream to wash away the mud that speckled her arms and legs.

She removed her dress, thinking she must find some clay to clean away the mud stains when next she came upon some. As she splashed off the grime and sweat, she thought of him, perfect and in motion. The need came upon her unawares. Her breasts ached and her body trembled. She wanted him in all the ways a woman needs a man but she knew why she couldn't.

She thought of all the men she had met at the fall gathering when they camped with the Wind Basin tribe and how none had chosen to court her. What if this man was her only chance to experience the coupling that her aunt and uncle obviously enjoyed in the night?

She crossed her arms over her heavy breasts,

her nipples hardening instantly. Then she splashed a fist down into the water. No, she would not repeat the mistakes of her mother. Storm was promised to another and Sky would never be a second wife. She must be strong and live alone.

She finished her bathing quickly and donned her dress over damp skin. Then she returned to camp to see Storm striking flint with a steel ring and sending a shower of sparks onto carefully gathered tinder of inner bark and the fluff pulled from the dry cattail flower heads. This method of fire starting was usually faster than the cord and stick, but it required steel, which she did not have. Her skinning knife was red flint that came from far to the east.

Storm glanced at her and then returned his attention to his work. Beside him lay three trout, two small and one enormous.

Soon one of the sparks caught and a wisp of smoke emerged from the nest of cattails. Expertly, he lifted the dry white fluff and blew into his hands. The dander caught, glowed, and then a flame erupted from within. He carefully set the flame inside the tepee of tinder and the flames began to catch and rise.

He had already gutted the fish, so she cut green skewers and returned to construct a simple rack for the whole fish. Then she peeled the cattail

tubers and cut the inner tender shoots into man-
ageable sizes. She left the cactus and thistle roots
for another meal but crushed several juniper berries and stuffed them inside the hollow cavities
of the fish.

When the fire had burned for a time, she set
her moccasins to dry but not too close to the
flames. They were precious to her, because, like
her knife sheath, they had been made by her
mother, the best quill worker in her village. Or
she had been.

When the larger logs began to collapse into
glowing embers, she raked the coals into a neat
pile and set the shoots to roast while he tended the
fish. Frost watched his every motion with hungry
eyes and a drooling mouth. Despite the warmth
of the fire, the air surrounding Night Storm was
still cold and he did not look at her.

"I am sorry," she said. "I meant no insult."

Finally he met her gaze. "It is why I do not
speak of it and why I do not want those in my
tribe to know. Then they will see me as you do."

"How is that?"

"Imperfect. Weak. Helpless."

Her shoulders sank at the truth of that. But she
also thought they might see him as dangerous and
frightening because of the owls.

"I am sorry. I know you are strong. I see you

are capable. But everyone has a weakness of some kind."

"I never did."

She turned the subject to something that troubled her.

"How have you kept the others from seeing you fall?"

"I spend more and more time away, alone."

She thought of him, unaided in a falling spell and frowned. "That is dangerous."

"No worse than losing everything I am," he said.

"Is your life worth any less?"

"Less and less every day."

She reached in her bag and drew out a leaf from the nosebleed plant she had collected. Then she crushed the leaf between her fingers and applied it to the scabbing wound on her hand.

"You have been alone during each spell?"

"But I usually have warning. I did not recognize it at first, but now I do and I move away from others."

Her anger faded as her curiosity was piqued. "What warning?"

"I smell the odor of burning flesh. Then my vision wavers as if I am looking through lake water or like staring through the bands of heat that rise from ground baking in the summer sun."

"You see movement?"

"A wavering or trembling of the world around me."

"Can you see the spirit world beyond?"

His brow furrowed. "I have not tried that. I think I see only this world. Sometimes it is just in one eye. I notice this because I closed one eye and then the other."

"Which eye?"

He pointed to his right.

"Is that all?"

"Once my hand began to tremble and I left the hunt. I found a place to hide, curled on my side and held my pounding head."

That was incredibly dangerous. If he had choked, none would know where to find him.

"When I woke, it was evening. My mouth was bleeding and my head ached."

He returned his attention to the fish, and she rolled the cattail shoots and tubers.

He offered her a stick with the two smaller fish and she passed him a portion of the roasted tubers and tender steamed shoots. He shared some of his trout with Frost, who gobbled without the bother of chewing. Once Storm motioned the dog away with a hand, his dog went with good nature and settled to sleep beside the fire and his master.

The fish was flaky and sweet and the tubers starchy and savory. The tart flavor of the junipers came through with each bite. As he ate he told her of the time that he and his brother had put a fish in his youngest sister's dress when she was bathing and she had thought the spirit of the deer had returned to its skin.

"She screamed so loud it brought the men to the woman's bathing place."

Skylark laughed at his imitation of his sister and then the escaping fish. She told of how she had once been so preoccupied finding a curative for burns that she had been caught in the forest at night and slept in the crotch of a tree because she was certain she heard wolves nearby.

"How did you keep from falling?" he asked.

"I used my belt to tie myself to the tree trunk. And do you know, there were wolf tracks all around the tree in the morning."

"You came down in the morning?"

"No. I didn't. I waited until I heard my uncle calling."

"That was wise. Wolves can run very fast."

"It was the first night I slept out in the forest, but not the last. My aunt and uncle are used to my wanderings."

"Most women stay together and keep close to the village."

"Most men hunt in groups, raid in groups, war in groups."

He smiled at her answer. Somehow the meal had changed them, made their conversation relaxed and more personal. She'd glimpsed a part of him that was comfortable. She felt content and even happy. It was wonderful to be away from the responsibility of shepherding after her father and helping her aunt tend their home. She did not want to think she was like her mother. But perhaps she was more like her than she cared to admit.

No, she was not like that. She wanted a man, a home and children. But she would heed her mother's words and choose a man who wanted only her.

She gazed skyward, seeing the pink bands of clouds beyond the aspen and pine. Still, she knew a part of her enjoyed her work and her time alone. Sometimes it was a struggle to be like other women. But it was important, too.

When she returned her gaze to the fire it was to note that their conversation had ceased and he was staring at her with a strange, speculative expression.

"What?"

"You look happy."

She smiled and nodded. "There is nothing like a fire against the growing darkness. A full belly and a full bag of roots and plants." She patted the bag at her side. "What about you? What makes you happy?"

His smile faded. "Riding. Riding, fast."

And now he walked.

The conversation that had flowed as naturally as a river came to a sudden stop. She glanced at him, his face glowing with the warm colors of the fire.

"You have more questions?" he asked.

"Many."

He drew up his knees and wrapped his strong arms about them. "All right then. Ask your questions."

"When you smell the searing flesh or your vision shakes or your hand trembles, do you always fall down?"

"Yes."

"Do you hear anything?"

"When the falling begins, I hear a hum."

"Like bees?"

"No, more like the ring, when you strike metal to metal. But it does not fade. It grows louder and louder, until I cannot hear anything else, and then I fall."

She thought on all he had said, trying to make some meaning out of it.

"You said that you never had unclean relations with a family member. Is that right?"

He sighed glumly. "Never."

"That eliminates illness brought by breaking a taboo. But we need to eliminate spirits and ghosts. If we can do so, that will leave only curses and illness. I can help only if you are ill. You understand?"

"Yes. How do we eliminate spirits and ghosts?"

"Spirits act out of offense. Have you failed to offer prayers of thanks or ignored any other required prayers and offerings?"

"I have not."

"Do you belong to a medicine society?"

"Black War Bonnet."

She paused at this. The men of that society were the bravest of warriors because they put the mark of death upon their shields. She was familiar with the unique design of this medicine society. A circle of black symbols on robe or shield meant this man held back death.

She lifted her brows and he endured her scrutiny. The owls. The Black War Bonnet society. Who was this man?

"And you perform all rites?" she asked.

"I do."

"That eliminates spirits. They do not attack the living without cause."

"Ghosts?" he asked.

"Ghosts are either enemies you have killed or

those you know who are not at peace. Sometimes if a life's circle is not complete, a soul can feel cheated and try to finish their journey with the body of the living. Have all those of your family been properly set to rest in either the ground or the sky?"

"Always."

"Possession of your body can cause ghost sickness. You would feel fevered, nauseous and sometimes have the sensation of suffocating. Usually those with ghost sickness see visions that are not there."

"I have seen things that are not there. But not the fever or suffocating sensation."

She nodded. They could not rule out ghosts then.

"Any recent deaths of someone near to you?"

"I lost a friend in the same battle when I was injured."

She straightened at this revelation as possibilities danced in her mind. "Injured. When?"

Night Storm hesitated, rubbing the back of his head as he stared at the ground.

From the lake, bullfrogs began their deep belching call. The burning wood popped and crackled as the fire consumed it, but Night Storm seemed to notice none of it.

Skylark was just about to remind him that she could do little without knowing what troubles he had and everything she could learn about his injury. Her grandmother was very insistent that she discover all she could about a person seeking care. That included minute details regarding his habits and all his past wounds.

At last he met her gaze and she again felt the punch of physical attraction hit her low in the belly. He held her attention and the pull to move near to him became more insistent. She set aside the remains of her meal, knowing that she had no further appetite for food. A different hunger gnawed.

His shoulders lifted and then settled as he blew out a long breath. Then he gave a little nod, as if he had decided something.

"We battled against the Lakota who were pursuing the white men who dress in the colors of the wolf. We had seen the white men who dress in blue cross our territory with people of a tribe we do not know. These warriors dress like the whites, but their skin was like the people and their hair was long and black and braided in the proper way.

All the white soldiers travel in groups and carry large guns, like the ones in the forts, and so we let them pass. We might have let the gray men pass, as well, but they brought our enemy into our territory. So we attacked. I have had many coups in battle. This I would say first. But in this fight, I was unseated and one of my horse's hind hooves struck me here." He pointed to the back of his head.

She drew air through her teeth at the image of him being kicked by his horse. "May I feel this place?"

Instantly she realized the problem with this request. She had touched the wounds of countless men and women in her tribe from the very old to the very young. But never had she anticipated the contact with such a yawning need. Eagerness, yes, that was what she felt.

He nodded his consent and she fairly leaped to her feet to close the distance that separated them. She knelt beside him and began as she had been taught, with a gentle touch to his arm. It was not right to immediately grope a place that might cause pain. She worked from the strong column of his neck to the base of his skull, trying to ignore the tingling awareness her fingers relayed with the contact of her flesh to his flesh. Her physical enjoyment of the contact ended when she found the place where he had been kicked. There was no lump. Rather, she found a shallow depression.

"Were you kicked or stepped on?" she asked.

"I was struck here with a war club." He pointed to the tiny red scar that sliced through one of his eyebrows. How had she not noticed that before?

"This was a glancing blow. But it caused me to lose my balance. Then our horses collided and I fell backward."

She examined the scar, her awareness of him now mixed with the need to solve this puzzle.

"Do you remember the blow or the fall?" She released him and sat at his side, turning toward him as he spoke.

"Neither. My friend, Two Hawks, saw the blow and watched me become unseated. He said I killed the man with my lance, but he hit me before leaving his horse. Two Hawks said that I did not fall like a man who knows he is falling. He said the horse's rear foot hit me here and that after they had chased away the intruders they came back for me, surprised to find me alive. I did not wake until late in the evening and I do not recall the battle or the blow or the fall or even the days that followed."

"I am not surprised. The bone of your skull was crushed. The swelling from this break should have taken you from this world and into the next."

"Perhaps it did," he muttered.

"Yet here you are," she countered. "How can that be?"

"I think I walked the ghost road and then came back."

They stared at each other. Owls…a death, his

death, and then his return to this world. She drew
up her knees and hugged them tight. Her heart
beat in her throat as she resisted the urge to draw
away from him. Had he walked across the sky to
the spirit world? Had he stopped on his own or
had the one who guards the road set his feet back
to the world of the living?

Was that why he heard the owl?

She shivered against the clammy chill that took
her.

"My shaman said he sang me awake," said
Night Storm.

"Did he give you anything to bring down the
swelling?"

"He called on the power of the spirit world to
heal me or take me."

"But no medicine?" She could not believe his
shaman had not given Storm something for pain
and to bring down the swelling.

"You said that someone close to you died?"
she said.

"Yes. My friend and cousin. We were raised together. We went on our vision quest together, and
we were inducted into the same medicine society."
He shook his head and looked truly miserable.

She did not ask the name of his cousin because
it was both impolite and dangerous to speak of
the dead. To do so was to disturb their rest and

risk inviting them to return to haunt the living. But some souls did not rest because they refused to walk the ghost road to the spirit world, lingering instead among them. These ghosts could cause havoc if measures were not taken to send them away.

"We can look into this possibility. Did he die a good death?" She was asking if he had fought bravely or, if captured, if he represented his people and himself with pride and dignity under torture.

"His death was good, quick. The gray white men shot him with their rifles."

"And his body was recovered?"

"Yes, and he was sent on a scaffold with his things."

"That is good. You said that you have seen things that were not there. Will you tell me of them?"

"Not tonight."

She pursed her lips at this delaying tactic and thought to remind him that he said he would be forthcoming. But he rubbed his forehead again, as he had done earlier when he said he had pain. She did not want to cause another fall by her questions.

"These wounds look recent." She laid an open palm on the scarred flesh at his chest. There were two ragged, raised places on each side of his upper torso that could mean only one thing. This man had tested his devotion and bravery in the most sacred of all ways.

"I have the honor of success in the sun dance," he said, his voice humble.

This was no small feat. She had watched the sun dance in her tribe. Young warriors volunteered to have wooden spikes inserted through the skin of their chest or upper back. The spikes pierced in and then out at a different place, like a bone awl through a buckskin. From these dowels, long rawhide tethers were tied. The other ends of these ropes were fixed to a tall pole, set deep in the ground solely for this purpose. Then the men would dance as sweat streamed down their bodies. They would dance and chant and blow whistles made from the bones of an eagle's wing. All the while they would stare at the sun and try to tear free of their bonds. This might take a day or more. Some men passed out during the dance only to revive to try again. Not all tore free. To voluntarily submit to such an ordeal was a true test of courage. And this man had succeeded.

"I was the first to free myself."

"The first?" It was a great coup. Skylark did not think she could be more impressed. "That is amazing."

"It was not. I tore free only because I fell."

Unease prickled.

"Your second fall."

Beyond the circle of their fire and past the open ground now fading with twilight came the hoot of a great horned owl. She stilled as the chill of night seemed to seep into every pore.

# *Chapter Five*

~~~~~~~~~~~~~~~~~~~~~~~~~~~~~~~~~~~~~~~~~

Night Storm did not seem to be bothered by the nearness of the owl, while she was completely unnerved by the sound. What had her aunt always said? If you hear an owl, ghosts walk near.

"The sun dance was my second fall," said Night Storm.

"Did you not hear that?" she asked.

"What? The owl?" He blew away a long, suffering breath. "I hear them…everywhere." He fixed his gaze on her and she wondered again who was this man?

"Would you hear of the sun dance?"

She nodded numbly.

"It was my hope that the sun dance would cure me. I blew my whistle, and I prayed for the Great Spirit to rid me of my weakness. That my prayers would rise up like the sacred tobacco smoke to the Great Spirit. I leaned away from the attachments in my chest."

She flinched at his words but he continued on.

"But the pain did not bring me closer to the spirit world. I smelled burning flesh and the ringing began. At first I thought it was the eagle whistles. But the sound was inside my head, and I fell before I could prove myself worthy of answered prayers."

"You fell in front of everyone?"

"I did. I was staring at the sun. Praying to the Great Spirit for his blessings. Instead, I had my second fall and the thrashing caused me to break free. I did not feel it. I did not suffer as I should have, and all who watched thought I was showing great strength, when, in fact, I was revealing my greatest weakness."

"How did they not know?"

"Many dance and twist and foam and bleed. It was all expected."

She nodded, wondering if she had been watching, if she would have known.

"You said you fell three times."

"The last fall came when I was walking by the river. The day was clear, and the water sparkled like the stars above. As the sun set, the colors danced from sky to water. I knew that time that it would come. I felt the urge to get away from my companions, but I could not run. The ground was shaking as it does from thunder. But I do not know if it really shook or if it only seemed to shake. I looked back and they all seemed as they did when I left them. They did not totter or weave. Then my vision went bad. I do not know what happened after that. Only you have seen." He waited, but she said nothing. "What did you see?"

She lifted a stick and poked at the fire. Eventually she did tell him what she'd witnessed.

"You stopped breathing and your skin began to turn blue. That was when I went to you. You went still, slack as if you had died. I listened to your chest and heard your heartbeat, but the wind of life had left you and blood filled your mouth. So I rolled you. You choked and then began to breathe. So I moved away and watched you."

"You covered me with my saddle blanket."

She nodded.

"And tied my horse's reins to a tree."

She stared at the fire, shy now to tell him how she had stood over him. Tended him. Washed him.

"Were you still there when I woke?"

She peeked up at him. "Yes."

"Why did I not see you?"

She pointed at the sky, now showing the glow of the first stars. "I was in a tree."

He chuckled. "I have not thanked you for saving my life. Instead, I attacked you and threatened you. I ask your forgiveness now and…" He hesitated, as if he had changed his mind about what else to say. "And…"

She cocked her head and waited, wondering what he wished to ask her beyond her forgiveness.

"And," he said again. "I owe you my life."

Her eyes rounded at the implications of that. For she knew that if the opportunity arose, he would give his life for hers. But, more than that, she was responsible for the life she had saved.

She stilled and stared in silence for a long moment. Then she nodded, shouldering this responsibility. It was what a woman did, lifted and carried, often more than she could manage. Skylark was small, but she was strong. Was she strong enough to bear this burden?

"And I will help you find the cause for this falling." She returned to her idle poking of the fire with the glowing stick. "I do not think you are haunted. But you may have touched the spirit world after your injury. You might touch it each time you fall. I think you should look through the shimmering light and see what is beyond."

Again the horned owl hooted, closer now. He looked to her and he thought he could see the hairs on her arms rise up as her face went ashen.

"I am haunted. They follow me."

She was on her feet now.

"Ghosts," she whispered.

He came to stand beside her, resting an arm across her shoulders. She wrapped her arms about his back and clung like a frightened child. He cradled her body next to his and was suddenly grateful to the owl for giving him a reason to hold her again. He dipped his head to breathe in the sweet floral scent of her skin. She carried the fragrance of everything green and alive. He held her and made a shushing sound.

"They are not here for you," he assured.

"But I do not want them to take you, either."

This surprised him. He was a stranger to her. Was it his words or her new promise to help him that made her say such things? She was so small, but her arms were strong and her determination rang clear in her voice. He petted the back of his fierce little defender, suddenly sad. He should be protecting her. But he could not because somehow fate had brought him this sickness or haunting or possession. But it had also brought him Skylark.

He did not know how she could help him, but he did believe that she would do all in her power.

The hooting came again. This time she released him and snatched up the glowing stick. Then she walked in the direction of the owl. It was an act of extreme bravery or foolishness. No one ever pursued an owl. In fact, most people he knew would have already run in the opposite direction. But not his little medicine woman. She shouted and shook her glowing stick as she ran toward the owl's call. A moment later the owl sailed silently through the trees, its body a dark silhouette.

She returned a moment later. "It is gone."

He could barely keep from laughing. She looked so serious, with her tiny glowing spear and fierce expression.

"What?" she asked.

"You are a very brave woman, unusual, but brave."

Skylark giggled and tossed the stick back into the fire. "When I get angry, it is my emotions that take over."

They stood there grinning at each other until the moment turned awkward and he glanced about at their camp.

"Let's bed down for the night," he suggested.

That made her eyes widen and she lost the brave expression she'd been wearing. She clasped her hands before her. The result was the unintentional drawing together of her breasts.

He looked away from this new temptation. She had not agreed to stay with him for that and he would not take what was not offered.

He went to his packs and withdrew the single

buffalo robe that suited him well for sleeping. Then he collected the rolled red woolen blanket, a prized possession he'd received for the trade of many beaver hides. He offered them to Skylark to see if she would make one bed or two. She made two.

Then she set to work crushing leaves between rocks and making a paste that she added to water in two separate horn cups.

"I wish I had my cooking kettle," she said. "I could steep this in hot water."

"What is in there?" He asked.

"Spotted Alder. This is very good for wounds." She pointed to the second cup. "This is Throw-wort. It quiets nerves and calms the blood. I have seen it used for trembling conditions. It might help lessen your spells."

Storm watched her work. He had shared a meal and a fire, and would shortly share his buffalo robe with this woman. And his most intimate secrets. That frightened him nearly as much as his falling.

She was all motion and sparkling eyes. She came alive with her plants, explaining each new withdrawal from her pouch, and he listened just for the pleasure of hearing her voice. Her familiarity with illness and cures impressed. Such knowledge was unusual for one so young. She divided the bounty into two groups, food and plants to heal. This last group she divided again into plants to help him and other plants for various conditions to restock her supplies. Some she hung to dry by the fire, others she carefully wrapped in bits of leather. It occurred to him that her skills must be highly valued by her tribe and that the Low River people were lucky to have her.

Her hands were steady and sure. She did not shake or tremble or fall down and foam. She was exactly the sort of woman he found physically appealing, with her slender frame and enough curves to keep a man interested in the day and warm at night.

He glanced at the sprinkling of stars, knowing that during this moon the nights were short and warm. But somehow he feared sleeping beside her would make the time bend back upon itself like a river. Despite the physical awareness they shared, he should not touch her. He could not. It was wrong to take a woman he could not provide for. And he did not think he could suffer the shame of having a woman provide for him. This was why he had yet to married Beautiful Meadow. He could not bring enough game for one wife, let alone two.

It was one thing, when one was old, for a son to hunt for him and a daughter to help move their tepee. But he was young and strong...or he had been. Was he well enough to take a woman if she asked?

"How long after the blow to your head did you fall?" she asked. She looked up from her plants and caught him staring at her backside. She tugged down the bottom of her dress and lifted her eyebrows at him.

He cleared his throat. "One moon. We fought the gray coats in the Fast Water Moon and afterward I was brought home to my mother's care. I do not recall very much of the Digging Moon. My mind was bad during this time, but I did not shake."

"Or fall?"

"I could barely stand. But, no, I did not fall until we met in the Many Flowers Moon." This time his words held no condemnation. How strange. When exactly had she turned from enemy to ally? "After the injury, I rarely stood upright. I was too dizzy and my head ached all the time. They carried me home. But now it has been four moons. People are asking when I will ride again."

She waved a hand, dismissing this, for now. He frowned. A woman knew that a man's best weapon was his horse. He needed to ride in order to hunt and war and feel alive. Without his horses, he was dying inside, like a plant cut from its roots.

"The injury caused the dizziness. But did it also cause the falls? That is what we must see."

He nodded.

"Your skull was broken. Four moons is not so long for such an injury to heal."

"Yes, that is what our shaman, Thunder Horse, said to me. He came to me often and sang over me. I do not think he believed I would live."

She returned to her potions muttering something about nothing for the swelling, nothing for the pain.

"One moon passed before I left my sleeping robe. During the Digging Moon I left my mother's lodge but, still, when I walked, the earth seemed to heave beneath my feet. I began to hunt on horseback with Frost beside me during the Many Flowers Moon." At the sound of his name, Frost lifted his head and thumped his tail. Storm stroked his furry coat and the dog closed his eyes to savor the moment. "My vision was bad and the sunlight bothered me."

"Headaches," she asked, guessing correctly.

"Yes. It was late in the Many Flowers Moon when I met you and had my first fall. I woke feeling sore and sick to my stomach. But I managed to get home. I told my shaman only that my stomach was still bad and he said it was too soon to ride."

"I agree."

"So I walked. But by the Little Rain Moon, my vision still moved like water in a river and my dreams were strange. That is when I feared you had cursed me. So I took part in the sun dance."

"That was not wise," she said, her voice low.

"I did not know what else to do."

"Stay in your buffalo robes and heal."

He made a face and she returned to her brewing.

"And the third time you fell?"

He scrubbed his fist over his mouth then told her what he recalled. "My first hunt after my injury, last moon. We stopped to fish on a lake and I managed to get away from the others before I fell."

"The same moon as the sun dance?"

"No. Not the Little Rain Moon. It was the time of the Ripening Moon."

She made a face. "So you fell during the dance and then decided to go hunting?"

She made him sound like a fool.

He did not succeed in keeping all of the irritation from his voice. "Do you want to hear?"

She motioned for him to continue.

"I was walking beside the river and the sun was low. I remember noticing the way the water flashed with all the colors of the setting sun. It was beautiful so I stopped to watch it. Then Frost started barking and I tried to get him to stop, but I could not speak. I had time to drop to my knees. The next thing I knew the stars were up and I was laying facedown and bleeding on the riverbank with my arm in the water."

Skylark felt the stab of fear behind her breast-bone, the kind she felt when she had accidentally cut herself but before she began to bleed, for she realized that on that fall he might have rolled into the river and drowned.

"What of your friends?"

"They found me. Laughing Jay and Two Hawks. I told them I fell."

"Did they believe you?"

He rubbed the back of his head. "I do not think so. But they did not speak of it when we returned to camp."

Likely because they knew how dangerous it would be for others to know of his weakness.

"They are good friends to you."

He nodded. "But I think they might have heard the owls, because they will not hunt with me now. That is why I go alone."

She decided that he could not be alone again until they learned what caused his falling and re-stored him to health.

She had been trying to heal her mother but she

continued to waste away and in the end all Sky could do was ease her pain. Was Night Storm just another incurable in a different body? Could she cure him or was she just fooling them both?

## Chapter Six

As the talk between them died away along with the rosy skies to the west, Skylark settled in her borrowed buffalo robe, folding it in half to act as bedding and cover. The sounds of the frogs by the lake and the flapping of the leathery wings of the bats filled the silence that yawned between them. She bade him sleep well and closed her eyes, but sleep was a long time coming. At least she did not hear owls.

To occupy her mind, she thought of all he had told her. Just two moons after cracking his skull he had tried to go hunting and met her. This was his first fall. One moon later he had taken part in the sun dance and fallen. Then last moon he went hunting again and again had fallen. The folly and bravery of that filled her with awe. But the battle seemed to have started his sickness. Was it his battle injury or the enemy's ghost that provoked his trouble? Sioux warriors were dangerous even in death, but it appeared a good death to Skylark. And he said all bodies were retrieved by the Sioux and the Crow.

Because of the injury, Night Storm had fallen before taking the scalp of the Lakota warrior. That meant the soul of his enemy might be trapped, unable to leave through the hole in his head. Could it have entered Storm through the crack in his? Such an enemy would have to be strong, because attacking a man during the sacred sun dance would require much power.

She shivered at thoughts of the strength of such a foe and tugged the heavy buffalo robe closer under her chin.

And what of the owls? She listened and thought the whistling was merely the wind.

Skylark dozed, dreaming of ghosts and owls and the shrill sound of the eagle whistle the warriors blew during the sun dance. She felt the vibration of the drums and pounding feet of the women as they chanted and danced in a slow circle about the suffering men.

She woke in a stupor, dreaming that her father was here, perched in the trees beside a snowy white owl. Skylark clutched her chest as she bolted upright. What a terrible omen. Was her father in danger?

She looked about, searching for Falling Otter, but then she recalled Night Storm and the obligation that came with saving a life. She drew her knees up to her chest. For a moment she thought she could still hear her father's laughter. She listened but heard only a small creature, skunk or raccoon, scurrying in the tall grass and the rising wind whistling through the treetops. Sky nestled back to the earth, curling on her side and longed for morning.

She woke again to the sound of distant thunder. Soon the flash of lightning revealed the dark clouds sweeping in from the west. She drew the thick hide up to her ears, glad that Night Storm had put them on high, open ground, well away from the tall trees that drew the lightning.

Thunderbirds, she knew, flew in the storm clouds, sending the lightning crashing to earth each time they opened their great yellow eyes. And there, trailing behind them came the Thunderhorse, his mighty hooves shaking the earth as he passed. The air smelled cool and sweet as it did before a rain.

With the next flash she saw Night Storm sitting up, eyes toward the sky, with his dog, Frost, huddling close to his master. They watched the flashing of the Thunderbird's eyes as the storm came quickly now. She heard the whine of the wind and then realized it was not the wind but his dog. She smiled. Many dogs cried out during storms. But Frost no longer huddled beside his master. Now he barked wildly, dancing before Night Storm, who pushed him away. The dog tried to get Night Storm's arm over his head, but it dropped loosely to his master's side. Skylark's smile fell away as the icy finger of unease prickled over her. In the flashing light she saw Night Storm's gaze fixed to the sky as Frost began to howl. She had heard that sound once before. Now she remembered when and where. Frost had done exactly the same thing the day she had met Night Storm. The day he had fallen.

She clamped her hands over her ears against the frantic howl followed by the crash of thunder. Frost rushed to her, barking and dancing, from side to side.

"Night Storm," she called, but received no answer.

She was on her feet as the first stinging droplets of rain struck her face. When she reached him, it was to find him already in a stupor. His expression was blank, his face slack, and his right hand shook. She put a hand on his shoulder.

"Storm!"

His shoulder yielded, but he gave no indication that he could hear her. But then she recalled him saying that sometimes he could hear. That meant she could not cry in hysterics.

"I will help you. I will keep you safe. Do not worry. I am here with you."

Again the lightning forked across the sky, striking something close. The boom made her jump. The trees now swayed with the power of Tate, the wind, and the rain came in sheets so hard and fast that it was difficult to breathe. Storm's body swayed like the treetops and then fell. He fell back in a contraction she remembered, his body arching like a strung bow. She stroked his forehead and used her body to keep the rain from his face. His expression was a mask of horror, like one of the newly dead. Was he there in the spirit world right now? His body remained taut as the thunder crashed and boomed all about them, and Frost whined at her side, his thin, wet tail thumping the earth with a hopeful optimism that made her throat catch.

"He will be all right, boy," she said, and gave the dog a quick pat.

As if her words had triggered some change, his body began to jerk. His arm flailed and he caught her across the cheek with the back of his hand. This sent her to her seat. Frost was barking again and she told him to be quiet, then was surprised when he did as she commanded. The rain drenched them all. She tried to hold Storm, but even when she threw herself across his body, he tossed her aside as easily as he might cast off his fine wool blanket.

Finally she folded the sodden blanket beneath his head as a pad and sat back to wait. The storm raged all about them, and inside Night Storm an internal wind blew. Blood and foam came from his mouth. She rolled him to his side, but he could not stay in that position. As the storm swept out over the lake and receded over the mountain, his jerking motions quieted and he finally went still.

Instantly she went to his side, rolling him so the blood and saliva drained away. Checking to see that he could breathe, she pressed an ear to his wide back and listened. Over the drum of rain she could hear the draw of wind and the beat of his heart. She sat back on her heels and blew out a breath. Her shoulders slumped and her head bowed.

The rain continued to fall, but this was no longer the punishing torrent. Now the rain came in a soft, steady stream. Frost nudged her with his head and then licked her face. Skylark shivered and hugged the wet dog.

She lifted a brow as a memory struck her. The day she had first seen Night Storm, hunting her in the dappled sunlight, Frost had given away their position. He had barked and she had heard him. It had spoiled Storm's easy capture, for she had run and he had chased. Frost had barked then and howled. Storm had told him to be quiet but his dog had not obeyed. He had howled as Storm fell.

Sky's spine stiffened and she realized that Frost had not been crying because of the lightning.

"You knew, didn't you?" she whispered, looking down into the soulful eyes of his dog. "You knew first."

Frost left her and approached his master, licking his unresponsive face and then curling up close to his back as if to keep him from rolling.

She recalled that on their second meeting, Storm had been staring at the trees with unfocused eyes and how his dog had poked him with his nose, drawing him back. Had he been nearing a fall then, too? How did his dog know?

Skylark looked to the gutted fire and the wet lump of blanket. Then she glanced to the buffalo robe. Only that would repel rain. She used a bit of wet buckskin to clean the mud from Storm's body and the blood from his face. Before she finished he was blinking his eyes blearily and trying to move. With his help, she got him up and to the folded buffalo robe. She tucked him in tight and then wrapped herself in the muddy blanket, shivering hard now.

His words were a whisper. "Sky?" He lifted the edge of the robe in an invitation. The strain of the simple action seemed to take all the energy he possessed.

She dropped the blanket and went to him, tucking her body between him and the back of the large buffalo robe. He wrapped one arm across her middle. This was better, she thought. She could listen to his breathing, feel any changes. She lifted the robe's edge once more and called to Frost who settled before her.

The hide had once covered a bull that stood twenty hands high at the shoulder. Even folded in two, there was plenty of room for a man, a woman and a dog.

Skylark stopped shivering. Night Storm's breathing grew soft and even. Frost lowered his head to his paws and Skylark knew from the dog's calm that for this night, at least, everything would be all right.

That was when she heard the laughter again. Frost lifted his head, telling her that the sound was not a dream or her imagining. She rose up on her elbow and searched the open ground for Falling Otter.

"Father? Are you there?" she called.

She listened and heard no reply. It was raining. A time to take cover. So, of course, her father was out in the storm. But he was far from camp.

Should she search the dark for her father or stay with the man she had promised to protect?

Night Storm's arm contracted as he dragged her closer to the warmth and security of his body. But it was a long time before Skylark closed her eyes.

"Father?" she called. "If you can hear me. I have food in my bag. There are roasted tubers, pemmican and prickly cactus."

The laughter stopped. Soon she saw the shadow moving through the tall grass beside their camp and with his passing came the sound of weeping.

Her father was happy.

# Chapter Seven

Night Storm woke first to find the sun shining low through the trees and the grass of the meadow glistening with droplets of rain. Had it rained? He didn't remember. His head ached and his body was so stiff. He shifted and felt something soft and warm.

He looked at the dark head of the woman sleeping tucked up beside him. *Skylark?*

When had she joined him in his bed? He glanced at the woolly fur of the buffalo robe and frowned. He had chosen the red woolen blanket. Skylark had picked the buffalo robe. So he had joined her in *her* bed? *That* he surely should be able to remember.

What was happening? But then he knew. It was the only reason he could conceive that would make his head ache so and explain the gaps in his memory. What did he remember? They'd shared a meal.

He had slept. Night Storm groped back through the mist and recalled a storm. At the first sound of thunder he had come awake. Then he watched the lightning from far away. His dog had been whining, upset by the impending storm. Then more streaks of light, closer and closer. The flash of lightning, flashing and flashing, first in the sky and then in his mind.

She came to him out of the lightning, just like the woman in his vision quest. Only now he knew with certainty this woman was Sky. She spoke. Her voice soothing. "I am here with you." And then the relief of knowing there was one person in the world who knew and still stayed to help him.

There had been so little warning. Would he have gotten away from the others in his tribe before it took him? He did not think so. This time again, he had been trapped by the flashing lightning as surely as a fly is trapped by a spider's web. And just like the fly, he could not move or cry out. He could do nothing but wait for the darkness that swallowed him up.

He had hoped he could master this weakness alone. He had prayed that killing the witch that had cursed him would set him free. But there was no witch, no curse. Only his dented skull and the sickness that made him fall and the ghosts that followed him. If not for Skylark he would have already died in his own blood and vomit.

He tightened his grip on Skylark, afraid that even she could not save him.

"Night Storm?"

Her voice was soft, just a whisper, yet it pierced right through him. He tensed.

"You are awake?" She spoke in a whisper.

"Yes."

"That is good." She rolled toward him, her cheek cushioned in the crook of her palm. They lay side by side, nose to nose. Her braided hair was mussed and she blinked at him with sleepy, alluring eyes.

Night Storm had lain with several willing women. Widows or women who did not wish a full-time man, ones who traded their attentions for whatever they lacked. But he had never slept with a maiden and he was certain Skylark was a maiden. He also had never woken beside a woman but now found his chest aching with the longing to do so again. One night more and then she would be gone. She was soft and warm and drowsy. The rising sun cast her face in golden morning light, and he thought she was the most beautiful thing he had ever seen. The need to make her his warred with the sure knowledge that she would never willingly choose a man who was unable to provide for her. Beautiful Meadow certainly would not. He knew that. No woman would. And he could not ask.

Except she had saved his life. Did she truly understand what that meant?

He had vowed to remain single until his recovery. And he had promised to make Beautiful Meadow his first wife as soon as he was well. If he was ever well. So why did he now want to pull the robe over them both and explore her body? He reached and laid a hand on her hip.

Her smile faltered. Chaste, he decided, her reaction confirming his belief.

"How do you feel?" she asked, her spine stiffening. She lifted a hand and brushed his forelock from his face.

A Crow warrior wore his forelock cut to only a few inches in length and used wax and tallow to make it stand up stiff and tall as the tail of a deer. But with the night and the storm, his hairstyle had fallen with his spirits and the rain had swept away the grease, leaving his hair soft as a woman's. She toyed with his bangs a moment longer and then retreated. His dog appeared from behind Skylark and stretched, then trotted off, nose to the ground.

Skylark lifted on one elbow to stare at him and

that was when he saw it. He startled up, throwing the robe aside.

The sudden change from reclining to sitting made Storm's head spin, but he was not deterred from his intention. Night Storm captured her chin in his hand and turned her face so he could study the blue-and-purple bruise on her cheek.

"Did I do that?" he asked, already knowing the answer.

"You did not mean to."

"But I did. I struck a woman." The shame of this caused him to sag.

She moved to kneel beside him, wrapping an arm about his shoulders. "I am all right," she said.

But he covered his face in his hands. First he could not ride and now he had attacked a woman. What had he become?

"I had another falling time," he said into his hands.

"Yes. During the storm."

"And I hit you."

"No, I got too close and you were thrashing. You did not hit me. I promise."

He felt he could breathe again. Frost returned and nudged at his arm and licked at his hands. He stroked Frost's head and found the strength to meet the gaze of this woman who was not like any he had ever known. Why hadn't she run away in the night?

"I do not know what I do, and when I wake my mind is in pieces like a shattered pot."

"Does your head ache?"

He nodded.

"I will fix you something. Stay here."

She set out with Frost trotting beside her, but his dog returned to him when it became obvious that Night Storm was not going along. Night Storm had time only to relieve himself, pray and wash in the lake before she returned. Her face was wet and her hair neatly braided. He was weaker than he cared to admit and that frightened him.

As she approached, she searched the web of tree branches, looking up into the leafy canopy.

Finally she met his curious stare.

"I heard my father last night and I think I saw him. I told him to take what food he needed and I see someone raided our supplies."

Now Night Storm was looking into the tree limbs with her.

"Where is he? He is welcome in our camp."

"Which is likely why he will not approach. Now if he were unwelcome..." She let the rest go and rummaged in her collecting bag. "I have Snakeweed for headache and dizziness. Also Trade Cloth Flower. The roots make a good tea to stop trembling and thrashing. I will show you how to make this medicine."

"Should we look for him?"

"We will not find him unless he wishes to be found." She gathered the green plants she needed.

"How fast do they work?"

"The headache will be gone very fast. But for the rest, I need to find which plant best suits you. There are many. Finding the right combination will be challenging."

"But you have only one more day."

She dropped the contact of their gazes. "Yes."

"It will not be enough."

"I will teach you what plants to try. We could find many right here." She motioned about her to the wide world.

"And which parts to use? And how to prepare them? And how much to take?" he asked.

Her shoulders slumped at the impossibility of it all.

"It is not enough time," she said, echoing his words.

They stared a long moment in silence.

"You do not think I am haunted?"

"I think you are wounded. The head injury has brought on the falling times. It may heal naturally, but I believe the correct medicines will bring on a faster cure. But the owls…"

"Yes?"

"You saw them before the falling. I wonder if they point you to some purpose."

"Death."

"No. A purpose here among the living."

"I am a warrior." He did not like the stubborn quality of his voice. "There is no other path for me."

"You are what you are. We do not choose our life path. It is chosen for us."

"What else can I be?"

"Now you ask the correct question."

"This is not my path," he said, pointing to the weeds she held in her hand. "I know my course, it is just—I have fallen. I must return to the warrior's way."

She stared at him with deep, thoughtful eyes, but she did not argue further.

"Do you really think you can help me?" he asked.

She did not glance away or hesitate. "Yes."

But did she mean to help him become a warrior or help him lose everything he was?

He drew a lungful of the sweet, moist air and let it go. Storm knew that to trust her required a different kind of courage, the kind that came from giving away the control he had always taken for granted. The command of his life he had achieved when he became a man. Now it melted away like snow in the thaw.

"Then you must stay with me."

Sky's muscles stiffened and she drew away. "I must return to my people."

"I will return you to them in time."

"You are promised to another woman."

"Yes."

"I cannot go with you."

"You have saved my life," he said, reminding her of her obligation. He knew it was unfair, but he was a desperate man. And a warrior fights with what is at hand.

Skylark cocked her head to stare at him. Something had changed. She felt afraid again, afraid of this man and the owls that followed him. His stare was too intense, his features too appealing, his body too hard. What exactly did he want from her now?

Night Storm was strong, but he was also weak. He needed help and had asked her. She cast a glance about for some other path, a way to return to her tribe. She looked a long time toward the east, in the direction they had traveled. She thought of the warriors who treated her with respect but never as an object of desire. Of her aunt and uncle, who had welcomed her into their lodge though she was well past the age to have built a home of her own. To the father who showed her people what path to take by doing the very opposite yet needed reminders to eat.

She had heard him cry last night. She was certain.

Skylark looked at Night Storm and saw desire and hope.

"Sky?" he said.

Why was her heart beating so fast? It made her ears ring and made his voice seem miles away. There was no future for them. But there was her promise to help him.

"You said it could not be done in a day. You need more time."

"Just because we shared a buffalo robe does not mean... Nothing happened," she insisted.

"Something happened."

She shook her head in wild denial.

"You saved me, again. If you wanted me to die, that was your chance. All you needed to do was leave me to drown in the rain and my own blood." His tongue ran the inside of his cheek. Was he feeling the gash he had torn there with his teeth?

"You do not wish to go with me. But you also do not wish me to walk the spirit road. You must choose one or the other."

"I have to go home."

He said nothing, just waited for her to recognize what he already knew. She had a duty to him now.

"No," she whispered, still clinging to her resistance even as it crumbled like unfired clay.

"You will come with me."

"Please," she said, her words whispered, weak now, for she already knew what must be done. He was like one still drowning. She did not know if he could be saved, but she knew she must try. She did not wish to fail again, as she had done with her mother.

She wanted to scream at him, thrash and cry like a child. Instead, she sat on her heels in perfect stillness as the truth of his words settled in her heart. *You will come with me.*

She would.

Skylark bowed her head. Her shoulders sagged and defeat settled on her like a heavy blanket. "Yes. But…"

She lifted her head in time to see his smile fade.

"But?" he repeated.

"How will you explain me to your tribe and to your woman, Beautiful Meadow?"

This time he was the one who hesitated. Then, with slow deliberation, he extended his open hands, palm up. "I have a lodge and I will trade skins for a cooking pot that will be yours. I have many horses. You may have your pick for your family. And from this day, I will protect you and provide for you."

Skylark's heart began hammering like a woodpecker on a rotted tree. Did she misunderstand him? For she did not trust what she had heard.

His words were so similar to the promise spoken by a groom to his bride that she gaped at him. Was he saying what she thought he was saying? Was he offering to marry her?

## Chapter Eight

The prospect of marriage to Night Storm both thrilled and terrified. Skylark knew he was promised to another woman. Would he set that woman aside for her? And what if she did not succeed? What if he gave up this woman he had chosen and she failed to restore him?

"What are you saying?" She wanted to know exactly what he expected from her.

His gaze was earnest. "When I first saw you here, I wanted you. It was the wanting that comes from here." He placed a hand low over his stomach.

Yes, she knew that kind of wanting. The ache of need unfulfilled. She knew this, for she now felt this desire for him.

"But now I also need you here," he said, and pressed his fingers against his forehead, lightly tapping the scar that sliced through his eyebrow.

His groin and his head, she realized. This was where he needed her. His hands fell back to his sides, never touching his heart. No, he did not need her there. That place was for Beautiful Meadow. The pain of that hurt more than she cared to admit.

Well, what did she expect—love?

He was speaking again. She forced herself to listen.

"I know there is something wrong in my head. I know I need help. It is something I have never needed before. So I am asking you to come with me to the village of the Black Lodges. I do not wish any of my people to know of my weakness, so I cannot bring you to them as a healer."

She waited, her heart pounding with a strange combination of hope and dread.

"So I will bring you as my wife."

She blinked at the words that brought sweet hope and also terror. "But we are strangers."

"No more. I know much about you. I know you are the kind of woman who helps a man who falls. I know you help your aunt run her home. I know you work hard collecting medicines to heal your people, and I know you have compassion, because you come alone into the woods to find your father and bring him home. And I know you are brave, because you chase owls with sticks."

She looked at him, recognizing that she wanted him in every way a woman wants a man. And believing she could grow to want him with her heart in time, knowing they would never have that time.

Time. Time to heal him. Fall in love with him. Lose him to his ghosts or this other woman. Time for her to give in to her need and become heavy with child.

Her mother said that a woman needs children but she does not need a man. Was that true? Could she be happy returning to her people with only this man's child?

No. That would break her heart.

She did not think she could speak. Her throat ached as she battled tears. She had dreamed of this moment since she became a woman and now it had come as a deception.

She shook her head, fearing how much she wished to go with him, be his, even as a lie.

"There must be another way."

"What way? Do you have some explanation for your presence? I would hear it."

"I could pose as your intended." Even as she suggested it, the notion fell flat. A man never promised himself to two women at once.

"Do you have relatives among the Black Lodges?"

She shook her head, seeing her idea crumble like drying mud.

"Such a woman would not leave her parents' home. I would court you at the gathering. But I might not live that long."

There it was again. Her obligation to the life she had saved. She did not regret helping him. But the bonds that tied them now seemed to have pulled tight as drying rawhide. She could not escape.

"But, my family… This is a time of gathering for winter. Without my help, they will have less tubers and dried berries."

"But more meat. If I live, I will hunt for them as I will hunt for you."

One elk could provide more nourishment than a basket of dried berries. She considered his offer. His eyes dared her to challenge his prowess to provide. But his inadequacy hung between them like rotting flesh. He could not ride—he fell, and his ability to fulfill the duties of a husband were uncertain.

But somehow she believed he could do it. He would provide for her or die trying.

"You cannot provide for my family and for Beautiful Meadow's. She is Wind Basin and I am Low River."

"Her father is chief of Wind Basin. He needs

none to hunt for him. And you are my first wife. I go to your people. Beautiful Meadow will leave her tribe when she becomes my second wife."

The same situation as had happened to her mother. A woman should not have to choose between her husband and her family. It was different for a man. They were expected to leave their tribe.

"Your wife? she asked.

"A wife?"

"*My* first wife."

Then Beautiful Meadow and, if his brother fell in battle, Night Storm would be obligated to take his brother's wife and child, as well, for that was a sacred duty. Somehow she found herself in the exact spot she had promised to never be, one of two or more wives.

"You do this, all to protect your secret?"

He nodded. "I would do anything to protect it."

Hope flared. "Anything? Will you set aside this woman you have promised to marry?"

He looked shocked that she would ask this of him and she felt ashamed.

"I have given her my promise."

And he was an honorable man.

"I will not be a second wife."

"You will be my first wife."

She shook her head. He had chosen another woman to make his home. She had no doubt that

whoever she was, she was accomplished and
beautiful. She was also the niece of the shaman
of the Black Lodges and daughter of the chief of
the Wind River people. Sky had no desire to leave
her aunt and uncle and father and go to the tribe of
her husband's other wife as her mother had done.
It was one of the things that made her mother most
miserable, losing everyone she knew and loved
for a man who had given her little attention when
she did not bear him a child.

"I will not share a husband with another. While
I am with you, you will not marry her."

"But why?"

She shook her head. "My mother's life taught
me that there is nothing more miserable than a
second wife."

"Then I will not marry her until after you are
settled. After I am well."

"If you are well, you will not need me."

"But I will still provide for you."

"And if I cannot cure this?"

"I will bring you home."

So, he wanted her only for her healing skills.
He was like the men of her tribe, only he was
more desperate.

"No."

"Skylark, I have promised to marry Beautiful Meadow. If you will not allow me to marry

her, then you must promise to break our marriage when I return you to your people at the winter camp. Any children would be yours, of course. You could take my lodge and all inside when you return to your tribe. Surely it is a fair bargain."

It was all any woman need do to dissolve a match, say publicly that the marriage was done and place her husband's possessions outside the tepee. Then he would return to his tribe and she would remain, with her children, in hers.

"Yes, but…" How did she tell him that she wanted a husband who loved her enough to make her his only wife? That she was tired of being valued for her skills and avoided for the same reason? The daughter of the heyoka. The odd one who wandered instead of tending the fires and helping her aunt keep their lodge. She flushed as full understanding came to her. She knew why he had kept his secret even when faced with death. The pain of an outsider was worse.

Still, she wanted to help him if she could. She had saved his life and she had a duty to him now.

"I will go with you. I will pose as your wife, if you will return me to my tribe before the Winter Camp Moon whether we succeed or not."

"Until the gathering?"

That left her what remained of the Hunting Moon and all of the War Moon before the Winter Camp Moon rose and signaled the tribes to gather. The four tribes of the Crow people would remain together for three to four moons, breaking apart when the Empty Belly Moon gave way to the Fast Water Moon once more.

"Yes. And you will not take a second wife until you are well or the time of the gathering. If you do, then I will set out your things and return to my people."

"I will be yours alone until you speak the words that end our union or the gathering comes," he said. "Then I will marry Beautiful Meadow."

"Is it a bargain?" he asked.

"Yes."

It was settled. She stared at this man who was now her husband and could barely breathe past the panic of what she had done. His face was serious, with no hint of joy or relief. Her stomach hurt.

She had imagined wearing a dress chalked white with clay and swinging with fringe for her wedding day. She had pictured his hand clasping hers as their wrists were symbolically tied together to signify their union.

Most marriages included a joining ceremony, a bride's dowry, a celebration of feasting and dancing. But that was not always the way. For many reasons, some duos just disappeared and returned as a couple. All that was necessary was that they agreed to be wed. And marriages could be broken just as swiftly.

Sky looked up at her husband.

She told herself she was strong, but she feared she was not strong enough to live with this man until the gathering and not fall in love with him. Still, that was what she must do.

Skylark rode the chestnut he called Gallop and he led the red roan he called Hunt. He had left his warhorse, Battle, with his brother's herd. Gallop was a good horse, strong and sleek, and she knew she had never ridden such a fine animal. It saddened her that he walked, however.

They had come days toward his camp and should arrive at his home before sunset. The day was still hot, so Storm wore only his loincloth and the quiver and bow crisscrossed over his back. He was a beautiful sight, but her gaze kept flicking to the trail before them, well-worn now.

With each step her nervousness grew toward panic. What would happen when they met Beautiful Meadow and her uncle, the shaman of the Black Lodges?

Sky glanced back across the wide stretch of open ground looking vainly for some sign of her father. Did he follow or had he turned back to their tribe? Would he be all right without her until the gathering?

Storm had spoken to Skylark in the evening when they made camp, but now, as they walked along, he was silent. She knew he watched for signs of the enemy Sioux who had been raiding earlier than usual this year. Likely her husband also hunted game so she remained quiet, but her nervousness got the best of her on more than one occasion. Frost seemed relaxed today, trotting happily at his master's side and then darting off after some sound or smell. As long as Frost was calm, she knew that Storm's mind was quiet.

But how did his dog know?

Frost dashed back to the trail they followed and touched Night Storm's hand with his nose. Storm scratched his head and Frost dashed off again. No danger, she realized. At least not for Night Storm.

As they rode, Skylark watched him carefully for any signs of illness or the falling sickness. She saw none. If she had not seen him fall twice, she would never believe there was any flaw in this powerful warrior. He moved with a steady, tireless gait while she admired the long muscles in his back contract and release with each step. He was perfection in motion and she found herself falling into her own kind of stupor, a mix of admiration and longing. His russet skin was smooth over the lean muscles of his shoulders and arms. His calves were firm. As he wore only the small breechclout on this hot afternoon, she had ample time to admire his form. Meanwhile, as his skin glowed with health and exertion, she perspired in her two-skin dress. She had made the dress with the help of her aunt, Winter Moon, from two buckskins. One draped over her arms, with a center cut for her head. The other formed the skirts. They were nicely tanned and smoked to make her garment resistant to rain. She had fringed the skirt but left the arms simple to keep the fringe from hampering her digging for roots. Now she wished she had taken the time to dye the garment green or red or sew a few shiny white elk teeth on the front seam. She had not even dressed her hair properly. As the sweat rolled down her back in the hot afternoon, she wondered why she had used simple cording to secure her braids instead of mink sheaths or red trade cloth, like the other women in her village. She fingered the strand of beads, her only adornment beyond her quilled skinning sheath. Her husband had given them to her.

Her eyes lingered on Night Storm. Her husband, she realized. He was her husband. Even if it were only a ruse she had a husband. She would make his meals and share a lodge. She would likely see him without his loincloth and he might catch a glimpse of her without her dress. Her heart beat so hard it drowned out the sound of the horse's tread.

He glanced back at her. "Are you thirsty?"

She nodded and he stopped to offer her a drink from a water skin, taking none himself.

"You are staring at me," he said.

How did he know? Of course she'd been staring at him for much of the afternoon.

"I am still trying to grasp that you are my husband."

There was a glimmer of a smile before he turned and returned the water skin to the packhorse.

"How are you feeling?" she asked.

His smile vanished and his face went hard. "Do not ask me that. If I have signs, I will tell you."

He took up the reins and continued along, his horse following behind.

Night Storm walked tirelessly, watching the trail ahead for any traces of the enemy Lakota and for any opportunity to hunt. Frost flushed several birds and harried ground squirrels, but nothing worthy of him drawing his bow.

He could still feel her eyes upon him, and when he glanced back it was to see her quickly look away. What did she think of him? Did she see only his weakness or could she also see his strength?

His wife. She was his until she spoke the words to break their bond. And she *would* speak them. He felt sure. Why had he not taken Beautiful Meadow before this? She wished to have her family with her for their joining ceremony, but he thought he could have convinced her. Now he would have to explain or try to explain why he returned from his hunting trip with a wife.

She would be furious, of course. Beautiful Meadow was generally sweet, but she had a temper. Perhaps if he had seen Sky before seeing Beautiful Meadow, he would have thought to marry her instead. His lightning woman. It had been his intention upon first sight to take her, seduce her and…he had not thought past that part. In fact, he had not thought at all. When he saw her alone, beautiful and distracted by her work, something inside him had broken loose. He always thought of what to do, but somehow this woman had made him forget his promise to Beautiful Meadow and the control of a warrior. He had thought only with his lower half.

How strange that his fate was now in her small hands. Was she right? Should he tell all of his tribe of his falling disease and let his medicine man attempt to sing away the ghost that possessed him?

He had seen Thunder Horse sing away many

illnesses. But he had also seen him tell their chief, Broken Horn, that a warrior could not be saved. That the spirits had marked him for death. Thunder Horse sang many men to their graves and Night Storm did not trust him. And Beautiful Meadow was his niece. If she knew of his weakness, he did not trust her not to tell her uncle. After his injury, that belief had kept him from speaking the words to make her his wife. She had been content to wait for her family and the gathering.

Now he did not know what would happen. But he thought it would be safer to meet an injured puma than tell Beautiful Meadow he had taken a wife.

Frost began barking. Before he could turn, Skylark was off her horse and at his side. He cast her an odd look and then went after his dog. He found Frost with his forelegs on a sturdy Lodgepole pine. Above him sat a porcupine.

"Good thing he treed him or his face would be full of quills," said Night Storm. "Hold him." He waited until Skylark had a firm grip on Frost. Then he notched an arrow and smoothly brought down the huge rodent. It was dead before hitting the ground.

No man ever turned away from a porcupine, for the quills were prized by the women for quillwork. Even one porcupine might keep a woman's hands busy all winter.

Frost barked as Night Storm used a bit of rawhide to lift the creature from the ground and carry it back to the horses. He gutted the carcass and let Frost have what he liked of the entrails. When he'd finished tying the spiny prize to the pack he found her staring again.

"What?"

Skylark looked away from Frost.

"Frost seems calm," she said.

He wrinkled his brow. "Do you do quillwork?"

She stiffened at his question. "Why do you think I do quillwork?"

Many women did such work, but to do the kind of work that she wore on her tall moccasins required a depth of skill rare among women. Such talent took much time and practice. He thought that might be why she had taken no husband, for he knew that women who specialized in such work sometimes did not marry or they lived with other women who quilled.

"Why, I said."

In answer, he pointed at her moccasins.

"My mother made these."

"Ah. Well, they are very beautiful."

"I cannot quill as well as she did."

"No matter. I have two sisters who would take

all the quills I can bring. Bright Shawl and Fills a Kettle can teach you."

"I do not wish to quill."

He tried to understand her, but the anger in her voice made no sense to him. "That is fine. I do not need decorative clothing. And you do not seem to wish it, either," he said, motioning to her plain dress.

This made her scowl deepen. "Not all women spend their time making pretty pieces. Some prefer to search for medicines to make people well."

He had obviously stumbled on some sensitive spot and, like a man discovering himself sinking in mud, he retreated. "It is a good purpose. I need no quilled adornments. I will throw it away, if you wish."

She hesitated, her scowl easing in slow degrees. "That would be wrong."

"No more wrong than making my wife unhappy."

She blinked at this. Had she forgotten she was his wife? She had said they were strangers and he never felt this was true so much as at this moment.

"I am sorry," she said. Her flushed face only made her more appealing. "My mother spent much time on her quillwork."

And had little time for her, he guessed.

He recalled that she mentioned that her mother

had walked the spirit road. He wished to ask, but it was impolite to speak of the dead. He knew that she worked quills and that she had been an unhappy second wife. But that was all.

"This knife and sheath were hers and these moccasins," said Skylark.

He tried to understand her and made a guess. "She was a second wife to your father?"

"Yes and no. My mother was married to a warrior who had a wife who was Low River. Then, after marrying my mother, he also wed his first wife's sister. My mother told me the sisters wanted his younger wife to gather all the wood and set the lodge. My mother said from that time onward she did all the hardest work. Also, neither had any children and her husband hoped my mother might bring him children but she did not. My mother left him and made herself a lodge."

"She did not move back to her tribe?"

"Her parents had not approved of her decision to marry, and my mother was too proud to return to their lodge."

He nodded. She believed Night Storm understood such pride quite well.

"It was not until after she left her husband that I was born. My father, Falling Otter, could not marry my mother because he is heyoka and must do the opposite. I remember a man came to my mother's lodge. He played the flute but my mother would not listen. Our shaman's wife, Starlight Woman, taught my mother how to quill so she could support us."

"She was talented," he said.

"Yes. When my grandmother grew weak, she joined us in my mother's lodge."

"Your mother's mother?"

"No. This was Falling Otter's mother. Also the mother of my aunt, Winter Moon. We lived beside my grandmother at every camp. We all worked hard. My uncle, Wood Duck, brought us meat. My grandmother taught me much about healing plants and many came to her for cures, but she left us in my sixteenth winter. When I reached my seventieth winter my mother grew ill. I tried, but I could not save her, either."

"So you moved in with your father's sister?"

"After a time. I had my mother's lodge, but my auntie did not approve. She said I was getting too thin and asked me to join her in their lodge."

This was what she must return to? A life with her aunt and uncle? Why had she not married? Surely others could see her beauty and her skill.

He waited for her to say more, but she did not. Frost finished his meal and returned to them, sitting beside Storm and panting with what seemed a wide grin on his face. Skylark was studying his dog again.

When she lifted her gaze to him, she must have read his question on his face.

"Frost has not been walking with you."

"He often dashes off after game," he said.

"But not the day you found me."

He cocked his head, wondering what direction her thoughts took.

"Or the night of the storm. Those days he walked so close he nearly trod on your foot."

That was so.

"What about the day of the sun dance?"

"I do not know. The dogs wander here and there."

"Think," she insisted.

He did. He recalled blowing his whistle and the sound of the drums. Had Frost been howling? He thought he recalled his sister saying so.

"Fills a Kettle said something about him." Storm had collapsed and had to be carried from the sacred circle. When he woke he remembered the dog. "Frost was with me when I woke, lying right beside me. My sister said he had to be tied during the ceremony because he kept charging into the circle."

"That is because your dog knows when you are going to fall."

# Chapter Nine

It had taken some convincing, but Sky thought Night Storm now believed her. Frost knew when he would fall. She did not understand it, but there were just too many signs for this to be chance.

"That means you might be able to ride again," she said.

Sky had dismounted to stretch her legs and so the horses could drink in a stream that was a short distance from his village.

"Ride?" The hope in his expression made her heart squeeze in joy. Clearly riding was important to every man. But for Storm, it seemed a mark of who he was.

"Yes. If you keep Frost close and pay attention to him, then you might be safe. If he starts to bark at you instead of at game, or if he howls or whines for no reason, you must not shush him. Get off your horse and lie on your side. Prop your back against a tree."

"I might still choke."

She knew that was so.

"Then take me with you."

He scoffed. "A man does not hunt with a woman."

"But I am your new wife. It is natural for us to want to be alone."

His brow quirked in speculation and her face went hot with the brightness of his gaze.

"Perhaps."

"And you could say that I am a healer, that I need to collect medicines and you do not wish me to go by myself."

"You could go with other women."

"I have tried that. I walk all day over rough ground. They cannot keep up."

He was staring at her legs now.

"What?" she asked.

"It explains why your legs are so strong."

She felt self-conscious. "Is that a bad thing?"

"I like a strong woman and I like your legs."

Now even her ears felt hot. Why had she asked? Everything he said, every look he cast her, seemed to make her skin heat and her muscles thrum. Even her fingers tingled with the desire to touch him. But she could not. He wanted her and he needed her. But he did not love her. She must remember that.

"Your face is pink," he said.

She placed her hands on her hips and he laughed.

"So fierce," he said, and then stroked her cheek with one knuckle. "My fierce, strong wife. Come, we are nearly home."

Without asking her permission, he took hold of her waist and swung her up onto his saddle. Then he leaped up behind her. His chest pressed to her back as he took up the reins and her bottom molded against the fold of his waist. It took all her restraint not to sag back against the firm, muscular body that enfolded her. She breathed in his masculine scent and found he smelled of smoked leather and sage. Then she glanced at Frost, who watched with an alert curiosity but no concern.

Night Storm pressed his heels into his horse's sides and set them in motion. She heard him draw a breath and sigh, as if this was finally where he wanted to be.

Was she right? Was it safe for him to ride?

"Your body is trembling," he said, his words coming with a warm breath that brushed her ear.

"I am worried that I am wrong. What if Frost does not know when you will fall?"

"Then you will have to catch me." He chuckled at that and they said no more.

Shortly, they splashed across the stream and

into a wide-open bank of an unfamiliar river.
Before them stretched the tribe's herd of horses.
The herd grazed with slow determination, tugging hanks of yellowing grass as their tails swept
back and forth in constant motion, doing battle
with the ever-present biting flies. Here and there,
boys sat on horseback watching over the tribe's
herd. The village dogs spotted them first, raising
the alarm with loud barking that brought cries of
welcome from the young guardians. Several boys
urged their mounts forward to greet Night Storm.
He sent one tall boy back to the village to alert
his family of his approach.

Night Storm moved through the herd and
down the sandy bank to the curve in the river.
There the ground opened up to a wide grassy
plain and before them lay the village of the Black
Lodges. She looked out at the five hundred tepees, the conical tips of each smoked black. It
was from this heavy smoke color that the tribe
had derived its name while her tribe, the Low
River tribe, received its name from their favored
camping sites.

She forced a smile as she saw the people moving leisurely between the lodges that each had the
distinctive blackened peaks of heavily smoked
leather. Judging by the thoroughly smoked top
portions of the buffalo lodges, she could tell

his tribe kept their lodges for several seasons. This black smoked portion of the lodge was very prized, she knew, for it was completely water-proof. When her auntie recently made a new lodge, she had cut Skylark's uncle a fine hunting shirt from the very top portion of hide.

As they drew closer, she did lean against him because the nervousness in her stomach had trav-eled to her lungs.

"You are trembling again," he whispered.

"What if your mother and sisters all hate me?"

He chuckled as if this were some joke. "Pretend they are owls and shake a stick at them."

She elbowed him in the ribs. "Do not joke. I want to make a good impression."

But why? So she could later disappoint them with her leave-taking?

Night Storm gave her a reassuring squeeze as if she were really his wife. "My mother has been after me to wed for three winters."

"But what if she finds out? What if she knows what we have done?"

"Now you sound like a nervous bride. Where is my strong medicine woman who can walk all day and sleep alone in the forest while the wolves circle her tree?"

"I think you left her back around that last turn."

He squeezed her arm. "I have said I will protect you, and so I shall, from everyone and everything."

Did that include Beautiful Meadow, she wondered.

"Lift your chin and sit tall. You are the wife of a warrior of the Black Lodges."

She shivered in the sunlight, and he tightened his arms about her as if to fortify her with his body.

Now in the Hunting Moon, the water slowed and the evenings turned crisp. The sunlight seemed deeper and colder, but most of the leaves were still green. She glanced about seeing a touch of red here and yellow there. Soon the War Moon would come and the trees would blaze with golden hues, like a fire just before the wood burns out.

As they neared the closest lodges, Skylark noted the women carrying loads of wood and water as they moved in groups on the opposite side of the river. They paused to look as she and Night Storm splashed across the wide, shallow stretch. She felt their stares fix upon her and tried her best to look calm and composed. But, actually, her heart pounded inside her chest as loudly as a charging herd of buffalo, and her face felt hot as a stone lying in the summer sun.

Which one was Beautiful Meadow?

He leaned close. "You are squirming like a babe with a wet breechclout."

She forced herself to stillness. "I have never been a wife and, anyway, a husband comes to his wife's tribe. You should come to my home."

It would keep her from Beautiful Meadow until the gathering. Why hadn't she thought to ask him to come to her tribe? But she had. He'd said he had to hunt for a widow here. If he could hunt, she thought.

"We are visiting here until the gathering, or that is what I will tell them. Besides, you have no reason to fret. You are pretty and smart and useful. My family will love you."

"Your mother?"

The hesitation did nothing to convince her. "Of course."

"I forgot their names."

"Why are you so concerned? It is only temporary."

That was right. She remembered that, but her stomach did not, for it twisted tight.

"I think I might throw up," she muttered.

"At least you do not have to worry about falling off your horse in front of everyone."

She gasped at that and her gaze shot to Frost, who trotted happily along at their heels as they cleared the river and moved onto the wide, muddy bank. A woman came toward them.

"Is that Beautiful Meadow?" she asked.

"No. I do not see her, yet." His words held a definite edge and she knew he dreaded this meeting as she did. "That is my sister. Smile."

Skylark forced a smile that felt tight and unnatural. Night Storm swung down from the saddle and then lifted Skylark to the ground beside him.

His sister was a tall woman who seemed about Skylark's age, but with eyes the same shape as Night Storm. She halted and lowered her burden of wood.

"Brother, welcome home."

Her dress was lovely, with fine beading across the yoke and fringe that had been twisted so that the strands curled like the tail of a buffalo. She had stained the bottom of her dress yellow. His sister approached her brother as Frost danced about her in pure joy.

She touched foreheads with her brother as she clasped his shoulders. Then she stepped back and turned her smile toward Skylark.

"And who is this?" she asked.

Night Storm took Skylark's hand and tugged her forward. "Bright Shawl, meet Skylark of the Low River tribe. She is my wife."

That announcement caused gasps from some and titters from others.

"Well, this is a surprise," said Bright Shawl. "Let me be the first to welcome you to our family." She quickly touched foreheads with Skylark and then motioned to the woman beside her. "This is my good friend, Many Blessings."

"Yes," said the woman at his sister's side. "And your husband has just broken my heart."

"Would you like me to bring Skylark to your lodge, brother?" asked Bright Shawl.

"I will bring her. Where are Mother and Father?"

"Mother is tanning a hide before our lodge. Father, I do not know."

Night Storm lifted the reins and set the two horses in motion. She wanted to ask Night Storm who that was, but before she could ask she saw a woman charging forward with her chin lowered and her hands gripped in fists.

"Beautiful Meadow," she whispered, certain she was right. Skylark sank behind Storm's body as the woman came at them straight as an arrow released from the bow.

The woman was taller than Sky and heavier. In a fight, Skylark thought she would lose. And this woman looked ready to fight. She stared at Sky now, pinning her with her eyes just like a hawk choosing its victim.

"Storm?" she whispered. Skylark had been in a few fights with other women but none had such a red face or dangerously glittering eyes.

Beautiful Meadow was certainly better dressed in a two-elk dress that was stained a becoming green at the bottom and had an expert band of green-and-white beading across the yoke. Her moccasins lifted dust as she stomped forward.

"Beautiful Meadow, we were just coming to find you."

Sky's gaze flicked from her adversary to the other women hurrying along to catch up with Beautiful Meadow and witness the entertainment that was certain to follow.

"Is it true?" she screeched.

"I would like to introduce you—"

She interrupted, fairly shouting. "Is it true? Have you taken this scrawny little nobody as your wife?"

Storm lowered his chin. "It is true."

She flapped her arms. "But you are promised to me!"

"It is a promise I will keep."

Beautiful Meadow gave him her back. "I was to be your first wife." She rounded on Sky, aiming a finger at her. "You are a thief."

"I am not."

"No? You stole my husband. You don't look like an elk to me." Her gaze lifted to Night Storm. "Isn't that what you told me? Where you said you were going day after day? To hunt elk. Yet you bring home nothing until today. You were hunting. But not for meat."

"Beautiful Meadow, you do not raise your voice to me," said Storm.

His fiancée's mouth dropped open and she sputtered. "I am going to tell my uncle of this. I think that woman has bewitched you."

Sky's throat went dry. This was worse even than she had imagined. Her uncle was the shaman. He had a great deal of power.

Beautiful Meadow aimed a finger at her. "I am not done with you. If you are wise you will set his things outside tonight and go back where you came from." If Sky set out his belongings, it would signal to all that their marriage had ended.

Storm took hold of Skylark's arm and drew her past Beautiful Meadow, who spit at her. The warm spittle struck her in the neck and oozed down below the collar of her dress. Sky pressed a hand over the spot and lowered her head. She let her husband lead her past the gawking women and the rows of tepees. She looked at the ground as he continued on and on, the shame burning deep inside her. All the while she struggled with tears.

What had she done?

# *Chapter Ten*

Storm did not stop and she did not succeed in keeping the tears from rolling down her face as they continued toward his lodge. Gradually she was able to lift her head.

"She hates me," said Sky.

"She needs time to get used to the idea that she will not be my only wife."

"You cannot marry her while I am here."

"Yes. I know. I will speak to her later."

They meandered through the series of lodges, some decorated with bright paintings, some patched and old, and others so new the hide at the peak had barely time to turn smoke-black.

Just as in her village, there was no set location for a lodge. The chief's wife set her lodge and then the council of elders chose a place in close proximity for the council lodge. Important men, such as the shaman, also camped close to the chief. But, after that, the village grew outward in all directions so that none had to walk too far to fetch water.

Night Storm drew up beside a small lodge of perhaps four buffalo skins.

"This is my lodge." Then he pointed to the larger one beside his. "This one is my parents', Red Corn Woman and Many Coups. Both my sisters, Bright Shawl and Fills a Kettle, are unmarried, though both are now women."

Which meant they lived with their parents and likely had suitors.

"My brother, Iron Axe married a woman from the Wind Basin tribe last gathering. My brother came to visit before my injury to say he already has a son called Firefly."

"That is a great blessing."

"He said Little Rain was very strong and needed no help birthing their child."

She wanted a child. Her gaze flashed to Night Storm and then away. Did she have the courage to go to his sleeping robes, knowing she must let him go?

"What?" he asked in response to her impolite stare.

"I was thinking of the plants I must collect." She looked away and began doing just that to take her mind to a different problem and one that she had some hope of solving. She was here to help him. That was all. She mentally made note of all the plants she must collect to help him as she shifted her gathering bag from her shoulder. Some of the ones she needed she already had on hand. But how did she know what other ones he needed? He went a full moon between his first and second falls. Could the moon trigger a fall? But there had been no moon last night. This was the most difficult problem she had ever faced because he was only occasionally ill.

Night Storm staked his horses and removed the saddle blanket from his chestnut as she unloaded the packhorse. She might be a new wife, but she knew her responsibilities. This night, she would likely not be preparing a meal unless perhaps her husband's mother expected to be served as a test of her skill.

Sky gripped her collecting bag close as a child clutches her doll.

Her breathing caught for, though she was excellent at foraging, she was less than adequate at preparing meals.

"You seem rooted as a tree," said Night Storm. He pried the folded rawhide parfleche container from her fingers, bringing her back to herself.

"This was a mistake."

He lowered his chin and gave her a hard look. "Sky. You promised me you would try."

She nodded. "Yes, but I am not a very good cook."

His brows lifted. "Most new husbands are not concerned with such things."

His smile faded, and his long look made her feel more inadequate. Her throat began to burn and ache. She swallowed at the lump forming there.

"My mother is a very good cook," he said. "She can teach you."

"No!" She had not meant to shout, but to have his mother teach her would be humiliating.

He frowned. A wife did not yell at her husband, especially in public.

She dipped her head in shame. "I am sorry."

He nodded his acceptance.

When he spoke she heard no hint of annoyance. "Bring that buffalo robe into the lodge."

Skylark was happy to do so and have a moment alone. She lifted the door flap, leaving it open and resting on the lodge's outer surface. Then she dipped to step into the circular opening. Inside she found a central fire pit surrounded by one buffalo robe. The second was in her arms. Extra weapons hung from pegs on the lodge poles and there was a tall stack of furs. Mostly beaver, she saw, but also wolf, fox and one that was quite obviously a puma. She had only seen one such hide before, but she recalled it well. This cat must have been at least fifteen hands long. What concerned her, as she turned about, was not what she saw, but what she did not see. There was an absence of containers for food. Also absent were the tools of a woman's lodge. There were no bladders for gathering water, no awls or tanned buckskins waiting to transform into clothing. No cooking pot. No strings of dry Timpsula tubers hanging in ropes or coiled like a lariat.

What would they do for food? It was late in the season to begin digging for roots and tubers.

Night Storm ducked through the opening and stood before her. She stared at him in horror.

"You are not pleased?"

"What will we eat?"

"My mother feeds me."

"But she will not feed your wife. She will expect *me* to feed you, as I should."

He set aside the pack frame and then nestled his fists on his hips and looked about as if the stored food might appear if he waited long enough.

"I was not expecting a wife."

She threw up her hands at this.

"Hello!" A woman's voice came from outside the lodge. Since the flap was open, their guest entered, because an open flap door was an invitation to visitors.

Skylark spun and watched an older woman glide through the entrance. Her motions reminded Skylark of Night Storm's. When she straightened, her smile changed to one of astonishment as she set eyes on Skylark.

"Who is this then?" she asked.

"Mother, this is my wife, Skylark of the Low River people."

Her mother pressed a hand to her heart and took one retreating step. Skylark noticed that her face was dark and round, with few wrinkles. Her hair had one distinctive strand of white that she had braided along with the rest, the white road weaving in and out of the rope of black.

"Wife?" The shock was gradually disappearing, changing to curiosity. She inched closer, her brows lifted. She did not look very much like her son, except around the jaw. They had the same square chin.

"Yes. My wife. We have come to visit until the gathering," said Night Storm.

"But I thought… What of Beautiful Meadow?"

"We met her on the way in. I have to go speak to her."

His mother stared at him with an owlish expression, the tension clear in the lines that flanked her face.

"I am certain she is upset. This will not be a welcome surprise to her. Son, most men have their wife's consent before they take another."

"Beautiful Meadow is not yet my wife."

"True, but she is your intended and, though her uncle, Thunder Horse, has joined our tribe through marriage, her mother and father are Wind Basin people. I am certain she intended to return there with her husband."

Night Storm gritted his teeth, following his mother's words and knowing where this trail would lead.

His mother held his gaze. "You have chosen two women from different tribes. So once you have wed Beautiful Meadow, will you live with the Low River people or Beautiful Meadow's family in the Wind Basin tribe?"

Night Storm stood silent. Clearly he had not anticipated this problem, either. A husband went to his wife's tribe. Generally a second wife was from the same tribe and often his first wife hand-picked this woman. She might be her sister, if her sister's husband died. Or a dear friend. She was not a stranger from a different tribe.

Skylark's eyes widened as they flicked from

mother to son. Her heart hammered so loudly she could barely hear Night Storm's reply.

"We have not decided. But Beautiful Meadow will go where I go," he said at last.

His mother stroked her chin between a thumb and index finger.

"Perhaps." His mother studied them.

Storm lifted one arm, hesitated and then set it awkwardly on Skylark's shoulder. The weight of that self-conscious embrace, combined with his mother's confused stare, made her wish she could sink through the dried yellow grass and slip under the lodge hide like a snake.

His mother came forward, her body slim and muscular, her grip firm as she took hold of Skylark by each shoulder and leaned forward to touch foreheads.

"Welcome, Skylark of the Low River people. Welcome to our family." Her voice was warm and her embrace seemed genuine. Skylark felt worse than if she had received the cold welcome she had expected.

His mother released her and turned to her son, who was speaking again.

"Skylark, this is my mother, Red Corn Woman."

His mother had her finger up, wagging it at her son as a grin lifted her features and deepened the crow's-feet at the corners of her eyes.

"Now I see. Hunting alone." She gave a snort. "Hunting, you said. Hunting for another wife!"

Night Storm's brow wrinkled at his mother's words as if he did not understand.

"You had me so worried. You stopped seeing your friends, you stopped scouting. You barely saw Beautiful Meadow. And, as for hunting, you brought little back to fill my kettle." She laughed. "To think I almost asked your sisters to follow you."

Night Storm's eyes widened, and he and Sky exchanged an uneasy glance before he returned his attention to his mother. His mother had recognized that something was wrong with her son, of course. Skylark was not surprised. Mothers always knew such things.

"Well, you were so preoccupied you barely ate and were not yourself. Even your father noticed, and Great Spirit bless him, he doesn't notice anything unless it happens in the council lodge or under our buffalo robes."

"Mother!"

"Well? You have a wife now. Such doings should be more familiar to you." She threw her arms up and actually twirled in a circle. Then she came to an abrupt halt.

"Oh, my. When you spoke to Beautiful Meadow, she did not set you aside?"

"No. But she…was very angry."

Sky touched the place where the spit had landed and then moved her hand down to cover her heart. Beneath her palm a pain shot across her chest. Night Storm might lose his intended because of her. He had said he would not marry Beautiful Meadow until he was well, but she might no longer wish to marry him.

His mother snorted. "I know her well enough to know she will not be pleased. I would suspect she will go to her uncle. I would anticipate a visit from him."

Sky gasped. Storm stiffened.

Red Corn Woman looked from her son's grim expression to Skylark's owlish one. She shook her head in bewilderment.

"Well," said Red Corn Woman. "I seem to have dropped a bug into the soup." She took Skylark's hand. "Please join us for supper tonight. It will be so lovely to have all three of my daughters about the same fire."

Skylark thought that Night Storm said he had only two sisters and then she realized that Red Corn Woman already included her among her inner circle. Just like that. A string of words, a lie, and she was wed to a warrior of the Black Lodges and a member of this stranger's family.

Skylark felt the terrible power of what she had

done, sliding like snow from a high peak, gaining speed until it obliterated all that fell before it. The foreboding chilled her and she wrapped her arms about herself. Night Storm moved up beside her, draping an arm proprietarily about her shoulders.

"We will be there," he promised.

His mother stepped through the opening of her son's lodge and closed the door flap, assuring their privacy. At least from prying eyes. But sound carried, so Sky must be careful with her words.

Her knees gave way and he caught her easily, guiding her down to the buffalo robe beside the cold fire pit.

"I had no idea she would be so thrilled," muttered Night Storm.

"What have we done?"

# *Chapter Eleven*

Skylark suffered through supper in Red Corn Woman's lodge, flanked by Bright Shawl and Fills a Kettle, who looked much more like Night Storm. Their father, Many Coups, was a warrior of the first order. Tall, strong and imposing, Sky knew from Night Storm that his father sat on the council of elders for the Black Lodges and headed the Black War Bonnet society. Now she discovered from Red Corn Woman that he had served many years as head man on the buffalo hunts and was now War Chief. He had distinguished himself against the Sioux and also the Blackfeet tribes. There was no doubt where Storm got his ambition to follow the way of the warrior. It was clear to her that Night Storm wanted to earn coup feathers and serve his people just like his father. But she thought of owls and wondered if his way might lead in another direction.

Red Corn Woman asked her many questions. When she discovered Skylark's talent with healing, she consulted her on various conditions, comparing what Skylark said to what she knew. It was the only time Skylark felt comfortable, briefly, until she began to worry that she was making a bad impression, with her many opinions of the uses of plants. But then she remembered that it would not matter because this match was predestined to fail. That realization freed her somewhat, until she also recalled that she would likely meet members of the Black Lodges after the marriage was broken. That thought saddened her because she liked Red Corn Woman.

As she stared about the circle of faces, she felt an unexpected longing for such a family. To have two sisters, a mother, a father—it was a fantasy she had held. This was so different than her life. Her aunt and uncle had no children and so would depend on her in their older years. It was an obligation of all daughters to look after their parents. And her husband must provide meat for his wife's family if an aging father could no longer hunt. Looking at Many Coups, she could not even imagine that ever occurring. But what of Wood Duck and Winter Moon? Would Sky's cures provide enough food for them when they could no longer see to their own needs? She glanced to

Night Storm, suddenly afraid of the burden that waited for her to carry alone. It would be easier if she had a husband, someone like Night Storm.

Red Corn Woman broke the gathering early, sending Skylark and her son to their lodge like children sent to bed. It was clear from her parting comments that she was hopeful to have another grandchild, which she was looking to her second son to provide. That seemed unlikely, as she and Night Storm now sat on opposite sides of the fire in his small lodge.

She thought of last night's storm, when she had slept beside him, safe and warm and happy. A person did not recognize unhappiness unless it was set against such a moment of perfect contentment. It brought to light all that she had missed and all she would likely never have. Because of her flaws and odd ways. Night Storm was best clear of her, she told herself, even as she stared out at him across the divide.

"Husband?" she asked. She told herself she used this title in case others listened. But really she liked the sound on her tongue.

"Yes."

"Your father is very…imposing."

"He has more coups than men much his senior," said Storm. "Should he wish it, I would expect him to be chief one day."

The silence stretched. Was he thinking of his father or his condition?

"My brother, Iron Axe, has earned many coups with his new tribe." He made a sound in his throat. "I have earned none since I fell."

How strange that a fall brought on his falling sickness. She told herself that it must be a sickness, because if it were not she could do nothing for him and all his efforts, even this sham of a marriage, were for nothing.

"Tomorrow we will begin searching for the plants to cure you."

Beautiful Meadow's words rose in her mind. She had told Sky to set out his things, publicly break the marriage. That would help smooth Beautiful Meadow's ruffled feathers. But she would be disappointed. Sky would not be setting Storm's things out from his own lodge.

He gave a long release of breath. She wanted to assure him that soon he would again defend his people and provide for his family. But what if he could not?

Sky wished she could creep across the distance that separated them and offer the comfort of her body. She wished she could experience the pleasure of sharing the night with this man. He was her husband until the winter camp. She was entitled to share his bed. He had promised he would not take her unless she wished. Should she take what he would give? Her pride kept her in place.

He didn't love her. They had made a bargain. That was all.

Would her father laugh at the predicament she was in or cry because it was funny?

Here, in the circle of this fire was everything she had ever thought she wanted. A strong man, a home, a family. All she ever dreamed of was here, and in one moon she would speak the words to release him and walk away.

There was a screeching sound from outside the lodge. Frost shot to his feet and growled. Sky clutched her chest thinking it was another owl. But then she heard the words in the screeching cry.

"Night Storm. Come out and face me."

She looked to Storm, who suddenly looked less brave, and she knew who called to him.

"Beautiful Meadow?" she asked.

Storm nodded and rose to his feet.

Night Storm ducked out of his lodge to meet the woman he had asked to be his wife.

"I do not see your things before this lodge," said Beautiful Meadow.

"You must trust me," said Storm. He was fully

aware that his parents, sisters and Sky could hear every word.

"Trust? You left on a hunt and returned with a wife. My uncle wishes to see you and your new wife. He thinks your fall has damaged your mind and that you are not well enough to marry."

"I am well enough."

She stepped closer and pointed at his lodge. "It should be me inside that lodge."

"You wanted your family from Wind Basin about you for the ceremony."

"And you could not wait two moons?"

He shook his head. "I could not."

"You said you were unwell, but you are well enough to take another. All this was a lie."

"It was not a lie. I love you. I will marry you at the gathering. And I will explain all to you then."

She glared, her fists stiff at her sides.

"If you love me you will give me until the gathering," he said.

"Is she going back to her people then?"

"I do not know." What did Sky think of that answer? He knew that their arrangement was for two moons, but some part of him already wanted her to stay. He just needed for Beautiful Meadow and Skylark to become friends.

"Would you like to meet her?" asked Night Storm.

"I did not bring my skinning knife."

Storm smiled and Beautiful Meadow did not. But her eyes now fixed on the closed flap of his lodge.

"Bring her out. I would speak again to the first wife of the warrior who promised to make me his first wife."

"I made no such promise."

Beautiful Meadow now turned aside and faced his lodge.

"Come out, Low River woman."

The flap lifted and thumped against the side of the lodge. Storm knew Sky was very good at gathering medicine and hiding from wolves and chasing after her father. He did not think she was prepared for a fight with Beautiful Meadow. In truth, he had never before seen Beautiful Meadow's temper and her tirade embarrassed him. He thought of his father sitting in his lodge shaking his head in disappointment.

Sky ducked out of the opening in the hide and stood, hands clasped upon her drab buckskin dress, her hair braided but unadorned. In fact, her only embellishments were her quilled moccasins, the sheath of her knife and the strand of white beads about her neck.

Beautiful Meadow, on the other hand, wore a finely made dress with many teeth upon the yoke.

She had multiple strands of beads about her neck, many of which Storm had given her. Her hair was glossed with grease and adorned with extensions of mink to make her braids seem to reach her waist. But her face was twisted in an ugly expression and the vessels at her neck bulged, making her face the color of a cherry.

Beautiful Meadow stalked forward, and Storm prepared to pull them apart.

"You little thief,"

"I am no thief," said Sky.

"Sorceress, then."

This insult held a hint of danger because of Sky's ability to heal and Beautiful Meadow's uncle being the shaman.

Beautiful Meadow turned to Storm. "She is plain as dirt."

"Then I offer no competition to you," said Sky.

Beautiful Meadow's head snapped back toward Sky and her eyes narrowed. She stooped to lift a stick from the firewood and raised it over her head.

Storm easily plucked the weapon from her hands.

"You will not strike my wife," he said.

Red Corn Woman stepped from her lodge and Beautiful Meadow turned to her.

"Do you see what he has done? He has made me the laughingstock of your entire tribe."

Red Corn Woman draped an arm about Beautiful Meadow's shoulders and steered her away from Sky and Storm. "But you are a strong woman. You must keep your head up. Such behavior as this does you no credit."

Beautiful Meadow glanced back at Sky. "I hate her. She will never be my sister."

"That will make for an unhappy home and an unhappy husband."

"I should break our engagement."

Red Corn Woman spoke in a voice filled with authority and calm. "That is your right. But perhaps you should think on this. I do not like to brag, but my son is very accomplished and has a bright future. He will serve his people well and his wives will be greatly respected. Of course, if you choose to go back to your people, we will understand."

Beautiful Meadow pulled away and looked back at Sky and Storm.

"I am not going back to my people. She is." Beautiful Meadow dashed away.

Red Corn Woman returned to her son. "You did not even tell her of this other woman?"

The next day did not go as planned. Skylark and Night Storm did manage to go foraging, which caused some good-natured kidding

among the young men of his circle. None believed
he trailed his new wife into the forest in order to
pluck flowers and dig roots. Unfortunately, all he
did was dig roots.

When they returned, it was to sly looks from
the men and tittering laughter from the women.
They received congratulations from so many people she was dizzy with it and wanted to turn right
back to the woods for some solitude.

"They want my father's favor," said Night
Storm. "That is why they offer blessings."

"Or they want your favor."

"Mine? I am no one anymore."

His words hurt her.

"You are and you will be again. Come, let's
make medicine."

Back at his lodge she set to work and he patiently drank the tea she made. He said it made
his stomach rumble, but he had no ill effects. She
had not anticipated Red Corn Woman's pride in
her new daughter would cause news of her healing skills to travel so quickly about the camp, but
before Skylark had time to put away the medicine
she had brewed there was an old woman before
her with stiff hand joints. Skylark made her a
salve with peppermint and wild ginger, then sent
her off. Next came a young mother with a child
who had a dry cough.

She treated poison oak and hornet stings, dry, scaling skin and itching feet. She treated cramps that come when a woman breaks her link with the moon, women with sore nipples from feeding their babies, stomach troubles, breathing troubles and one child with eyes running with pus.

Night Storm went to see Beautiful Meadow and her uncle Thunder Horse, and returned scowling.

Gradually over the next several days, women came for their men, who would not seek the advice of a woman but sent their wives and mothers to do just that. She had so much work that Red Corn Woman set her youngest daughter to help her create her cures and learn all she could. Fills a Kettle was bright and learned quickly, but she was so eager to learn that she asked to come along on the foraging trips with her brother, and Sky was running out of excuses.

The morning of the waning quarter moon, Sky peeled the outer skin of the large burdock roots she had discovered the previous day and Storm sipped his tea.

"Beautiful Meadow wishes for me to ask your permission to come with us today."

Skylark groaned. "She'll likely slit my throat when we are alone."

"She says she wants to learn where to find the

medicine plants and how to identify them and thought if I asked, you might allow her to come."

"Has she ever shown an interest in healing?"

"In truth she is most interested in beads and sewing."

"For herself?"

"Well, so far she has only needed to sew for herself."

Sky managed to keep from rolling her eyes.

"Do you think that is wise?" What if he had a spell before them?

"How would you have learned if no one showed you? Besides, she has made a gesture, a first step. Skylark, when you are gone, she will be my wife."

That comment hit home and lodged like a thorn. Why did it hurt so much when he spoke no more than the truth?

"Or you could stay," he said.

"I will not be a second wife. Or a first wife." Sky had seen more than a few families with two or more wives. Most women in this circumstance were not happy and some wives were miserable. Her mother had chosen to live alone rather than be a second wife. Sky had taken her advice to heart. To have a husband would be wonderful. But it was preferable to be alone than to watch your husband crawl from one sleeping robe to the other. In addition the thought of sharing a lodge with Beautiful Meadow gave her the shivers. She might become more like her father and stay out all night just to avoid being in the same tepee with her.

"I will go at the gathering," she said.

"More reason to let Beautiful Meadow come along."

It was a mistake. She felt it in her heart, but still she nodded her acceptance.

"All right then. If you wish it," said Sky.

"She has found three other women who wish to join you."

Sky's hands stilled as she considered the implications of this request. Three women, friends of Beautiful Meadow, and Skylark. She did not like those odds.

"What do you suggest?" she asked, turning the slippery root in one hand and the skinning knife in the other.

"There is no sign of enemies in our territory. So, they should come," he said. "But I should not. My friends have stopped teasing and begun to give me odd looks once more. They know something is wrong. It is nearly the War Moon. They are eager to raid the Sioux camps and take all the horses they can find."

He did not say the rest. But she knew. He wanted to go, too. He wanted to gallop along with his fellows, take her back to the Low River people and make amends with Beautiful Meadow by bringing her many horses. She felt the pain in her chest bubble up inside her until she could barely breathe. Their eyes met. Why did this man have to be promised to another?

Because he was one of the most eligible men among his tribe. Of course he had women to choose from and he had picked the prettiest, most accomplished woman of the Wind Basin people. One with a powerful uncle and a warrior father who could help him rise among his new tribe. She also had a temper to rival a wolverine's.

What did she have? A heyoka father with much power and no power. A lodge she shared with her aunt and uncle and a bag of healing herbs. If they had met first, she knew that Storm would not have chosen her.

"We will talk about the raid this evening."

"I have had no further falls."

"Perhaps the tea is working."

"I could test this cure."

"How?" she asked.

He motioned toward his bow. She felt the fingers of fear grip her heart. When had his welfare become more than part of their bargain? She swallowed back her dread because the hope in his eyes made her hesitate from giving her denial. A man should not have to wait for permission to ride.

"I could go for a hunt with the others."

She nodded, ignoring the tugging in her middle. "Keep Frost with you. Watch him carefully."

His eyes twinkled with excitement as he dropped the pestle he had used to grind leaves to pulp and lifted his bow.

"If your dog barks at you, howls or even whines, then you must leave the others—"

"Yes. I know. Find a tree."

If he had time, she thought, as unease crept over her like a thick mist. He stood, looking taller suddenly and more alive.

Storm slung the bow over his back and Frost leaped to his hind legs, then spun in a jubilant circle. She watched them dance, Storm holding Frost's front paws. Finally he released his dog, that dropped back to all fours. Storm reached for her. Before she could protest he had her up and in his arms. He spun her in a circle so fast that her legs lifted up behind her. She feared she might overturn the tripod that held the cooking kettle Storm's mother had given her.

Finally he set her back down, but then hugged her again until they were both laughing and Frost barked. They drew apart instantly and stared at the dog. Frost sat down and stared back, his tongue lolling. It was enough to remind them both of the danger.

"He seems all right," said Storm.

"So do you," she replied.

He blew away a long breath and she worried her lower lip, regretting encouraging him to go. She waited as he gathered his hunting things and then walked with him, carrying the buffalo bladders she would fill by the stream. At the river, she hugged him and they touched foreheads. She had meant the gesture only for show, but found her emotions genuine as she wished him luck and worried over him as he took his leave. Frost trotted after his master. She stared after them until they were out of sight.

"Keep watch over him, boy," she whispered. When she could no longer see him, she resumed her duties, filling the bladders and returning to her tepee to discover Beautiful Meadow waiting with four women. One was familiar. Storm's sister, Fills a Kettle, greeted her wearing a freshly made carrying bag that looked remarkably like hers, except Fills a Kettle had died the buckskin of her bag an appealing dark green.

"My brother told me you were collecting medicine and invited me along," said his sister.

Sky's mouth quirked. Had Storm sent his sister as protection against trouble from Beautiful Meadow and her friends?

"You are welcome, of course."

They set off on the journey to the wooded area. Sky did her best to identify the plants and their uses to her companions. Fills a Kettle gathered many things, but Beautiful Meadow seemed more interested in asking questions.

Over the journey she discovered all about Sky's mother, her aunt and uncle and her father, Falling Otter. Sky was more exhausted from talking than from gathering. At last Beautiful Meadow left her to speak with her friends who also did not gather anything but food.

"She is making trouble for you," said Fills a Kettle. "You should send her away and don't answer any more of her questions. I am sure that she is up to something."

Sky lifted her chin, feigning a confidence she did not feel. "My husband loves me. She can do nothing to me."

"She has a tongue like a whip," said Fills a Kettle. "I do not trust her. I am even wondering if my brother should reconsider his offer to wed her."

"He cannot break his promise."

"Yes. That is so and why I believed that he brought you home to make Beautiful Meadow break the engagement. Instead, she seems to plan to send you back to your people."

Sky thought she could save her the trouble. But Beautiful Meadow's efforts might give Sky the easy excuse she would need to leave Storm at the gathering.

"I hope she does not involve her uncle in this. Thunder Horse is a fearsome shaman. I know some who prefer to take their chances than to call him to their lodge."

"But why?" asked Sky. Their shaman, Spirit Bear, was kind and very powerful. He had visions that helped him know what the people should do and his words were very respected among the tribal council.

Sky had looked forward to meeting the shaman, Thunder Horse, but now that she knew he was the uncle of Beautiful Meadow, she was much less anxious.

Throughout the afternoon Sky pointed out various useful plants to Fills a Kettle as the other three women trailed behind them, collecting roots and firewood. Sky thought she should be listening to their words. Their harsh laughter was clear enough.

But her mind was on Night Storm. Was he all right? Had he fallen again? She was so worried that he might need her. But she couldn't very well go chasing after a hunting party.

Before the sun had reached the treetops, she led them back to the camp of the Black Lodges. Beautiful Meadow said the she did not like digging in the roots of trees like a wild pig and disliked dirt under her fingernails. But she said it was a job that suited Sky, since she was already low to the ground.

"Maybe your mother should have named you Dirt, instead of Sky."

Her friends tittered at the jab. So much for becoming friends, thought Skylark.

"Thank you for keeping me company, Beautiful Meadow."

She snorted. "There is still time to set out his things before he returns."

"Good night," Sky said.

Fills a Kettle looped arms with her and Sky felt immensely grateful.

Fills a Kettle whispered to Sky, "I'm going to tell Storm how mean Beautiful Meadow is. It's lucky to learn this now, before she is his wife. That woman is insufferable."

"But he loves her. I heard him tell her so."

Fills a Kettle groaned. "Men can be so stupid."

Sky laughed and squeezed her new sister's arm. "Thank you for watching over me today."

They returned in time to help prepare a meal with Red Corn Woman, who showed Sky how to make her elk stew.

When Frost appeared at Red Corn Woman's tepee, Sky was on her feet and running toward the river where the warriors kept their horses.

# Chapter Twelve

Skylark found Night Storm dividing up an elk with the other men. She was so relieved she gave a little shout. Storm turned and had time to drop his steel knife before she leaped into his arms. He caught her easily and held her tight. It was only when she heard the men's laughter and bawdy comments that she recognized how forward her behavior really was. He grinned and set her on her feet. He leaned close and whispered in her ear, "You even convinced me that you are a new bride who is anxious for her husband's attentions."

She blinked and flushed. She had been so relieved to see him safe that she had let her emotions take over. She let her hands slip from around his neck.

"Are you all right?" she whispered.

He grinned and motioned to the bounty before

them. "I have brought you a fine elk skin. Since the Great Spirit blessed me with this kill."

She beamed with pride. Not only had he not fallen, he had taken an elk. As customary, a hunter shared with the tribe. Sky was so honored to be with him when he distributed generous portions to friends and family. He did not forget the old women who had none to hunt for them or the woman and child that he had been assigned to provide for by the chief. The task of hunting for those who had none to hunt for them would soon be reassigned. Now that he was married, that duty would be given to another unmarried man. She could understand why Broken Horn, the chief, had picked her husband to hunt for a family in need. He was a good provider.

She slowed as reality sank in. Soon she would give him up. If he was really and truly well, he would not even need her.

Instead of filling her with joy, that possibility filled her with despair. She did not find his company tiresome, as she did with many of the men of her acquaintance. In fact, she craved it. But how could she find a way to be a real wife to him without losing her heart before the gathering? He was clearly not willing to set Beautiful Meadow aside, and she would not share a lodge with a woman who hated her. Storm easily captured her elbow and righted her.

"My bird is not usually so distracted that she would fall from a tree," he teased, his smile making her stomach tighten and her breathing catch.

"I was thinking about Beautiful Meadow."

"Oh, how was your trip today? Are you two becoming friends?"

She could not hold the smile on her face and his brow wrinkled.

"Skylark, what did you do?"

"I tried. She does not like me."

"We will go see her together."

"No. I think you should go there alone."

"If you are sure."

Sky thought he looked taller. Then she realized it was the pride at fulfilling his purpose that lifted him up and filled his chest with the winds of life.

"You are a good husband to bring so much meat," she said.

It was easy to be the wife of such a man and if she was doing any pretending, it was pretending that her feelings for him were not becoming real. Sky recognized as he touched his forehead to hers that this game now threatened her heart. She was not so foolish as to let herself fall in love with him. She drew back as the longing warred with the knowledge that he had captured her to cure him, not to be his wife.

"I will meet you back at the lodge."

His frown grew deeper but he let her go. "I will see you soon."

But he was not home soon. She sat alone in her lodge and waited. Red Corn Woman called out to her to join them for their meal and she went.

As the sky grew dark and the sparks of the fire danced above the flames like fireflies, she glanced to those gathered around the circle. His father, Many Coups, rested on his seat back, his belly full as his daughters shared stories of the day. Members of the extended family had come to share her husband's kill and some of his pride shone on her as the wife of the one who had taken such a large elk.

But Storm's absence was there with them. He had stayed with Beautiful Meadow. Taken her meat and remained to feast with her, while leaving his new wife to his family. They did not understand and she could not explain that their joining was a lie, real only in her fantasies.

Finally Red Corn Woman called an end to the celebration, giving cooked meat to their guest to use in stews or eat cold the following day. Then the women stretched the skin on the large wooden frame, where it would remain until the morning, when they would gather again to clean the hide.

Sky touched foreheads with Red Corn Woman and wished the others good-night.

Inside their tepee, Sky sat upon her sleeping skin. She did not remember dozing, but she woke to the sound of murmured voices. A woman and a man. At first she had a fear that Storm had brought Beautiful Meadow back with him despite his promise to take only her for the two moons of their agreement. But then she recognized the voice of Red Corn Woman and Storm. At last the words fell to silence and Storm ducked inside the lodge with Frost. The dog found a place beside the dying fire and curled into a ball.

"Are you awake, wife?" he whispered.

"Yes."

"I just spoke to my mother. She says that our lodge was very quiet at night and asks if everything is all right with us between the buffalo robes?"

Sky's skin went hot at the news that his mother had been listening for sounds of their lovemaking in the night.

"That is not her business."

"I'm afraid it is. She has asked me to find out if you need instructions on your duties."

"Oh, no."

The idea of making grunting sounds and the shouts and cries she had heard coming from her aunt and uncle's robes made her stomach flip.

"What should we do?"

"I do not know. I could tell her you are very quiet. But when you break your link with the moon, she will know you do not carry my child."

Sky's hand went to her empty belly and the sorrow was so deep she hunched around it. Was that how he felt to have lost his way on the warrior's path? Empty and sad.

The Hunting Moon was waning and there was but one more moon until the gathering time. It was long enough to get with child. "Your mother will have to listen and wonder."

"Do you find me unappealing?" he asked.

She hesitated before speaking. "I do not."

"Then why will you not let me touch you? Why will you take no comfort from my body or let me take comfort from yours?"

She hesitated, debating her answer. The truth or some version of the truth. The trouble was that she did want him.

"Were you just with Beautiful Meadow?"

"Yes."

"Did you take her to your buffalo robes?"

"She is still chaste."

"So am I."

"And you wish to remain so for your real husband?"

She wished to sink into the ground and vanish beneath the buffalo robes.

"Until the winter camp, we said. And you would return me as a maiden."

"If you wish. But I would perform my duties with my wife. I am a good lover or so I have been told. Gentle and generous."

That thought made her tingle all over.

"Would you like a child?" he asked tentatively.

Her throat closed so fast she did not have time to stop the little mewling cry that escaped her. Tears rolled from her eyes as she struggled to breathe. She could do it. Raise a child alone. She made enough to support herself just with her salves and herbs. Her healing brought her more hides and meat than she needed.

"Sky?" he whispered.

But she could not have answered even if she knew what to say. Of course, she wanted a child. And she knew that she could make the choice her mother had made. Sky's stomach cramped and her breathing grew raspy.

He moved to her now, settling at her side and drawing her against him. He cradled her in his arms with such tenderness that she cried harder.

"I want a…a husband and ch-children," Sky

managed. "But I do not want a man who loves another woman and does not love me."

"I am sorry." He stroked her head and back, rocking her like a mother comforting her child.

Finally her tears slowed and her breathing became steadier. She felt like a fool, but she did not draw a way, just swiped at her eyes.

"I want to touch you, Storm." There was no one she wanted more than Storm. And she had him only until the Winter Camp Moon. Should she take what he offered?

Sky's pulse began to pound. She could share his buffalo robes, explore his body and discover if what the married women said was true. That in the arms of a man there was found a pleasure beyond all others.

He took her hands.

Sky sat beside him in the dark deciding what to do. He wanted her. That alone was enough to make her say yes. And she wanted a man. Or she had to know the attentions of a man. Now she only wanted *this* man.

"Would you not rather lie with Beautiful Meadow?"

He stroked his fingers over her neck. "I wish to sleep with you, Skylark."

With her, also, she thought. It hurt in her chest. She did not know why she was so jealous. She had no right. He had told her of his proposal to this woman before they made this bargain. She just had not expected to want him so much.

"Do you wish for me to touch you?" He went very still except his hand that slipped beneath her loose hair and stroked the column of her neck. The shivering reaction told him without words what his touch did to her.

"I do, but…"

"But?"

"I think to do so will make it harder for me to leave you."

"Would that be so bad?"

"Night Storm. You told me you could not take a woman until you could provide for her."

"And today I brought down an elk."

He acted as if this somehow made him well.

"You are not well."

"How do you know? I have not fallen. I ride. I hunt."

She threaded her hands in his hair, finding the weak place and adding the slightest pressure. He flinched and drew away.

"You are still healing. Riding, hunting and lying with a woman are all dangerous."

He snorted. "They are also the only things that make a man feel alive."

Storm moved to his sleeping robes and sat facing the sputtering central fire.

"You are a talented healer. I have seen you with the ones from my tribe. Even the men are speaking of your skill. If it is in the power of a healer to cure me, you will do it."

His confidence filled her with pride, as did his admission that her skills were recognized and appreciated.

"If you heal me, then I could be a husband and take a wife to my sleeping robes. I want a wife and many children."

A wife? Or Beautiful Meadow. That was the wife he wanted. Whether or not she healed him, he would set her aside for Beautiful Meadow.

Sky lay quietly as her throat ached. Her tears ran down her face and were absorbed into the tanned hide.

"Sleep well, Skylark," he whispered.

Why had she ever agreed to this bargain?

## Chapter Thirteen

Sky woke to a familiar cold nose poking at her face. She groaned and tried to push Frost away, but he whined and she went stock-still. The lodge was dark except for the glowing embers. How long had she been asleep?

"Storm?"

She received no answer. Sky threw back the buffalo robe and pushed herself up. Cold air rushed in to fill all the warm places and she shivered. Frost whimpered and she rested an arm over him.

Gradually her eyes adjusted to the darkness and she saw him seated just as he had been when he had bade her sleep well.

"Night Storm?" she said, and crept to his side.

He did not move but sat still as the poles that held the lodge. It was frightening to see that his body was no more than a dark silhouette. The night was still, without even the comforting rustle of the wind. That was why she could hear the call of the owl so clearly. Her hand was just inches from his shoulder and she withdrew, pressing her palm to her own beating heart. Frost whined and nudged her.

She steeled herself and reached again, placing her hand on his shoulder and finding it cold as the air about them.

"Storm!" She shook him. His body lolled and she thought he would topple like a badly stacked pile of wood, but instead he pulled himself up and drew a great breath.

She sat back, staring at him as his head pivoted, searching his surroundings as if just awakening.

"I was dreaming," he said.

Frost moved to his side and nudged him. Storm threw an arm over the dog's back and patted his side. Frost's tail thumped as he sat beside Storm.

"I do not think that was a dream," said Sky. "You were staring at the embers. Your eyes reflected the orange of the fire."

"My eyes were open?"

"Yes." She inched away and swallowed back her dread. "And the owl was hooting again."

He cocked his head, but there was now no sound from outside their lodge.

"What did you dream?"

"I dreamed of horses. Many, many horses and

my friend Charging Bull, slipping from the herd of the Sioux with two fine mounts." Storm's voice trailed off.

"What happened?"

"They killed him. Also Two Hawks."

"A vision?"

Storm tucked himself between the buffalo robes. "I do not know. It seemed very real."

Frost lay beside his master and lowered his head to his paws.

"You did not fall or froth or twitch," said Sky.

"What?"

"Your mind disappeared, but you did not fall."

"It was only a dream. Go to sleep now."

Did he really believe that, or was he afraid to admit that he had finally looked past the veil that separated this world from the next.

"Storm? Do you think you should tell your shaman of your dream?"

"No more talk now. I must sleep."

Sky woke before dawn to the chanting song of her husband greeting Wi, the sun. She rose to birdsong but when she exited the lodge, Storm had already left for the river to bathe with the men.

Sky met Bright Shawl and Fills a Kettle as they were leaving their mother's lodge to collect water for cooking at the river and to gossip.

Beautiful Meadow arrived and looked down her pretty nose at Sky, then made a gibe about how Sky should be called Dirt because her hands always stank. Before Sky could say a word, Storm's sister Bright Shawl reminded Beautiful Meadow that her brother would want his wives to live in peace and since Skylark was already wed to her brother, Beautiful Meadow had better mind her manners.

"Thank you," said Sky.

"Do not thank me," said Bright Shawl. "She had no right to say such hurtful things. And it is not even true. You smell like cedar and fresh growing things."

"Besides," said Fills a Kettle, "you are our sister now."

Sky felt a tugging in her chest. If only it were true.

"Perhaps this one may stay with you and Storm after the gathering," said Bright Shawl, giving her younger sister a little shove. "She's a woman now and I know the Low River men are very handsome."

Fills a Kettle beamed. "I could come help you with your healing and learn to be a healer, too. Then I could come home with a fine husband and the skills to help the Black Lodges."

Sky worried at this suggestion. She had not really considered how she and Storm would separate and she had never given a thought to how much it would hurt his family.

"I think Storm plans to live with the Wind Basin people."

"Well, I don't want to live with Beautiful Meadow. I already know how to braid my hair," she said, and giggled.

When they returned from the river it was to see many women rousing their cooking fires before their lodges. The day began.

Today was a council meeting. She remembered Storm telling her that he must attend. Something serious had happened and she knew she would hear all about it from the other women later on. Some of the elder women always sat before the council lodge to listen to the men. When the council broke at midday for their meal, the men would consult with their wives before returning to make decisions. In this way the judgments of the council reflected the will of all the people. Sky had hoped to see Storm before the meeting. She wanted to hear more of his dream. But he went directly to the lodge of their chief, Broken Horn, who was the son of the previous chief Lone Horn. So Sky decided to sneak off alone to gather roots.

If she could just find Peachwort, then she could

make a true tincture to add to his tea. She thought it should be easy to spot by the stream because of its high slender stems and small pinkish flowers. She recalled her grandmother saying it could quiet the winds of the mind.

She said farewell to Frost, who sat before the council lodge. She paused and considered staying. Something was not right with Storm, and she feared the possibility of him having a fall before the tribal council. In the end she decided she could not keep this from occurring and went to do what she could.

Sky gathered her shoulder bag and set off. She did not make it out of the village alone, however. Frost found her and followed. She was worried at first but decided that if he thought it safe to leave Storm, then it was safe.

As she searched, she felt free and happy away from the gathering of women. Sky came away with a full pouch and a full belly as she had found a patch of blackberries and some lovely beech-nuts.

She returned home at sunset and was met by Fills a Kettle, who was most unhappy to have been left behind.

"You missed all the excitement today," said Storm's sister.

Sky paused, hoping that Storm was not the cause of the excitement. "What has happened?"

"Thunder Horse told Broken Horn that Winter Bear is unfit to ride."

"Who is Winter Bear?" asked Sky.

"Oh, I forget you do not know everyone yet." Fills a Kettle smoothed her hair and then began again. "He is a new groom, but such a good hunter that our chief allowed him to continue to provide for one of the old men who has no living sons."

A hunter for the tribe. Just like Night Storm was now.

"Anyway, Winter Bear fell from his horse in the Fast Water Moon. Thunder Horse prayed over the break, but it was bad and his hand has shriveled." Fills a Kettle drew in her arm tight to her body and curled her fingers until they resembled a claw. "It looks like this."

"Did no one treat his arm?"

"Yes. Thunder Horse had him rest and keep still and he prayed and burned sage and sweetgrass. But the break healed badly. Thunder Horse says that Winter Bear has broken some taboo and that now he is unfit to be a warrior of the Black Lodges."

The pit of Sky's stomach dropped. Where was Night Storm? She glanced around for Frost and found him gone.

"What will happen to Winter Bear?"

"Mother said that Thunder Horse said he should be exiled as he is of no use to anyone and is another mouth to feed. Even the chief, Broken Horn, was in favor of sending him away, but Lone Horn spoke for Winter Bear. There are few who can sway our chief, but his father, Lone Horn, is one who can. His father continues to be his most trusted advisor. The old chief said that Winter Bear has been a diligent man and should have until the Story Moon to learn some useful skill. If he can learn to paint medicine shields with his one good hand, then perhaps he will survive."

Sky realized that without the help of Lone Horn, the man had been handed a death sentence. Only the very strongest of men could survive the winter moons alone. A man with only one useful arm had no chance at all.

Sky understood clearly now why Storm had avoided seeking the help of their shaman.

Sky found Night Storm before their lodge knapping flint into arrow points. She had seen his arrow points and knew he crafted fine, thin points with edges that were exceedingly sharp. He was so skilled that she thought she had never seen more elegantly fashioned arrow points. This

was why she slowed when she saw the bits of
flint flying up in all directions and the result-
ing tortured flint looking worse for his efforts.
He did not look up as she approached but spoke
to her.

"I did not tell Thunder Horse of my vision,"
he said.

She could see why. Thunder Horse had just had
a warrior of status stripped of all he was.

"That was wise."

He paused in the destruction of his flint to stare
at her.

"He seems dangerous," she said.

"Yes. He has much power."

And he was the uncle of Beautiful Meadow.
She bit her bottom lip as she worried over this
new powerful enemy.

Skylark did not believe that Thunder Horse had
the sort of power that comes from the world of
the spirits, but rather the kind that comes from
the misuse of his position. That made him very
dangerous, indeed.

"I am sorry, Storm. But Winter Bear is not
you. His arm, well, it cannot be fixed. But you
are healing and showing signs of a new spiritual
power."

"No. I do not have visions. I am a warrior."

She pressed her lips together wondering why,

as a fighting man, he fought so hard to avoid what seemed to be happening to him. He had revelations. They might be important visions.

"But what if your friends are really in danger?"

He stopped his work. "I will watch over them."

She wanted to remind him that his injuries weakened him and that he might not be capable of this.

"Does Winter Bear have a wife?"

"No longer. She has set out his things from her lodge and told him to return to the Shallow Water tribe. But she left enough pemmican for him to last until the full moon."

"Has he no brothers, no sons?"

"No brothers. His son is very young and he has a sister who had no husband when he left his tribe. Still, she might be married and he might go back to her, I suppose."

The rest went unsaid. Winter Bear would be a burden. In the cold moons, when food was scarce and stores ran low, such people often starved. His sister might have to decide between feeding her brother and feeding her child.

He lifted his chin and looked at her.

"He and I walk the same road. Only they can see that he is weak."

The denial sprang to her lips. "You brought down an elk."

"The Hunting Moon gives way to the War Moon. Our time grows short."

"You have not fallen."

"But last night my mind went away again. I did not know what happened about me. A warrior must always be aware of his surroundings."

"You did not fall," she reminded.

A woman approached and called a greeting. Night Storm introduced their guest as Prairie Flower and then went back to butchering the innocent piece of flint. Prairie Flower watched a moment and then lifted a brow as she exchanged a look with Sky, who shrugged. The woman had a son who was ill. She begged Sky to come and see him. Sky asked her husband if he needed her and he waved her away. So she gathered her things and followed Prairie Flower to her lodge.

There she found a child of perhaps four winters, lying upon a piece of buckskin. They had lifted all the sides of the lodge and an old woman fanned him, but despite the cool breeze, sweat ran down his brown skin.

"What are his troubles?"

Prairie Flower described a hacking cough and burning skin. Sky laid her ear upon the boy's chest and listened. His heart was strong but his breathing gurgled and his skin felt wet and hot.

Sky made a tea of birch for the boy's burning

skin and a syrup from berries and Blue Ginseng
for his cough. She showed his mother how to prepare the mixtures and said she would visit the following day. Before she left, Prairie Flower asked
her to look at a growth on her husband's face. The
lump was so large it was interfering with Broken
Arrow's vision. Prairie Flower said that she was
afraid, after what happened to Winter Bear that
their shaman might find her husband unfit.

It was enough reason for Sky to consider helping him.

"I could remove it."

They both agreed so quickly it made her angry
that this shaman who was supposed to bring help
brought terror, instead.

She washed her skinning knife and sliced a
bit of wild ginger to clean her knife and then she
spread the healing juices over the skin. Broken
Arrow sat still as she made a cut through the skin
above his eyebrow. When the skin gaped, she saw
a fatty tumor beneath. There was no difficulty
removing the yellowish mass in one piece except
that the facial wound bled so much. She stitched
it with a fine bit of sinew soaked in the juice of
the ginger root. The stitches helped stanch the
bleeding.

"These must come out in half a moon's time."
She gave instructions for cleaning the wound

and covered it with fresh white sage leaves, then promised to check back the following day.

When she returned home it was to find Night Storm sitting in the darkness before their lodge. Frost lay quietly beside Night Storm. The dog was not upset, but it concerned her that the hound clung so close to his master. Night Storm told her that he would be joining the raid on the Sioux.

He looked to her and his eyes dared her to object.

"I think you must go."

He brightened. "You do? You think I am well enough."

"No. I think it is a risk. But you must follow your vision and protect your friends."

"It was just a dream."

She shook her head. She did not think so.

Over the next few days and nights Sky treated many people. Prairie Flower's boy improved and Broken Arrow's wound did not fester. Storm went on another hunt, but this time it was his friend Charging Bull who took the meat, a pronghorn that he shared with Red Corn Woman. They joined his family and Sky had to listen to plans for the raid that was fast approaching.

After the meal, they said their good-nights and returned the short distance to their home. Night Storm and Sky sat before their lodge staring up at the starry sky. The new moon was rising. The orange sliver growing larger each evening reminded her that their time together trickled away. Frost stuck close to Storm and Sky watched them both, feeling a kind of anxiousness over his dog's behavior.

She asked him about the hunt and his condition. Finally he admitted that the day's ride had made his head hurt and so she roused her banked fire and made him a simple tea to help ease the pain.

Sky then sat beside him wrapped in a buffalo robe. He lifted the edge and slipped in beside her. They sat side by side as she tried to pretend this was natural. Sitting next to her husband.

But the feel of him and the warmth of his body made it hard not to lower her head to his shoulder and wrap her arms about his middle.

The rising moon shone yellow as it crept higher in the night sky. She stared up at the heavens and noted that Storm did not look at the moon or the fire. Instead, he looked out into the darkness. A shadow of an idea began to form in her mind.

"My father has asked how many horses I plan to give your parents," said Night Storm.

"Since we will end our marriage at the gathering, you do not need any horses."

"Would you like to explain that to them?"

Of course she could not. A man was expected to generously give to the family of his intended. The number of hides and horses was a mark of her value. Since they would separate soon there was no need except the perception of others and their curiosity should Storm not gather a dowry.

"My mother crossed the sky road to the spirit world three winters past. My aunt and uncle will expect no dowry because I am not their child."

"You have a father," he said.

"And it is traditional for the father to accept the bride's dowry, which is the very reason my father will not accept it. As a heyoka, he cannot."

"You will care for your aunt and uncle and father in their winter years?"

"Of course."

"Then they have good reason to receive reassurance that the man you marry can provide for them, as well."

Of course, her aunt and uncle would expect that. They would not know that Night Storm would not join their tribe but instead go to the tribe of Beautiful Meadow after Sky set out his things, bringing their marriage to an end.

"I will provide for them," she said.

He nodded. "I know you will do so, but would you have all know that I feel you are of no value?"

Sky's mother had seen to their needs with only

her quillwork, refusing the offer of the chief to have his sister, Snow Raven, hunt for them. And when Sky showed an interest in healing, her mother had arranged for the shaman's wife to help teach her, building on the knowledge of her grandmother.

He let the robe slip from his shoulder and rose, offering her his hand.

"We should go in," he said.

She smiled at the quickening inside her at just the touch of his hand. He assisted her and then laced his fingers with hers as they ducked into their lodge. If she did not know it, she would think this man had real feelings for her. But he was just playing a part. Wasn't he?

She readied their robes, setting hers beside his. He lifted a brow.

Sky told him that she wished to sleep beside him as they had that first night, and she tried to say this but then felt anxious.

"In case you need me in the night."

His warm expression died and she felt sorry she had protected her pride at the expense of his. He said nothing to this, but the corners of his mouth dipped and he settled in his robes. Frost lay beside him and she beside Frost. He did not need her in the night and she wished she had never said that he might, for it touched off a yearning for foolish things she would never have. The yearning now grew past the need to know a man. She wanted this particular man and not just until the winter camp. The bargain she once saw as a blessing now seemed a curse.

She had only the War Moon left before their people made preparations to gather. Then he would return to his path and she to hers. He was healing, becoming stronger, and soon would have no need of her. But her need for him grew greater night after night. Soon the longing would be too powerful and she would abandon her pride and ask for what she most wanted.

In the darkness of their lodge Sky began to wonder what it would be like to make him her husband for the time they had left. Living with him and beside his family made her consider she might not really be as odd as her own people believed. Here she found Storm's sister willing to learn from her, and only Beautiful Meadow and her friends disliked her—and with good reason. Was it possible that she had not found a husband at the fall gatherings, not because she was odd but because she believed she was odd?

One thing she had not changed her mind about was sharing him with Beautiful Meadow. But she saw now an opportunity. She cared for him, respected him and was more than attracted to him.

Why then should she not take him to her buffalo robe?

If the Great Spirit allowed, she might leave this marriage a woman in all ways. She stared across the darkness, wondering if she might convince Storm to give her a child.

Sky dozed and tossed, unable to find a comfortable position or quiet the thoughts that grew like clouds in a summer sky. She woke to find Storm up. She rose, fuzzy headed, to see that he had already stirred the fire to life, a job that was hers.

"Good morning, wife."

She rubbed her eyes.

"You see I did not need you in the night?" He spread his arms wide to show himself fit and whole.

She wished she could say the same.

"That is good," she murmured. She excused herself and scooped up the water vessels. Frost accompanied her. She was halfway to the river when she became aware of a commotion behind her. Sky turned to see Prairie Flower running along beside the tribe's medicine man, Thunder Horse. Sky knew him from a distance because of his buffalo horn cap threaded with hundreds of brown weasel tails. Between the twin horns stretched a bit of sinew threaded with what looked like the

vertebrae of snakes. His shoulders were draped
with a green medicine shirt with the symbol of
lightning blazing and forking across his chest.
In his hand he held a staff fluttering with blue
feathers that came in trade from the people of
the Pueblos far to their south. Below the leather
grip hung many sacred objects including a small
turtle rattle, the head of a hawk, eagle feathers
and the skull of a raven. On the very top was the
claw of an eagle holding a smooth rust-colored
stone. Pipestone, she knew, was also sacred and
powerfully connected to the spirit world. All in
all he was a fearsome sight.

The medicine man ignored Prairie Flower,
who trotted beside him with her son clasped to
her chest. She was pleading with her shaman and
Thunder Horse turned to shake his medicine staff
at her. Skylark pressed both hands to her chest.
She did not know why the medicine man was so
angry.

Prairie Flower fell to her knees and wailed and
sprawled before him. But her son pushed himself to his feet, then squatted beside his wailing
mother and tugged at the shoulder of her dress.

The boy seemed fully recovered and that made
Sky smile until she noticed that Thunder Horse
barreled forward with his eyes fixed on her.

Sky shrank away from the shaman. His face

was nearly purple and the look he shot at her had all the sting of a slap. Behind him, Prairie Flower drew up and ran away. Sky watched her go, wishing she could do the same.

It was clear from the shaman's fixed stare that she was the object of his journey. Sky drew herself up and prepared as best she could. She did not know what he wanted but knew it would be bad.

"You are an evil woman," he said.

# *Chapter Fourteen*

Sky had been called odd and worse. But never evil. She frowned. The insult stung and then she realized that this arrow had a barbed tip. If others believed everything this man said, he was threatening her now. Reflexively her hand went to her skinning knife and she wrapped her fingers around the quilled sheath that lay centered between her breasts.

"I am not."

"Do not speak to me. I have heard of your ways. You used sorcery to bewitch a warrior of the Black Lodges. Did you also make him fall in battle?"

Sky noted that his barking words were now drawing the attention of others. Several of the tribe stood to watch the unfolding scene. One of the faces beamed with a wicked smile. Beautiful Meadow.

Her appearance at this exact moment could not

be coincidence. This was her uncle, after all. Sky now saw a double threat.

Frost began to growl. Thunder Horse lifted his staff and the dog slunk back.

Thunder Horse spoke to the gathering now.

"This woman has tended a warrior. Drained him of his power and made him useless."

Was he referring to Broken Arrow? If so, that was a lie. She had only removed a simple fatty growth from above his eye.

Thunder Horse continued on. "She has interfered with forces she cannot understand. The boy was marked for death and she has changed his path. Now I have ghosts demanding his spirit. She is bringing ghosts to our tribe."

Was that so? She had never heard such a thing. At home, her healing talents were sought after and she had never been chastened for saving a life.

"She endangers us all."

Sky looked from one face to another. More than one of those gathered had requested her help for a remedy. Yet none came to her defense.

"She is dangerous. You must all avoid her medicines. The spirits tell me that it is because of her that Night Storm fell in battle. I have heard the owl and followed it to their lodge." He pointed at her. "This one can call ghosts."

The people shrank back. Skylark's stomach

clenched as she realized she was alone in this. None here would speak for her, a woman of the Low River people.

If her father were here, he would likely fall down before Thunder Horse and cry to show all that their shaman was behaving as a child who had lost a favorite toy. But she was no heyoka and could never speak to a shaman in such a way. In fact, she should not speak to him at all.

The people exchanged nervous looks and she could not tell if they were frightened of her or for her.

A voice came from behind Thunder Horse.

"Thunder Horse, if you have issue with my wife, you should first speak to me."

The man turned and Sky saw Night Storm striding forward, with Prairie Flower jogging along at his side still clutching her child.

Thunder Horse glared back at her and then directed his attention to Storm.

"You have been ill. Now I see the cause."

"You said the cause was a crack in my skull, which is still healing."

"Such a crack is like a tunnel opening to all manner of evil. This woman you have chosen as a wife is no healer. Only I see what she is."

Storm moved to stand between her and the medicine man. Sky knew that he now placed himself at risk for her. He had gone to great lengths to keep his people from seeing his weakness. Now his defense of her brought that weakness to everyone's attention.

She glanced to Beautiful Meadow to see her scowl deepen as she glared at Sky. Clearly she had not wanted Night Storm to come into this.

Storm spoke. "I will promise Thunder Horse that my wife will not treat any of the warriors here and that she will help only those who seek her remedies."

"None will seek them," said Thunder Horse. "They are bad medicine."

The words hung like the vibrations of a struck drum. No one moved or spoke.

Storm stepped too close to Thunder Horse and leaned in. His words were a whisper and even Sky could not hear them.

Thunder Horse stiffened and his face turned purple. He backed away and aimed his staff at Storm.

"You should break this marriage. She will not help you. If you keep her, she will ruin you." He turned to the others and swung his staff in a wide arc. The turtle shells, skulls and talons rattled ominously.

"Keep clear of this one. She speaks to owls. This is owl medicine and it brings death."

They all stood as Thunder Horse stalked away. Beautiful Meadow waited until he was far ahead and then set out to follow. No one else moved. Sky narrowed her eyes upon Beautiful Meadow and realized that men were not the only ones who went to war.

Prairie Flower looked to the retreating medicine man and gathered up her son and ran in the opposite direction. Broken Arrow remained in the circle of onlookers, his stitches raw and angry above his brow. All could see the warrior she had dared to treat, and she hoped they could see he was better for it. But he said nothing as he retreated back and out of her sight.

Why had she not considered that by healing the boy that Thunder Horse had condemned to die that she had shown his mistake to all? And in the process she had made a powerful enemy.

The people gradually returned to their morning routine and Storm led her toward the river, where she filled her buffalo bladders with clean, cool water.

He walked with her on the way to their lodge, speaking to many along the way. They returned his greetings but cast her only nervous glances. At their lodge they found Prairie Flower, her child and Broken Arrow.

"I cannot have her remove these stitches," he said to Storm.

"Can you tell me what to do?" asked Prairie Flower.

Sky gave instructions for the timing and how to make a salve to keep the wound free from pus. The couple departed.

"This is very bad," said Storm.

"What should we do?"

"I cannot let you journey out alone. You must stay with me until the gathering."

This made her tremble. Clearly Storm thought the threat to her very real to take such a precaution.

"Thunder Horse is afraid. I see now that he is not a strong medicine man and he dreads that others will also see him as he is. He fears you because you are a greater healer than he will ever be."

She sucked a breath between her teeth.

"He will hate me."

"Yes. It is good you will not be here long."

"He saw the owl," she said. "If he sees you fall…" She understood his need for secrecy. Why did the council fail to see that their shaman was not a holy man? "Storm, you are risking everything for me."

He took her hand. "And you are risking much to stay here, Sky. You have come to heal me. You left your family to do this. It is my duty to protect you. I must stay with you."

"But you must go on the raid. Your vision. Your friends. They need you."

This time he did not deny his vision, but his mouth grew grim.

She started to cry. "What should we do?"

He gathered her in his arms and held her tight as the tears choked her.

"Hush now." He lifted the flap to their lodge and led her inside. There he held her, stroking her head and keeping her close to his side.

She did not know how or when it happened, but gradually her tears ceased but his caresses did not. His hand moved up and down from shoulder to hip. She rested her palm over his heart and looked up into his eyes. His smile was tender. She pressed her mouth to his cheek. He held her then and lowered his lips to hers. Sweet, gentle kisses covered her face, brushing away the tears.

Her breathing increased and she lifted her arms to hold him. Their kisses changed as the heat flared. She needed to touch him and had the urge to press herself tight to his chest. Her breasts grew heavy with an exquisite aching pressure that even the grasping pressure of her embrace could not assuage. She needed him in the most desperate and intimate way.

"Storm," she whispered. "Make me your wife."

His hand slipped beneath her dress, his fingers dragging up the sensitive flesh of her inner thigh. She gasped as her head lolled back at the feathery touches that made her ache.

"Skylark? Are you there?"

She glanced to the entrance and realized they had left the flap up.

Storm released her and slipped away an instant before his sister's face filled the opening. Fills a Kettle motioned over her shoulder and Sky saw two people behind her.

"May we come in?" asked Fills a Kettle.

"Of course," said Sky, tugging down her dress and trying vainly to still the furious thumping of her heart.

Instead of his parents, the two faces that next appeared were Winter Moon and Wood Duck. What were her aunt and uncle doing here?

Sky shot to her feet and Storm rose beside her.

"My aunt and uncle," she said.

"Terrible timing," he muttered, and lifted a hand in welcome.

Sky greeted her aunt with open arms. To have a familiar face here was greatly comforting. She realized as she hugged her uncle and invited them to share a meal that had they arrived a few moments later they would have received a very different welcome. This night they would share their tepee with her family, of course. From the forced smile on Storm's face, she knew he was well aware of this.

Her uncle had presented her with a horn ladle for cooking. Her aunt gave her a fine two-skin dress with decorative white elk teeth across the yoke and the long fringe she never before thought she wanted.

The gifts only made her feel worse, especially when she saw the pride her aunt had in her marriage and the relief on her uncle's face. When had she become a burden to them? Sky straightened. If they were both here, who was looking after Falling Otter?

"Where is my father?" she asked. "Is he well?"

Her aunt's smile faltered. "Truly, I hoped to find him here with you."

Sky's eyes rounded with concern. "I heard him my first night. And once since. But I have not seen him."

They exchanged a worried look. The men took their leave of the women soon afterward to gather together and smoke and talk with the other warriors. They would exchange information and smoke well past dark. Meanwhile, she introduced her aunt to Storm's family and the women went to the river to bathe, as they did each afternoon when the weather was good. Her aunt took special pleasure in washing away the dust and sweat from the journey.

That evening the men returned for their meal and then departed again, leaving Sky with her aunt. She wondered how much to tell her. She decided to speak of the trouble she had with Thunder Horse.

"You should come home with us. There is no need to remain here with his people until the gathering."

None except she had given her word to do so and Storm's vision of his friend's death on the upcoming raid. He must be here, so she must be here.

"I will speak to my husband about that." When had she begun thinking of him this way? When had the lie become a reality to her?

"This shaman is dangerous. Tomorrow I will help you strike your lodge and we can go."

But she would not go. Sky knew that.

Late in the evening Storm returned with Wood Duck and the men settled beside their wives. Wood Duck's familiar snore filled the air a few moments later, followed by the soft breathing of her aunt.

She told Storm what her aunt had said.

"I would have you go with them," he said.

"Will you come?"

"I have to raid with my friends."

"Because you need horses for my bride-price or because of your vision?"

"Both."

"Would you wish me to set out your things to-morrow?"

His grip changed from relaxed to possessive as he drew her tight against his hip. "I would not."

She longed to ask if he wanted her to stay for herself or because he needed her medicines. Her fear of his answer kept her mute.

"Then I will stay until the gathering as I promised."

"But I will be away for several days on the raid."

She tried to keep her breathing even, but the thought of being here without him frightened her. But she also knew that he had a vision, even if he would not admit it aloud. He had seen his closest friends killed. If he could stop that, he must try.

"And I will be here when you return." She thought her voice held a note of calm quite opposite to the whirlwind of emotion spinning within her.

He squeezed her and then rested his mouth beside her ear. "I wish you would stay to be my first wife."

The ache in her heart hurt so much she had to rub her knuckles over her chest. She wanted this man, but she did not want to make both herself and Beautiful Meadow miserable.

"But I will not."

He kissed her temple. "Until the Winter Moon then," he said and sighed.

He had made a promise to Beautiful Meadow and she had made a promise to herself.

Sky closed her eyes and tried to relax in his arms. She was weary but the gentle rush of his breath against her temple and his hand, familiar across her hip, kept her from finding rest. Storm's breathing grew even and his hands twitched as he dropped into slumber. But she could find no rest and that was why she heard the first tiny sounds from above.

A scratching sound came from the tops of the gathered lodge poles. She stilled and looked up through the opening of the tepee. The hole that was intended to funnel away the smoke was open to the moonlight. So it was easy to see the silhouette of the bird that had landed on their tepee and now gnawed at the sinew that held the poles fast.

Sky threw her hand over her mouth to keep from crying out. The owl rotated its head completely around and stared down at them. Beside her, Storm roused, his body going stiff and his breathing changing. She knew he was awake.

Sky folded her arms over her heart and shuddered. Storm drew her in. Both stared toward the opening of the lodge and the bird perched there.

Death had come for a visit.

## Chapter Fifteen

Sky recalled the words of Thunder Horse. He said that she called the owls. Was that possible? Had she called the owls to him?

She listened to see if her aunt and uncle roused but, judging from their breathing, they did not. Eventually the owl vanished while she lay awake beside her husband for much of the night. It was clear from his absolute stillness that he had not found slumber either, but neither wanted to disturb the other or their guests. His nearness and his warmth drew her, and she struggled to keep from reaching out to touch that velvety skin sheathing the iron of his muscles. He smelled of tobacco and wood smoke from this evening and the familiar scents comforted. She had not realized the security that came from sleeping beside a man.

His breath caressed the skin of her neck, making her feel as if her body were on fire. Why had no one told her of the terrible temptation and yearning that would come with wanting a man and not being able to have him?

Well, that was not exactly right. She would have him until the gathering and then she would let him go. She could have him. She just could not keep him.

Out beyond their lodge an owl hooted and Sky shivered. Her husband reached out, pulling her close. He rhythmically stroked her back as the terror that gripped her gradually ebbed.

"Go to sleep, wife," he whispered.

"What if it is ghosts? I cannot help you if it is ghosts. What if it is the one who struck you, the one that died?"

*And what if their shaman was right and she called the owls?*

He squeezed her tight and she rested her head on his muscular arm.

"It is not his ghost. They have followed me since my vision quest. But tonight I have been dreaming of them, the owls."

The terror was back, gripping her heart. Across the lodge her uncle's familiar snores gave the appearance that all was normal. But she knew better.

"What dreams?"

"I have seen a child lying upon a yellow buffalo robe. I have seen the prayers for his cure rise up to the spirit world with the smoke of the burning sage. But the owls whisper in the trees that it is not ghosts or spirits who plague the boy."

"What does it mean?" she asked.

"I do not know. I only know I wake as he dies."

She pushed up on an elbow. "Do you know this boy?"

"I cannot see his face because it is already painted black."

A death mask, she knew made of bear fat and charcoal.

She was still thinking about the dream when slumber finally took her. In the morning she woke fuzzy headed as Night Storm slipped from their sleeping skins. The birdsong told of morning, but through the hole above her she still saw the stars.

She dozed and then woke again to the familiar chant of her uncle's prayer to the rising sun.

Her aunt rose and together they made a meal of the remains of the elk mixed with the cattail tubers she had found. The men returned from their bath and the day began. She said goodbye to her aunt and uncle. Her aunt said she hoped to find Falling Otter and would keep watch for him at camp. She was glad to see her niece a happily married woman but worried over the troubles she was having with their medicine man.

"I will speak to Spirit Bear of this," said her aunt. "We will see if we can help you."

They touched foreheads and Sky resisted the urge to cry. After all she would see her soon.

"I am so happy to see you with a good husband. It is clear he cares very deeply for you," said her aunt. "I hope you will come to live in our camp. But, if not, we will see you soon at the winter camp."

Sky's smile faltered as she added her aunt and uncle to the list of people who would be hurt when her sham of a marriage dissolved with the rising of the Winter Camp Moon.

She and her husband accompanied them out of the village, with Frost walking close to Night Storm's side. Storm gave Wood Duck one of the promised horses to carry the hides he had given for her dowry. She waved as her family departed and watched until they were gone.

"I will see you get them back," she said.

He said nothing to this but his jaw clenched. Frost sat beside them and whined. Both of them looked at the dog and then each other. When Sky looked back, Frost's tongue lolled and he panted in the rising heat of the day.

"We will leave tomorrow for the raid," he said.

That pronouncement made her stomach jump. She gripped the strand of white beads in her fist, squeezing them hard as she tried to stop herself from begging him to stay.

"How can I help you prepare?" she asked.

"Fill my water skins with the tea you make me."

She nodded and set to work as he prepared his weapons.

"I need more Peachwort."

"I will come gathering with you today, and we will go alone."

The way he said alone made the hairs on her arms lift up as she shivered in anticipation. He was leaving tomorrow and this would be their last day before he went on a dangerous journey. She knew well that the Sioux were a strong and vigilant enemy.

The thought of his capture or death filled her with a new kind of terror. She was so afraid for him, but she could not ask him to stay.

"I would welcome your company today," she said, and earned a smile.

Sky gathered a water skin and collecting bag. Storm took his weapons and saddle. When they left the lodge, Fills a Kettle was there, but Storm told her to stay home. Frost was allowed to trot along with them. Together, they walked back to the herd of horses hobbled in the high grass across the wide river from the camp. Storm accompanied his wife to the river, where they removed their moccasins and forded the wide waterway, leaving their footprints on the sandy shore.

Sky waited as Gallop was saddled and bridled. Storm mounted and swung his quiver across his shoulders. She walked beside their dog as they wove through the herd.

"Do you look forward to rejoining your family?" he asked.

"I look forward to being at peace with my tribe. It is difficult to fight with Beautiful Meadow and her uncle frightens me. It will be good to be away from them."

Somehow just mentioning their parting made her weary all over and Storm went quiet, keeping his thoughts for himself.

They walked until it would be time to turn back or consider camping for the evening. She stopped only to take the most irresistible and rarest of plants. She found the Peachwort and took enough to last her many days. Frost darted here and there. Storm left her and the horse to pursue their supper. He was not gone very long, and when he returned he carried two ducks on one arrow and Frost carried one in his mouth.

"He is a good retriever, that one," he said, and Frost wagged his tail. His coat was wet and he gave another shake, making the droplets fly, and the duck lolled in his mouth.

She approached and Frost dropped the duck at her feet, sat and wagged his tail, clearly pleased. She stooped and praised him for the wonder that he was and he basked in the attention.

Before long, Storm had chosen a place to camp and it was lovely, on the shore of the pond with soft tall grass sprinkled with yellow and orange flowers and the cover of spruce and cedar trees beyond. By the time the fire was right for cooking, Sky had the ducks gutted and plucked. She stuffed the cavity with cedar and sage for flavor and set several wild onions to roast. Of course, she saved the most colorful feathers. Frost did not wait for the cooking and gobbled up the leavings as she prepared the birds to roast.

Sky had not brought a cooking pot, so they skewered the birds and sat to wait. Fat dripped hissing into the fire. The aroma of roasting duck was heaven, but the meal tasted even better. After they had finished, Sky stored away the extra food in a parfleche pouch she kept in her bag. The rawhide was colorfully decorated and inside she kept reeds she had filled with various dried herbs and plugged with wax. She steeped his tea and offered it to him.

"You must learn to make this yourself soon,"

she said. She tried and failed to hold her smile. Their separation, tomorrow and then at the gathering, forever yawned before her.

The wind came up making their fire flare and then sputter. He added more wood and wrapped a blanket about them. His body heated her as much as the fire and soon the chill had left her.

"Sky, when I first saw you I wanted you. Then when we began this bargain, I wanted only for you to help me. But now I find myself searching for a way to have you as my real wife and still keep my promise to Beautiful Meadow."

"I see no way for that to happen."

"I cannot convince you to come with us to the Wind Basin people?"

She bowed her head. "Even if she wanted me as her sister, I would be among strangers again and I would be a second wife."

"My first wife," he corrected.

"The one you took out of necessity. How do I explain?" She looked up at him. "I want a husband. But I want my freedom, as well. I do not wish to make a lodge or keep the fires or tan hides. I am a medicine woman. So it is best for me to live alone."

"Or have a husband who has a wife to do all those things."

"She would resent me for not doing my share of the work and I would resent her."

"For what?"

"For having to share you."

He startled and she could see he had not expected that answer. She regretted her honesty and wished she had not told him that.

"Do you have feelings for me, Skylark?"

She looked away, but he captured her chin in one strong hand and turned her head until their gazes met.

"I will not stay. You will not leave Beautiful Meadow. The rest is just the aching of a lonely heart."

"I made her a promise before I met you."

"And you should keep it."

He nodded, but his eyes glittered with a dangerous light and she felt herself bracing for what she knew would come next. Her mind cried out a warning as her body moved toward him.

Her last coherent thought was to wonder what it would be like to remain his wife. The possibilities flitted before her like a firefly, winking on and then out.

After that it was too late for words, because his mouth was on her throat and his hands slipped under her dress. Her thoughts were scattered, pushed aside by the rising need. Her head lolled back as he lavished attention on the column of her neck, his teeth grazing her skin in a way that made her entire body buzz to life. She felt an unfamiliar throb and hum awaking deep inside her that grew until her skin flushed hot and prickled.

He wore no hunting shirt, just the leggings that tied to his loincloth, the breechclout and his moccasins, so when he pressed her back against his chest she felt the contact of his muscular torso with her exposed arms. He slipped her dress up over her thighs. She shed the unwanted garment and soon he had swept it up over her head. She wore nothing beneath and so sat facing their fire and wondered if she burned hotter than the glowing embers. But she was wet, too, her skin damp, and the place between her legs ached. Was that normal? Her aunt had said that a woman's body prepares for the coupling with a man. But Sky had not thought to ask how.

Behind her, Storm released the leggings and kicked away his moccasins.

"Turn around, Skylark," he whispered. "I would see my bride."

Now her skin went cold and then hot. Would he find her appealing? She had compared herself to other women at the bathing area. She was average height. A little skinnier than some, shorter than others. All the rest of her was ordinary. That was why, when she turned and his breath caught, she felt suddenly embarrassed.

She lifted one arm to press against her breasts, smashing them together, but covering her tightly budded nipples. That was when she realized that her breasts felt different, too. They were heavier somehow, full and very sensitive.

He reached and clasped her wrist and gently drew it away.

She watched him as his eyes cast over her like a net thrown over the water. Who would have guessed that even his stare could bring her to trembling?

"You are beautiful."

She shook her head. "I am not."

Sky slipped off her moccasins. She looked at Storm. He still wore his loincloth as he knelt before her. Her breath caught at the sight of him, poised and coiled in preparation to take her to his blanket. But he did not hurry her or press her down. Instead, he waited until she lifted a hand. She placed it on the wide, flat muscle of his chest and let her fingers glide downward. He shivered and she smiled, pleased to know that he also endured this internal storm. When her fingers reached his naked hip she paused, one finger resting on the tie that kept his breechclout in place. She lifted her gaze and met his. His mouth quirked, but the muscles at his jaw bunched as if his stillness cost him much. She lifted her brows in a silent question and he inclined his head just the slightest bit.

Sky tugged at the soft moose-hide waist cord and felt the knot release.

## Chapter Sixteen

Storm could not stop the groan of pleasure as Skylark's cool fingers skimmed over his bare hip. No other woman had made his body sing the way this small woman did. Even the woman he had chosen as wife did not tempt him like this. He had selected Beautiful Meadow not because of her pretty face but because her father was chief and her uncle a powerful shaman. Now his ambitions to marry well had captured him like a rabbit in a snare. The more they kicked, the tighter the sinew grew until it choked him.

He glanced to the moon that had become his enemy. The near-perfect circle was waning now. It diminished with his time with her. How could he keep her and avoid breaking his promise to Beautiful Meadow? Would he really lose Sky forever?

He wondered, if he showed her how perfect they were together, if it would make any difference.

Her hand slid away, and he opened his eyes to see her staring down at him with wide hungry eyes.

"May I touch you?" she asked.

He nodded. He tried to stay still as she wrapped her small hand about him, but it was impossible. His erection jumped and his hip rose to meet her touch.

She gasped. He drew her up to meet him, pressing her naked body to his. The contact rocked him and she released a breath that sounded like a hum. Then he was kissing her and licking and taking small nips with his teeth along her neck and jaw. Her head dropped back. He moved downward, kissing and stroking her fine, firm breasts.

"That feels wonderful," she murmured, and when he took her nipple in his mouth and sucked she gave a little shout and arched up to meet his eager mouth. Her fingers threaded in his hair and she pulled him even tighter to her breast. Now her hands moved over his back, her nails scoring his flesh and arousing him to greater lengths.

He stroked her belly and the thick dark hair between her legs, finding her wet and wanting. He toyed with her swollen flesh until she began to glide up against his palm. He moved faster and her breathing changed to gasps and moans. He slipped a finger into her body, sliding in and out in a motion he planned to repeat very soon to find his own satisfaction. Her eyes opened wide and she sucked a breath between her teeth.

"Something is happening," she said.

"As it should. It is good. Let it happen."

"Yes?" she gasped, still uncertain.

"Yes." He nodded and her eyes dropped closed as she lifted her hips to meet his hand. He wanted to kiss her there, but he would be patient. Her first time should be full of pleasure because a happy woman will return.

He planned to make her happy. So happy that she would never want to let him go. He had to change her mind until she wanted him so badly she would stay and be his wife.

Her release began with a high whine at the back of her throat that blossomed into a cry to break with the contractions that squeezed his fingers with rippling waves. The sensation was so erotic that he almost lost himself right there. That would not do. He wanted to feel her all around him.

Sky collapsed back against the bedding, floating in the lethargy he wished they shared.

He lay beside her, hot and wanting, gently stroking her belly and the outer curve of her breast. His fingers danced over her shoulders, memorizing the line of her collarbone until she began to touch him with greedy hands.

"There is more," he said.

She met his steady stare.

"I want it," she whispered.

He rolled on top of her, using his knee to spread her legs. She knew enough to plant her feet and bend her legs, letting him settle between her strong, soft thighs. He drew a ragged breath, trying to take control of that which no man ever completely mastered. She was too sweet and he was too ready.

A thought occurred to him and he paused. If he gave her a child it would be hers. He would lose both her and their baby. He stared down at her, realizing that instead of making her want him, he had accomplished just the opposite. He did not think he could let her go.

"What is it?" she asked.

"I was just thinking…what if there is a child?" he asked.

Her eyes widened and her mouth twitched. He knew then that she wanted his child. But not him.

He felt as if he might cry.

"If you give me a child, I will cherish it."

But she would raise their child alone or with another man who would make her his only wife.

He felt the need then to make her his in the only way he could.

She looked down between them, at her body

ready for his. He wanted to make her his wife
in all ways. Watching her, feeling her hand as it
stroked down his bare thigh in invitation, was one
of the most erotic moments of his life.

He eased gently into her slick, wet folds, but his
medicine woman was too impatient. She wrapped
her strong legs around his middle and rose up to
meet him, taking what he would readily give. Her
head fell back and she gasped. He held still, waiting for her to withdraw or move.

*Please, let her move.*

She did. Away and back, up and along.

She captured her lower lip in her strong white
teeth as they moved as one. Her eyelids fluttered
shut and then opened wide. She met his gaze with
one of wonder and he thought that if he died right
now, this instant, his only regret would be that
he'd only had her once.

Then her head tossed from side to side as she
arched. An instant later her cry came deep in the
back of her throat and her body began to contract
all around him. The sensation was otherworldly
and he came with her in a rush of heat. He collapsed upon her and she gripped him tight. She
moaned a protest as he turned to his back but quieted when he gathered her against him and let his
fingers caress her back in light feathery strokes.
She nestled close. He watched her eyes close, and

her breathing deepened as she fell into slumber. He followed her into the land of dreams and slept more soundly than he ever remembered.

Storm woke to the sunrise with the clouds above them bathed in hues of purple and magenta. The light of the day stole across the ground until it touched her face. She held one of his hands with both of hers and her cheek pressed to his upper arm. Her mouth was pursed in slumber, and her cheek was flushed from their lovemaking.

Another day gone, he realized as the regret tugged at him.

He did not wish to wake her. But he had to return to prepare for the raid.

"Sky?" he whispered, squeezing his hand about hers.

She made a sound of protest, unwilling to leave her dreams.

"Sky. Look."

She opened her eyes and made a sound of wonder as she saw the clouds changing by the moment in the rising light.

"Beautiful," she whispered.

The early sunshine filtered down through the trees. It would be a bright sunny day and already the birds and insects flitted about their camp. A dragonfly landed on a stone beside their gutted fire and then flitted off. It was a good sign. Dragonflies represented water and life. Much better than the owls who usually followed him.

He rolled to his side, so they lay nose to nose. She smiled. His gut twisted at the mix of joy and sorrow she brought. He had to find a way to keep her.

"How are you feeling?" he asked.

She grinned at him and blushed. Then she stretched and her brow wrinkled. "Oh, my muscles are stiff."

He nodded. "You are not used to that sort of riding."

She rolled to a seated position and giggled. "That is so."

He excused himself to say his morning blessing to the sun and to wash. He heard Sky moving about the camp and walking to and from the stream for water. When he returned she had the pemmican ready and two horn cups of icy water waiting.

After the meal, Sky began to break camp. He found her at the stream, filling their water skins. Frost trotted along with him, but, instead of catching frogs, he sat beside his master on the mossy bank. Sky watched his dog and him with interest. She tied the opening of the skin to keep the water from draining away and then came to join them.

He looked across the lake, watching the swallows darting up and down as they caught bugs over the water. The sunshine glittered on the surface in sparks of light. He shook his head and directed his gaze to her.

Beside him Frost whined and lay down with his head resting on his paws.

Sky drew a long breath, pressing her generous mouth into a line of grim determination. He felt the first trickle of unease in his belly spread to grip his heart.

"How are you feeling, Storm?" she asked.

He tried to answer that he was well. But, instead, he stared at the shafts of sunlight that glittered like mica on the surface of the water. Frost barked. Beside him, Sky shouted and pushed at his shoulder. But the water held him tight.

# Chapter Seventeen

Night Storm felt it coming this time. That was why Frost had been barking. Storm knew he should lie on his side. But the water before him shimmered, and he almost felt as if he stared up at the sun from beneath the water.

He could feel Sky right behind him, yet her voice came from far away. Her hands covered his eyes and he felt himself drifting. The vision he saw now was of men, creeping through the tall grass along the river, there where the women of his tribe were bathing. They waited and watched. He knew them as enemy, Sioux warriors, a small party. And he knew the women, his women, of the Black Lodges—the wife of Fire Horse and his two older daughters Yellow Bird and Pond Flower. But they did not see their enemy. The raiders waited until all but three had gone up the hill. Then they sprang upon the women, who were taken with hardly a sound. The warriors dragged away their prizes into the grass and toward the horses, more than they would have brought. That meant they had somehow taken women and horses in broad daylight, and the dogs and their scouts had seen nothing.

The vision faded to blackness and Storm saw slivers of light. He blinked, realizing that something warm and soft pressed to his face. He lifted his hands and found two more hands already covering his eyes.

He tried to speak and found he could. "Sky?"

"Yes!" The relief in her voice was obvious. "Storm, can you hear me?"

She did not remove her hands from his eyes. "Yes. Of course."

She laughed.

"Did I fall again?"

"No! You did not fall." She kept one hand tight over his right eye and slowly removed the other. She peered around him. "Can you see?"

He looked at the lake and realized the sun was higher now, because the light did not break on the surface in a shimmering band.

"Clearly," he said. "I had a vision. But I did not fall. I knew you were there with me the whole time. But I could see other things. How did you do this?"

"Frost knew the spell was coming. You were

staring at the water again. It was as if the water had captured you. I could not get you to turn your head or look at me and I could see your face go slack. So I covered your eyes to block the water from your sight."

He took her hand. "And I did not fall." His voice held astonishment.

She shook her head.

"Why did I not fall? Why did covering my eyes keep the moth madness from consuming me?"

"I do not know."

"But how did you know to do this?"

She shook her head, seeming as bewildered as he.

He looked to the ceaseless motion of the lake brushed by Tate, the wind spirit that blew over the earth and in and out of a man's body. The wind of Tate was the breath of life, the same force that stirred the leaves and brought the whirlwinds. Tate was a great spirit and there was power in the stirring waves, dangerous power. Storm quickly looked away. There was some magic there in the dancing water.

Storm turned to look at Sky's beautiful smiling face and jubilant expression.

"I had the vision and did not fall." He took her hand. "Perhaps that means we can control this."

She squeezed his hand and giggled. "Perhaps."

He stared at her in wonder. "How did you know what to do?"

"I didn't. I just knew it was the water that had charmed you somehow, so I shut it out."

Unfortunately, he could not take her riding and raiding with him. He thought back to the night of the violent thunderstorm when the mighty Thunderbirds had sent much lightning crashing to the earth. There had been no lake then. Yet he had been captured. His head still ached, dully, and he could not think as he wished. Was it Tate, the spirit of the wind, that gave him the moth madness?

Then the vision flooded back and he stiffened abruptly. He started to rise and she pressed him down.

"Wait."

"I cannot wait. There are Sioux warriors in our camp. Or they will be there soon. I saw them."

"Are you sure?"

"I am certain. They are coming or they *are* there."

"But you nearly had the moth madness. You must rest."

He straightened. "I am a warrior of the Black Lodges. It is my duty to protect my people."

"But…"

"We must go."

\* \* \*

They galloped back to camp. The journey that had taken them much of yesterday flew past on the back of his charging horse. Storm wore his right eye shielded beneath a bit of buckskin tied with sinew and Frost ran, tongue lolling as they went.

She believed his vision held meaning, but neither knew if the raid he foresaw would take place today or had already taken place or might occur in some far-off moon. Storm did not lower her to the ground when they reached the village from the south, below the bathing place. Before them the horses of the tribe's herds had scattered far along the opposite riverbank. It would be easy to steal the ones who wandered the farthest from the boys who were lax in their duties guarding the horses.

Storm shouted to them to gather the horses into a group and he sent one boy to find Fire Horse and bring him.

He let Sky slip to the ground here, on the shore closest to the village.

"Should I raise the alarm?"

"If I am wrong or if I have the wrong time, what will we say?"

She stared back at him, as uncertain as he felt.

"Go home," he said. But she did not. Instead, she ran toward the woman's bathing area, keeping above the cattails and reeds that lined the bank. At this season the grasses were well over her head and she knew they made good cover for a private bath, but also for the enemy to sneak up upon the women unawares.

She reached the bathing area to find many of the women had already left. Several stood on the bank of the river using bits of soft tanned buckskin to draw away the water from their damp skin and then ringing them out to use again. There were five still bathing. She did not know them but saw an older woman beside two younger ones. Was that the family of Fire Horse?

She looked to the opposite bank and saw the grasses move. Something was there. Two more women left the water, so only the three remained. Just like his vision, she realized, and the hairs on her neck prickled.

Sky clutched her skinning knife and called to the women to come out. They paused and turned to her, their conversations ceased. She motioned frantically and their expressions went from calm and cheerful to worried as they trotted in her direction, using their arms to paddle toward the shore.

The first cry came from behind her. She swung about to see Night Storm leading a charge, with his lance lowered. Beside him rode his father and another man who carried a war club with a spiked piece of metal across the shaft.

The women now screamed and rushed toward the men. At the same time four Sioux warriors leaped to their feet and ran from the river, in the direction of the grove of cottonwood on the far bank.

They reached the grove, where she assumed horses waited, as the warriors of the Crow splashed across the river and up the far bank.

The women ran screaming back to the village, and soon more men flooded the riverbank. Most were on foot, but they carried their weapons and hurried across to assist the three in the vanguard.

Sky waited for what seemed eternity, there on the bank of the river beside the others who had come to wait and watch. Bright Shawl introduced Sky to Velvet Dove, Fire Horse's wife, and his two daughters, Pond Flower and Yellow Bird. Yellow Bird was crying.

"How did you know?" asked Bright Shawl.

"I—I saw the grasses moving on the opposite bank."

Bright Shawl cocked her head. "That might have been only a village dog. And Night Storm said there were intruders. I saw father mount his extra horse."

"Owl magic," whispered Pond Flower.

Sky met the woman's eyes and felt the trickle of dread at her look of absolute horror.

Bright Shawl quirked a brow at Pond Flower and took hold of Sky. Before Bright Shawl could press her for answers she did not wish to give, the men returned in triumph carrying the bloody trophies of war. These enemies would not be able to haunt the living, Sky realized with some relief, because their spirits would escape through the hole in the tops of their heads where their hair once grew.

She greeted her husband, who no longer wore the scrap of leather over his eye. He pulled her up onto his horse for a hard embrace and a lingering kiss. At last he drew back and she nestled into his arms, her cheek pressed to his. He turned them back to the tribe's herd, having wisely decided not to join the scouts who even now searched for more enemies.

"It was a vision of the future," she said, hugging him fiercely as she whispered into his ear. "You are a far-seeing man."

It was a great gift, to be able to look forward and see what was to be. Such a gift should be shared. But when she drew back it was to find that Storm was not smiling.

"Do not say so," he said.

"But you must tell your chief and your shaman. Why, you are a shaman, too!"

Storm shook his head. "I am no shaman. I cannot cure or sing a man back from the spirit world. I know nothing of such things. I am a warrior. It is all I ever want to be."

"But…but…your gift."

"A curse."

"Not a curse. You saved them." She pointed toward the river. "You touched the spirit world. You saw what was to be."

"I saw the evidence of raiders on our journey home."

She drew back to arm's length and stared in shock. Was that what he would say? Then she recalled her lie about seeing the grasses move, which she had, but only because she was looking for raiders because of Storm's vision.

"Storm, you must tell your chief."

"Sky, Thunder Horse has his ear. Our shaman is already threatened by your healing skills and he is angry with me for taking you before marrying his niece. What will happen if I tell the chief that I have visions?"

"He will…" Her eyes rounded. "You will be a threat to Thunder Horse."

He nodded at her understanding.

"He is powerful and he will fight to keep that power. You must tell no one of what has happened."

"But you are…"

"A warrior. That is what I am. It is best for me to get you to your people and for me to leave the Black Lodges with Beautiful Meadow. That will keep you safe." He glanced back toward the village. "I wish I could stay. But I must go on this raid."

"But you just had…" She paused. He had not had a fall exactly and seemed in perfect health. But that was only because she had prevented it somehow. But on the raid he would be alone. "You must not look at water."

He nodded. "Sky, if I can feel the storm rising inside myself, I can close my eyes or cover my face. If I can control this, then I can ride, hunt and raid again. I can bring many horses and enough buffalo robes to make a large lodge.

"But to deny your gift. It is wrong."

"If you have healed me, then I can return to my path and you can return to yours."

"You could marry Beautiful Meadow."

His face was grave as he nodded. "Yes."

The wife he wanted, she thought. Just not her. Sorrow filled up her heart until it ached. He took her in his arms and kissed her fiercely on the mouth. She stiffened and then wrapped her arms about him and deepened the kiss. At last he drew back and set her aside.

"I must go to the council meeting."

He left her there, mouth dropped open and the tingling excitement of his lips still on her own.

Sky had to press her hand over her chest in a vain attempt to stop the squeezing grip of sadness. He might want her only with his gut and with his head, but Sky found to her deep sorrow that she wanted him with her heart.

She watched him go, knowing that she would never feel for another man the way she did for Storm. She cradled her hands over her flat stomach, lifted her face to the sun and prayed.

When she opened her eyes, she knew what she would do. To go on like this was to fall more hopelessly in love with him. Sky's throat ached as she walked back toward camp.

## Chapter Eighteen

The scouts returned and Red Corn Woman told Sky they had found no evidence of more raiders. The raiding party from the Black Lodges had formed and they were preparing now to depart. Red Corn Woman and her daughters joined the women of the Black Lodges to bid farewell as the raiders rode along on parade.

Night Storm led the group, mounted on his warhorse, Battle, a strong black-and-white pinto with long legs and a powerful chest. Storm wore his finest war shirt. Sky had never seen it before and, when he appeared with the others, she was struck speechless by his splendor. But she could not see them, for she had eyes only for Night Storm.

His mother laughed at Sky.

"Look, daughters, she is blinded by his beauty."

And it was true. He wore his moccasins and new leggings, but these leggings were so heav-

ily fringed that the twisted strands pooled on the
ground. His shirt had been dyed a rich blue on the
bottom. It was a color that came only from traders
and was called indigo. The white-and-black beading that swept down his wide chest in two vertical
bands only added to the imposing figure he made.
Over the shirt he wore a breastplate of elk, leather
and wide white beads, punctuated with blue and
black along the center. At each shoulder he had
painted a medicine symbol of lightning on a black
sky. A night storm, she realized. She lifted her
gaze to see that the elk skin sheaths that covered
his braided hair held many eagle feathers, each
carefully wrapped in blue trade cloth and tufted
with the soft underfeathers of the eagle, then tied
with strands of cascading white horsehair.

She stood beside Red Corn Woman, feeling
suddenly as plain as a female mallard duck beside
her iridescent mate. He was so striking a figure
she could only gawk.

He spotted her and smiled. Across the way
a woman shouted his name and she saw it was
Beautiful Meadow rushing to Storm's horse. She
held up something and he took it with words of
thanks, then looped the beaded red trade cloth
sash over the front of his saddle. His future wife
had made him an ornament showing to all her
skill and talents.

"Don't look so glum," said Fills a Kettle. "She can't even remove a splinter without getting dizzy."

Red Corn Woman clapped her hands. "See how beautiful that sash is with his blue shirt. And so many feathers," said his mother. "More than his father had at his age, I can tell you. This one will soon be on the tribal council. I know it."

The raiders paused before their chief, who stood with his council, including Storm's father. What would his father, the leader of the Black War Bonnet society, say to his son if he knew of his visions?

Many Coups stepped forward wearing a head-dress with so many feathers that he might have been chief. About his neck were multiple strands of white beads from which hung the tails of mink, taken in winter so the fur was snow-white and tipped with black. His war shirt was not dyed, but instead of fringe, the arms were also hung with the tails of mink. From shoulder to wrist lay a thick beaded band so complicated that Sky's mother might have made it. Beneath his war shirt he wore a double-beaded apron showing a geo-metric pattern in red and green and in his hand he held a feathered plume.

Night Storm's name was spoken and Broken Horn summoned Night Storm. Storm dismounted and came forward to be presented with an eagle feather by the chief. Lone Horn told the gathering this was for saving the women of the Black Lodges from capture. He extended the mark of honor in two open hands to Sky's husband. Storm took it and touched it to his forehead, bowing to his chief. Then he raised his feather to the gathering and they cheered. As the cheers died away there came a howling, hooting cacophony of sound. Heads turned, people stared; some gasped and others laughed as someone made their way through the gathering.

Sky could not see the individual clearly. All that was clear was that this person had painted half his face white and half black and seemed to have a live duck tied to his head. Children began to laugh and chase after the man who stepped into the circle at last. He was painted yellow, or mostly yellow on his bare chest. Her smile died as she realized who this was.

Her father.

"I am Falling Otter of the High Mountain people."

Of course, there was no High Mountain people, but instead of saying he was from the Low River people, which was proper, he said the opposite.

"Do you know him?" asked Fills a Kettle, leaning in to be heard over the crashing sound of her father beating the iron lid of a kettle with a stone war club.

Sky could only nod. "My father."

The duck objected to the din and wriggled free of its tethers, then used Falling Otter's head as a takeoff platform, pushing hard against his nose as it flapped away.

The group howled with laughter.

Sky tried and failed to sink into the earth.

"I have another feather for you," said Falling Otter, casting away his pot lid and dancing in a very good imitation of the woman's coming-of-age dance. This shocked some of the women who now looked disapproving at the goings-on.

Her father stopped before Night Storm.

All about them, the people strained to see. Sky wondered how a man with a duck on his head had managed to slip past the sentries and into their midst.

"Here is your feather, my son." Falling Otter held out a beautiful white feather.

Of course, Night Storm was not his son.

Night Storm reached for the gift and then paused as he noticed the distinctive ruffled edge. Sky knew that only one bird had such feathers as that one. Her blood chilled and the hairs on her arms and neck lifted as the shudder rolled through her. An owl feather, the very mark of the spirit world, ghosts and all things unseen.

Storm's hand had stopped moving forward and remained fixed over the object as if suddenly frozen.

It was the shaman who put an end to the drama by striking her father's arm with his staff and so knocking the feather to the ground.

It was a very disrespectful way to treat a heyoka and Skylark started forward. But Red Corn Woman stopped her by gripping her arm.

"That is no fit feather for a warrior," said Thunder Horse.

"It is for *this* warrior," said her father.

"What feather?" asked Broken Horn.

Thunder Horse pointed a bony finger at the feather. A claw hung tied to the end by a cord. A second cord held a small skull with huge eye sockets.

*No*, she thought, pressing her hand to her chest. How could her father even have suspected?

But there it was, the small skull of an owl, the talon of an owl and the snowy white feather of an owl.

"Owl feather," said the shaman.

The gathering backed away as the taboo feather lay in the center of their gathering. No one knew what to do. Such an object could bring all sorts of trouble and this heyoka had brought it right into their midst.

"Pick it up," ordered Thunder Horse.

"No. It is for him," said her father.

"Pick it up, I say, and take it away." Thunder Horse's voice cracked, revealing his fear.

"If you are so powerful, then you can touch it." Falling Otter waited. But when Thunder Horse shrank back, Falling Otter began to laugh, showing all about him just how upset he was.

Then he turned in a circle until he found her and waved.

"Daughter! You should come home."

Her smile fell. Why did he want her to stay?

"I must find another duck," he said, and hopped to the edge of the circle as if his legs were suddenly bound together. The crowd parted and he disappeared.

When she turned back toward the center of the circle, it was to see Thunder Horse glaring at her. Her husband stooped and lifted the owl feather from the dust, placing it with the eagle feather. The gathering breathed a collective gasp. Then Storm mounted his horse and led the raiders from their midst.

## Chapter Nineteen

Night Storm moved through the darkness with his favorite raiding horse, Shadow, who was small and fast and black as the dark side of the moon. For night raids, Shadow was the best choice. The men had removed their war shirts and finery and left them with their second horses back at their camp. Also at camp was Frost. He could not bring the dog among the enemy's herd without spooking the horses and alerting the sentries to their approach.

It felt good to be astride a horse and in the company of men, but he worried about Skylark alone at camp. Her father's antics had frightened his people. Even his fellow raiders did not like that Storm had touched the owl feather and still kept the offering.

He had tried to explain. It was given to him by a heyoka and so it was sacred. But it would mean the exact opposite. An owl feather from the hand of a heyoka would mean life instead of death.

His fellows urged him to leave it behind, bury it deep in the earth. It had not helped that they had heard the hooting of owls as they rode through the forest, reminding Storm of the vision where he saw his two closest friends killed. He had stopped the Sioux raid back at camp. Prevented the capture of their women. Could he also save Two Hawks and Charging Bull?

His unease grew as he wondered what was happening at the camp in his absence. He had asked both his father and mother to be vigilant and see that his wife was safe from both Beautiful Meadow and her uncle. He trusted them. But he did not trust Thunder Horse. Now that Thunder Horse knew Falling Otter was Skylark's father, Storm thought his rage might be directed at her. It was one thing to help his niece. But it was another to defend his position among the people. Storm felt himself tugged in two directions and wished he had sent Sky home with her aunt and uncle. With a heavy heart, his horse moved forward, carrying him away from her and in the direction he had chosen.

There was no water here to attack him, but he knew the Sioux camp was situated on the river's bend. His scouts had told him where.

They dismounted and each man now walked with his horse, to be sure their mounts did not whinny a greeting to the enemy's herd. One of them would have the unenviable task of staying with the horses while the others slithered through the grass like snakes in an attempt to steal many horses. He knew he should be the one to take that duty. It was all he was good for, but if he fell and the horses escaped, then they would all die. It seemed he was not even fit for that.

One of his men drew up beside him.

"Why have we stopped?" Charging Bull whispered.

Night Storm had not even realized he had stopped. He should turn over the party to Laughing Jay. He was a good friend and strong leader.

Charging Bull pointed. "There," he whispered. "The horses."

Neither man could see or hear them, but the scent of them was strong. Night Storm called Little Elk to him and told him to stay back. He promised to soon return and relieve him of his duties so he could raid, as well.

Night Storm crept forward with the others. This raid would be silent. This time, they did not want to kill their enemy, only steal horses. Charging Bull moved to his right and then off on his own. Each man would slip into the guarded herd and then out with all he could take. The trouble was that the horses might give them away at any moment forcing them to flee. Storm watched the grasses move all about him as his men fanned out. He hoped Charging Bull was lucky, for he had ambitions to marry a pretty woman from the Wind Basin tribe and needed a dowry to claim her.

Night Storm realized with shame that he had stopped again. The herd of horses rested in a tight group. He could see the sentries closely spaced. But one of the sentries had left his place to go speak to another guard. The two men stood together, creating a larger gap between them and the next patrol. It was through the larger gap created by their conversation, through which Charging Bull slipped.

Storm watched him move past the Sioux scouts and into the herd. Some of the horses shifted but none whinnied or ran.

Still Storm watched. He wished he had brought Frost. Standing in the sliver of silvery moonlight Night Storm realized he had lost his confidence. Even if he did not fall, he now realized his secret placed his men—good, brave, worthy men—in danger. He was not fit to lead.

One of his men was already moving from the herd with two horses. He could not see which man as he walked between two mounts, each tied about the neck and nose with a single leather lariat. Another man emerged with three horses. Charging Bull, he thought, taking a risk to earn more of the bride's price. They would be easy for the sentries to spot now. Storm moved toward the warriors, pausing close. He reached back and slipped an arrow from his quiver and notched it. As he had feared, the scouts noticed the movement of the horses from the herd. They could not see his fellows but they were not fools. Horses did not leave the herd, especially at night. Both men started in the direction of the horses.

Storm let the first arrow fly. His enemy fell from his horse and before his comrade could disappear into the grass, Storm's next arrow was protruding from his chest. The Sioux sentry turned and looked at Night Storm as he fell.

*Two more ghosts to follow me with the owls*, Storm thought, moving forward to lift the scalps and make certain that the spirits of these two men left their bodies and found their way to the spirit world. He did not take their fingers or disfigure them, as some did. It was good that an enemy was not whole in the spirit world. It would be one less enemy to face upon death. But he had no stomach for it. So, instead, Storm took their weapons and offered a prayer to soothe their crossing.

He knew in that moment that he would never be what his father had become. He could never earn enough feathers for a flowing warbonnet with a train that followed behind him when he walked.

He knew all he would not be. But he did not know what he *would* be. The path ahead was unclear and he felt like a young boy lost in the woods. He did not know his true path, only that the one he had intended to journey was gone. Storm reached into his pouch and drew out the talon, skull and feather ornament that the heyoka had given him.

He tugged at the cord holding a single snowy white feather and it fell free. Then he wrapped the cord around the bottom of his braid and tied it fast. If the owls wished to follow him, he thought, let them come.

Clouds now swept over the moon, racing like horses across the sky. He stared up at the flickering light and heard the ringing of metal on metal. He tried to look away, but he could not. What was he supposed to do? He tried to remember, but the ringing was so loud he struggled to think. His eyes. Cover them. His arms did not respond to his urging. But he managed to shut his eyes. The ringing went on and on but he kept his eyes squeezed tight. The ground bucked and his knees gave way. This time he felt the contact with the ground. He heard the ringing recede. His stomach heaved and he lost all he carried there. But still he kept his eyes shut. How had the moon taken him? The moon had not danced on waters and was small now, less than half-full. But she was still powerful.

He regained his equilibrium first. His stomach was still bad, but he managed to stagger into the herd. He was clumsy and thick-witted. But the gap between sentries meant that even a boy could have stolen horses. He managed to take three, not really caring to select the best. Then he returned for Little Elk, relieving him of the duty of watching their mounts. This was bad, he realized. He had nearly fallen.

Storm scanned the herd for signs of trouble, his bow now gripped in his hand. Gradually his men began to emerge from the gathered herd, bringing away their prizes.

He would have to tell his chief. Sky had said so. She had tried to tell him. But how could he do it? How could he stand before all and admit that he was no longer a warrior?

Charging Bull returned as Little Elk disappeared into the tall grass. Storm followed to cover his escape and that of the other raiders.

One by one, the men returned. All came back and no alarm was raised. Storm did not wait and even though his headache was gaining momentum, he led them all to a safe distance before the party mounted up and galloped away, guiding their strings of ponies. They were not out of danger. The Sioux would pursue them like angry hornets the moment they discovered the missing horses and missing men.

But luck was with them, for they were well out of the Sioux territory before sunrise. Storm's head continued to pound and his body trembled. When had he become as weak as an old woman?

They rested long enough for the horses to graze and drink and for his men to eat. Two Hawks told the others that the reason they had such success was because their leader had killed two of the sentries as silently as a puma and bragged that Night Storm would earn two more feathers for his bonnet.

Why did that not please him? He thought of Sky, working so hard to help the ill and injured to survive. Then he thought of the owl feather her father had offered him, calling him son, as if he, too, believed that he and Sky were husband and wife.

Perhaps he called him son because he somehow knew that Storm was not his son; that his daughter would not stay with her new husband. He wished he had never offered for Beautiful Meadow. The choice he made now haunted him like the owls. She was powerful but used that power to hurt Sky and reveal that she had a jealous heart. Should he blame her for fighting for what she felt was hers? Would he not do the same? He could not take back his promise without losing all honor and dignity. But in his heart he admitted the truth. He no longer wanted Beautiful Meadow. He wanted only Sky.

He must be mad to covet an owl feather and the daughter of a heyoka.

They rode the next day through Crow territory and stopped in the afternoon, resting and then changing into their finest war shirts for their triumphant return to their village. Frost found him there and trotted beside his horse as they returned home, his pink tongue lolling.

Storm continued on with the others, looking for Sky. But she was not among the faces that shouted and cheered a greeting.

When he reached his family, it was to find his sisters, mother and father waiting with grim faces. Beside his mother stood Beautiful Meadow— the only one smiling. His head swiveled and he searched for the one face he longed for. But did not find her.

He swept down to meet his family. His little sister took charge of his three new horses. Frost trotted from his side to greet his sister and then his mother and father, who did not seem to notice him. But Storm did. Frost's ease meant he was in no danger of falling. Instead, he faced a different kind of danger.

Beautiful Meadow stepped out to greet him. Something about the triumph of her smile washed him cold. He pushed her away when she threw herself into his arms.

"Where is Skylark?"

Her pretty smile widened. "Gone."

"What!" Cold fear squeezed his heart and his mouth went dry. He could barely speak. "Where?"

"Thunder Horse said that her healing was owl medicine. He drove her out. Do not worry, Night Storm. Before going, she has set out all your things outside your lodge. So she is no longer your concern."

He knew by the nausea he felt at her announcement that Skylark would always be his concern, whether she chose to be his wife or not. Storm set Beautiful Meadow aside and went to his parents.

"Where has she gone?"

"Back to the Low River people," said Red Corn Woman.

He turned to his father, whom he had asked to look after Skylark.

"Who accompanied her?"

"Her father. But she went on foot for she would not take any of your horses."

On foot with a heyoka as a guard? Storm thrust his hands in his hair and tugged to keep from screaming.

"I asked you to watch over her."

His father lowered his voice. "She uses owl magic. I hear them in the night. Thunder Horse said she is calling you to your death. Let her go, my son."

Was his father afraid to face Thunder Horse or to risk his position for a girl who could heal and a heyoka who gave his son the feather of an owl? He did not know, but for the first time, he saw fear in his father's eyes. Fear for his son, Storm realized, and an enemy he could not fight.

"The owls are here for me, Father. Not her."

Red Corn Woman grasped his arm. "Let her go, son. She is no longer your wife." His mother motioned to Beautiful Meadow. "This one is waiting to be your bride."

Storm tugged free of his mother's grip and his father's beseeching stare. They didn't know what had happened to him and still wanted him to walk the warrior's way. But he could not.

A tingle of dread rippled through him. A woman alone, making such a long journey, was madness.

"When did she go?"

"Two nights have passed."

Night Storm swept back up into his saddle, and Frost raced along beside him as he headed toward the herd. There he collected Battle, tying Gallop behind. Perhaps Sky had come into his life, not to curse him or to cure him, but to guide him to a new way to walk the Red Road.

And perhaps she would never again be his.

But he had promised to protect her until the gathering and that was what he would do.

Once he found her.

# *Chapter Twenty*

Sky continued along the river in the golden sunlight of the cool afternoon. Her father's meandering pace slowed her and if she did not know better, she would have suspected he did so on purpose. She disliked being out in the open, exposed. But she did not know how else to find her people, other than to follow the river. Despite her father's dancing and crying and swimming in the dirt, they were finally close to the camp her aunt had told her they had left. She knew this place along the river and felt the reassurance of familiar ground.

She wondered if Night Storm had been successful in saving the lives of his friends and if he would be relieved or angry to find her gone. She had promised to stay until the gathering but had been forced out before the wind had even begun to eat away the War Moon.

Now she would return to her path. Not the direction of her choosing but the one she must walk. There were others who had worse situations, husbands dead in battle or from disease. Children lost. But these women had husbands and children. Her hand went to her middle and then she forced it away, afraid to even hope that she carried his child with her. Her father lifted his head from the tall grass by the river and then gave a warning cry of a frightened deer before disappearing again.

Had she been her father's greatest trick?

It was not just her father who lived the opposite. Her mother had behaved like a contrarian, refusing to take up the responsibilities of other women. She had rejected offers to wed and did not gather food but relied on making what she loved, to see to their needs. And, oh, her quillwork had been a marvel.

Sky's tread was heavy as she continued on until she found her village spread out on both sides of the wide stretch of water.

She was home at last. She could see her life stretch before her like the river and it was just as cold and solitary.

She glanced back to find her father had vanished into the grass. But her eye caught movement. At first she thought it might be Night Storm and her heart raced with joy. A moment later she realized the warriors bearing down upon her were not Crow warriors, but Sioux.

She turned back toward her village. The distance seemed impossibly far. But still she gave the warning cry. Off on the distant bank, the boys guarding the ponies began to move. The women at the river straightened and then ran. Help was coming. She saw it. Then she turned toward the warriors and knew in her heart that help would arrive too late.

Night Storm heard Sky sound the alarm, a high trilling call that traveled well across the distance. He had no doubt that the Sioux would reach her before her warriors. She had done the right thing and likely prevented her capture because a woman, even a small one like Skylark, would slow their retreat. And the men must retreat, for they would be badly outnumbered in a very short time. So the men had two choices. Withdraw or kill the enemy woman and then flee.

Sky turned to face the men, drawing her skinning knife. His little healer was preparing to fight and to die. He thought he would never forget the defiance in her stance as she drew her shoulders back and stood tall.

He pressed his heels into his horse's sides and the horse exploded into a smooth fast gait. He did not give his war cry yet. He needed to be closer to keep the element of surprise. Three to one, but he had the advantage because he had Sky to protect. Nothing would stop him from reaching her.

The warriors were upon her. His horse was fast, but not fast enough to be there first. Night Storm gripped his bow and notched an arrow, feeling the smooth gait of his charging horse and sighting his target. He aimed for the heart of the warrior last in line and released the arrow that flew straight. The Sioux warrior arched and cried out, toppling from his mount. His fellows turned to witness the fall and then glanced back, seeing Storm riding on their heels.

The lead man lowered his lance at Skylark, who turned to run. Then out of the grass leaped her father, Falling Otter. Was he brandishing a dead rabbit? Night Storm could not think of a more useless weapon, which was the point, he supposed. The warrior turned his lance toward the new target and Falling Otter threw his rabbit. The rabbit struck the warrior in the face and the lance dipped, so instead of hitting Falling Otter in the center of his chest it sliced into his shoulder and stuck forcing the warrior to release his weapon. His fellow was now firing an arrow back at Night Storm, who had already taken a position on the side of his galloping mount.

Falling Otter fell laughing to the ground as Night Storm reached the archer and drew his war club, swinging it high. The warrior lifted his rawhide shield as they passed, but Storm succeeded in contacting him in the center of his back, unseating him. His opponent rolled along the grass and then to his feet, but without his horse or bow he was no threat. The last man chose to retrieve his fallen comrade rather than finish Sky or her father. Then the two remaining Sioux raced past him. Storm recovered his bow and planted one arrow into the second rider's back before the two charged over the rise and out of sight.

"Come!" Storm shouted. "There are more of them."

He reached and captured her, pulling her up behind him. From the ground, they located her father, who shouted, "Stay. Stay. Stay all day!"

"He wants us to go," she said.

Storm looked back and found the warrior he had engaged now returning with many more.

He pressed his heels into Gallop's sides and dashed for safety, passing the warriors of the Low River people. Beside him the river sparkled and danced in the bright sunlight and his mouth filled with the taste of blood. He knew what was coming and he did not stop. Did not close his eyes because he had to get Skylark to safety.

"Sky," he said, his words thick and awkward on his tongue.

She pressed tight to his back. "Yes? I am here."

"I do not want…" He tried again. "I still wish you to be my wife."

"What?"

"My wife. You. Only you."

The ringing was so loud now that he could not hear his words. Had he even spoken? His body began to tremble. He could see men ahead of him. The mounted warriors, preparing to fight should their vanguard fail. The women waited for orders to flee. The lead warrior rode a warhorse that was as white as the fur of a fox in winter. He knew this warrior, for a female warrior was a rare thing. It was the sister of the chief of the Low River tribe, Snow Raven. Beside her on a red roan galloped her husband, the mighty warrior, Iron Wolf.

Night Storm's vision narrowed as if he rode through a day that was morning and night together. He urged his horse on, but his legs had grown slack. Behind him, Skylark gave a yelp and wrapped her arms about him, clutching the saddle horn before him.

"Sky," he said, but his words were a gurgle. He had saved her. She was safe. Night Storm let go and allowed the moth madness to consume him.

\* \* \*

Sky gripped Storm even tighter as he went stiff in her arms and then slumped forward. She knew what came next but still she held on. If she let go he would fall and his horse would continue on, without him. She knew his skull was still healing. She knew a fall could kill him and she knew that if she succeeded in reaching the village she could find help. That also meant that the people of her tribe would see his weakness. He would not thank her if she let the men of her village see him twitch and shake.

She clung tighter and steered his horse with her legs, pressing with the heel closest to the river as her uncle had taught her, sending the horse back in the direction of help. Her uncle, Wood Duck, reached her first and dragged Night Storm toward him, but still she clung.

"Let him go, niece."

She did. But she knew what would happen. Night Storm's mouth began to foam and his body began a wild jerking. Her uncle just managed to bring Night Storm to the ground before he stepped away in horror.

"What is this?" he asked. "Is he injured?"

Bright Arrow, the chief of the Low River tribe, remained on his horse as the warriors who had remained behind circled the downed man. Night

Storm's attack went on and on. Skylark tried to go to him, but her shaman, Spirit Bear, ordered her back.

Her stomach tied itself in tight, painful knots as her gaze swept from Night Storm to the men watching with a mixture of horror and disgust.

"He has moth madness," said Little Badger.

"He will swallow his tongue and die," said Laughing Crow.

"Niece," called Wood Duck, but she did not heed him as she dropped to her knees beside Night Storm. His madness passed and he went still. His face turned purple and Sky pushed until he rolled to his side, his head lolling and his eyes fluttering.

"That one is dead," said Little Badger.

"Or soon will be," said Laughing Crow.

Off in the distance came the shouts of the warriors as they engaged the enemy. From the opposite direction came the answering cry of the women, still safe behind the line of men guarding the camp. Sky knew that the Sioux were crafty and might send a party to a camp and lead away the best warriors only to attack from another direction with a larger force. But if she knew this, her chief also knew it. So he had kept most of his men back and close to camp. This only gave a larger gathering to see the worst falling spell of them all.

Even on his side, he did not breathe. So she pried open his mouth, releasing the blood and saliva that blocked the sacred wind of Tate from flowing in and out of his body.

As his breathing returned to normal and the purple color left the skin of his face and neck, Skylark sat back on her heels and let her shoulders sag. He had survived again.

When she lifted her head to meet the stares of the onlookers, it was to feel their shock and unrest. Did they find his fall disquieting? A reminder of their own vulnerabilities? Or was it that she had pried open his mouth and snatched him again from death. She felt them measuring her and found herself lacking.

She threw herself over Storm's body, wrapping him tightly in her arms and weeping. From somewhere behind them came the sound of a warrior singing his death song, mixed with short intervals of the women's harvest song. She lifted her head, recognizing her father's voice. He sang a death song, so he thought he might live.

"Falling Otter," she said. "He was wounded trying to save me."

Hunting Wolf, a member of the council of elders, ordered Little Badger to retrieve Falling Otter from the field. Then he called for a travois to bring the fallen man to their camp.

"I would have Spirit Bear attend this one," said Hunting Wolf as he motioned to Night Storm. "Perhaps he can do something or sing him to the other world."

Spirit Bear was the shaman of the Low River people. She was honored and terrified that the elder tribal council member had asked for the help of one so holy. Perhaps Hunting Wolf believed that Night Storm needed to be helped to cross the spirit road.

That only made Skylark grip Storm more tightly. She would not let them sing a death song.

The first travois passed them on the way to collect her father. Before long a second arrived. Sky was happy that Storm was still unaware as they placed him on the travois and carried him behind a horse through the village.

She walked beside him, her head up and her hand upon his chest as it gently rose and fell. There would be no more hiding now. All would know. Certainly his tribe would strip him of his position, as they had done to Winter Bear. But would they also cast him out? Storm's moth madness would give Thunder Horse the weapon he needed to attack Storm. She feared for him now more than ever before.

If they banished him, could he survive? Few ever had, because the task of hunting and gathering wood in the harsh cold moons was too much for just one person. But what if he brought a woman, a certain kind of woman who knew how to gather roots and berries and make medicines?

A man like that might have a chance of surviving. Was she seriously considering going with him?

Yes, she realized—if he would let her—because she would rather walk with him than stay here without him.

The cheering women and children parted as their chief led the procession of warriors back to the village, their bodies gilded by the late afternoon sunlight. They were followed by a travois carrying her father. She walked beside Storm, past the curious stares. Behind her, Falling Otter shouted from the travois, hurling insults at the Low River People, calling them cowards and fools, proving just how proud he was to be returning to them.

Winter Moon stepped from the gathering to embrace Sky and then fell into step beside her niece. The cries of the women greeting the returning men filled the air, making speech impossible, and Sky was relieved.

They stopped before the lodge of Spirit Bear. The hide that stretched over the frame had been painted with a series of medicine wheels showing the four directions in black, red, yellow and white. Spirit Bear called often to the power of Waki—the son of Tate, or the Wind—to heal and teach.

The travois had been detached from the horses and her father began to laugh. His sister, Winter Moon, knelt at his side and took his hand. Spirit Bear's wife stepped from her lodge. Starlight Woman greeted her husband first and then her guests. Her face was smiling and well wrinkled from the many winters she had walked the earth. Sky suspected she had been married to Spirit Bear for longer than Skylark had lived. Yet the medicine man, who was capable of taking several wives, had need only for this one and had kept only her even when she had born him no children. Skylark felt a prick of jealousy as the woman leaned to press her forehead briefly to Sky's and then repeated the greeting with Winter Moon. Starlight Woman left them then to assist her husband, who still rode a horse, but he was stiff and the joints of his fingers each swelled like the burl on a tree branch.

Sky took her place beside Night Storm and Winter Moon moved to stand by her brother.

"Welcome home, brother," she said.

His laughter was the only thing that succeeded in bringing Sky from Storm's side because it told her that her father was in great pain. His shirt was soaked with blood. Someone had removed the spear point and the blood flow was too heavy for him to live for long, unless she stopped it.

# *Chapter Twenty-One*

Sky removed a bit of buckskin from her pouch and folded it into a pad. This she pressed over her father's wound, using the weight of her body to stem the flow.

"Get my things, please, Auntie. The yellow bag and my sewing kit. And my cooking kettle." It was her prize possession, the small iron pot in which she brewed her medicines.

Sky was still holding the bandage tight to her father's wound as he made sounds like an owl. The medicine man made his approach to Night Storm.

"Where was he injured?" he asked her.

Yes, that was the question.

"I do not know."

Spirit Bear's snowy brows lifted.

"He was injured in a battle during the Fast Water Moon," she offered. "His skull broke inward. Since then…he falls."

Spirit Bear's brows rose even higher and his attention went back to the fallen warrior. He felt Night Storm's head, his long gnarled fingers pausing on the place at the back where the bone had been crushed.

"This one should have died," said Spirit Bear. He looked to her. "How is he called?"

"Night Storm."

His forehead wrinkled. "Are you sure? That does not seem right to me."

Now her brows lifted as she recalled all Storm had told her of his vision quest and the owls. She was spared from answering by her father's laughter.

Spirit Bear looked at the feather tied in Storm's hair with interest.

"What is this?" he asked, lifting one of Storm's braids so that the feather fluttered in the breeze. The wavy white edge marked it for what it was, for only one bird, a silent hunter and messenger of spirits, had a feather of such an unusual color and formation.

"My father gave it to him," she said.

"Your father?"

"Your sister is bringing something to ease the pain," she said to Falling Otter.

"She is not my sister. I hate her. Hope she is very slow." He closed his eyes and seemed to be concentrating on breathing, which worried her greatly.

Spirit Bear spoke to his wife, who ducked into their lodge.

"She is bringing a Black Hemp tea for Falling Otter's pain. This is very strong medicine and will make him sleep."

Sky smiled, pleased at the choice and the knowledge that her shaman worked with both body and spirit. She knew he was more forgiving and tolerant than Thunder Horse, who had frightened her. Still Spirit Bear also had the authority to banish a warrior, though she had never seen him do so.

"Do you approve?" he asked.

Sky still leaned on the folded pad covering her father's wound, relieved to see the bleeding ebbing. But Spirit Bear's question so shocked her that she sat back on her heels, releasing her hold on her father. Was the shaman of the Low River people actually asking her opinion? She could think of no reply.

To her knowledge the shaman had never asked the opinion of a woman before. Her stomach ached as she considered what to do.

She glanced at her father and knew what he would do. If it were inappropriate to speak, he would speak. She cleared her throat.

"Well?" asked the holy man.

"That will ease the pain. I would add Cranes-bill to slow the bleeding."

Had her answer been impertinent? She waited, scarcely breathing.

"If I had some, it would be an excellent addition."

"My auntie is bringing that." Before she knew it she was in a conversation over which plants she preferred for wounds and when she would stitch a wound and when she would leave it opened. The entire exchange seemed like a dream and she could not really believe that her shaman cared what she thought.

"Well, all I have heard is true. You are an excellent healer and becoming as lovely as your mother." His smile seemed sad and his gaze lingered on her longer than was polite.

She blushed at the compliment.

Her father, who kept his eyes pinched shut, still managed to speak. "My daughter is very lazy."

The shaman chuckled. "High praise, indeed."

His wife emerged with the tea and Sky helped her father drink. Black Hemp was strong medicine, so Sky was not surprised to see that soon her father's face relaxed, and a few moments later his eyelids drooped.

"Wide-awake," he muttered, his words slurring.

Sky checked on Night Storm, who seemed to be only sleeping now, his breathing soft and regular through his open mouth. It gave her time to treat her father's wound. Her auntie returned and Sky set to work, sending her aunt to find fresh leaves from Ground Ivy. When Sky was done, the gash was cleaned and stitched loosely to allow the flow of fluids. The lance tip had not entered the joint of his shoulder but only pierced the bone of his upper arm, slicing away the muscle. On exploring the wound, she had found the tip of the flint point still embedded and carefully worked it out. Her aunt arrived with Sky's things and Sky made a mash of the bruised leaves to encourage tissue healing.

When she finally returned to Night Storm the sun had dipped below the horizon. She found him blinking wearily. He tried to rise, but Spirit Bear pressed him back to the travois.

"All is well, my son. Rest now."

He said one word in a slow, slurred speech. "Sky?"

She took his hand. "Here."

He gave her a weak smile. "Safe?"

She stroked his forehead. "Yes. Because of you."

He relaxed back to the ground, and for just one instant she thought his breathing stopped.

She gave a shout of panic and pressed her ear to his chest, hearing the steady beating of his heart and then the slow draw of breath. So slow, she thought. Too slow, she knew.

"We have to sit him up."

With the help of her aunt and Starlight Woman, they propped Storm up. His breathing improved. The bluish tint receded from his lips and Sky thought she herself could breathe again. Warriors from the Low River tribe arrived to stare at the falling man from the Black Lodges people. Sky remained at his side.

Her aunt asked her to come home, but she would not. Her uncle returned from the chase and reported that all was clear. Lately there had been many more skirmishes between their tribe and the Sioux snakes, and her uncle said he looked forward to winter camp when the snow would be too deep for the Sioux to consider attack. Until then, the men would raid and fight because it was the War Moon.

As twilight turned to evening, her aunt insisted that both Falling Otter and Night Storm be moved to her lodge. The transportation was easily arranged and once the men were safely tucked inside by the fire, Winter Moon insisted that Sky eat. Later, with her stomach full, Skylark turned to face her aunt and uncle's questions. Why had she come alone across the distance between their tribes? Why had her husband been chasing them? And what was wrong with her husband?

Sky felt weary before she even began to answer. There was no reason to lie now. She had set out her husband's things, ending the marriage, and all had seen him fall. The truth he had dreaded had been revealed. So Sky told her aunt and uncle everything that had happened since she had left their tribe, and then she added a truth she had not spoken aloud.

"At first I was only trying to help him. But over the days and nights I began to wish he could love me and that he was not already promised to another."

"A man can take two wives," said Wood Duck.

"Her mother told her never to be a second wife," said Winter Moon. "Second wife, second life, second love, second from his heart. Isn't that right?"

Sky nodded.

"But if it is the only way to have him."

Sky shook her head. "She hates me. It was by her efforts that I was cast out. Their shaman is her uncle. Her father is chief of the Wind Basin tribe. And my father is…"

"A man of great power and well respected by all."

Sky lowered her head.

"But your father is powerful, as well."

Sky placed a hand on her father's forehead and smiled.

"Skylark," said her aunt. "He is powerful and you are powerful, but your power does not come from Falling Otter."

"What?"

"You're power is not of chaos but of healing."

Sky squinted, trying to make sense of her aunt's words.

Winter Moon placed a hand to her mouth and met Sky's gaze. Then she lowered her hand. Sky knew that what she would say next was important and she straightened.

"My brother is a great teacher and he loves you very much, but he is not your father."

Sky blinked in astonishment as she tried to tell if Winter Moon was teasing and saw that she was not. Her mind struggled to understand but it made no sense. Her gaze flicked to her uncle who was not her uncle.

"I don't understand. My mother told me…" But what had she actually said? That her father loved her. That her father was a great man. That her father could not live with them like other fathers. She fixed her attention on her aunt. "Who?"

"This man, who is your father, I wish to say

that he asked your mother to be his second wife.
And his first wife agreed to bring your mother
into her lodge. But your mother had just left her
husband and his wives. She had been very unhappy there and had no interest in becoming a
second wife again. Also, she once told me that she
knew this man loved his first wife with his whole
heart. He was much older than your mother then,
perhaps twice her age. She turned down his offer
and asked him not to claim you. This was a hard
thing to do because this man and his wife had no
children then or now."

Sky's eyes widened as a possibility rose in her
mind.

Her aunt continued. "When you were born he
asked again, begged to claim you as his daughter. But your mother reminded him of the promise he made."

"Aunt, who is my father?"

"A healer, like you. A leader and a husband
who has no child but you."

"His name?" And then another thought struck
her. If he had been an old man when she was born
he might have already crossed the spirit road. If
her father was dead, then her aunt would not,
could not speak his name. To discover her father
was not her father and that her real father might
be dead—it was too much. The tears began to

leak from her eyes and roll down her face. "Has he crossed over the way of souls?"

"No. He lives. Your father is alive."

"Spirit Bear," said Wood Duck.

"The shaman?" she whispered.

"Yes," said Winter Moon. "I discovered from my brother. It is easy when he speaks in opposites. I asked your mother and she admitted the truth but asked me never to tell. I have kept that promise."

Sky thought of Spirit Bear, seemingly an old man even then and then recalled the man who she remembered as if in a dream, from her earliest memories, when her mother still walked out in the forest and Sky used to chase butterflies. There was a man with white hair. Had it been Spirit Bear?

Sky looked to Falling Otter, still blissfully unaware thanks to the Black Hemp tea.

"But why did my mother not let Spirit Bear claim me?"

"She said she did not want the tribe gossiping about her and Spirit Bear. She did not wish to bring pain or shame to his wife, who was unable to bear his children."

"Strange the man who can heal so many could not heal my mother." Just as she had been unable to find a cure for her. At the end she could do nothing but ease her pain, and she recalled Spirit Bear had come and sung her to the way of souls, so she could cross safely to the spirit world.

As she sat beside the woman she had known her entire life, something occurred to her.

"If Falling Otter is not my father, then you are not my aunt."

Winter Moon paused and gave her the look of exasperation that she had seen so many times after returning from the forest alone.

"I was your mother's best friend. I helped deliver you and I raised you after her death. I *am* your aunt, by choice if not by birth."

Sky hugged her.

When she drew back her gaze turned on Falling Otter.

"Did Falling Otter think I was his child?"

"He told everyone that you where his child. I don't know why they believed it. Falling Otter was the only one who ever shared your mother's lodge but only when it was very cold, so it made sense. Everyone just assumed."

Why had she never noticed that Falling Otter called her daughter the same way that he called a rabbit a bird?

"I think your mother preferred her freedom and solitude to the responsibilities of a wife."

"So Falling Otter is not my father." That truth

filled her with a real aching sadness for she loved him. She swallowed.

"Not all relationships are forged in birth," said Winter Moon.

Sky nodded her agreement as she looked at her father. He had been there, helped raise her, taught her how to climb trees and catch frogs, and made her laugh so hard her sides ached. He had carried her on his shoulders and lifted her so she could pick the highest fruit. He had followed her to the Black Lodges and he was always close when she needed him.

She rested a hand on his uninjured arm.

"This man, Falling Otter, *is* my father in all ways that matter. He claimed me and in his own way, he raised me. And today, he saved my life," she said, looking at Falling Otter with new eyes. "He threw a rabbit at a charging warrior."

"A live rabbit?" asked Wood Duck.

"A dead one. It hit the Sioux warrior in the face."

Wood Duck chuckled. "I would bet good tobacco that that surprised him."

Sky laughed. "Indeed. It changed the direction of his charge from me to him.""

"Worst weapon imaginable," said Wood Duck.

"It worked," said Winter Moon, defending her brother. "She's alive and he's alive."

"I'm dead," said Falling Otter without opening his eyes.

"Have you been listening all along?" asked his sister.

"No," he said.

"Are you hungry?" asked Winter Moon.

"No."

"I'll get you something."

Sky moved to Falling Otter and took his hand. "Thank you, Father, for rescuing me."

He smiled. "No. You are dead and I am dead." He began to chant as a shaman might do over the body of a dying warrior, but then he groaned and pinched his eyes shut tight.

She stroked his forehead and checked his wound. Then she kissed his brow.

He smiled. "Go away."

"Yes, I will stay with you," she said.

He nodded his head and gave her hand a squeeze. "No."

Falling Otter drank some broth and Wood Duck helped him rise and leave the lodge for a few minutes. Inside the lodge, Sky helped her aunt set out the sleeping skins.

When they drew apart, her aunt looked down at Night Storm.

"Does he usually sleep so long after falling?"

Sky moved to his side. "No. Not usually. But this fall was a bad one."

She studied him, seeing his color was good and his breathing normal. She noted something else. Beneath his closed lids, his eyes moved fast.

"Dreaming," said Winter Moon. "Should we wake him?"

Sky shook her head. She caught movement and looked to the circular rawhide door of the tepee that was reinforced by a frame of wood. At first she thought it was Wood Duck and Falling Otter, but the flap lifted only a few inches. Sky reached for her skinning knife but relaxed when she recognized a certain long furry snout and wet black nose.

Frost poked his head into the lodge.

"Who is this?" asked Winter Moon as the dog slipped into the lodge uninvited.

"An honored guest. His name is Frost."

Sky smiled. She was not surprised that Frost had found his master and thought she should have expected it. Frost greeted Sky with a wagging tail, then politely greeted Winter Moon with a lick of her extended hand and finally moved to Night Storm to sniff at him. Then he folded in close to his master, resting his head on Storm's stomach.

Some relationships are not forged in birth but in love.

## Chapter Twenty-Two

Night Storm woke in the darkness to find his head aching and his body stiff and sore. The metallic taste still clung to his tongue. He stared up at the poles of the lodge, trying to grasp a thought or a memory of how he came here and where he was.

"Sky," he whispered. Something had happened to Sky.

And then she was there, her face glowing warm in the light of the dying central fire.

"Shh. All is well."

On his opposite side something cold and wet touched his neck. He startled and then found Frost resting his head on his master's chest, so it was easy to lift his arm to the top of his dog's head.

"Safe?" he asked.

"Yes. You can rest. We are all safe."

Storm closed his eyes. "Dreaming," he murmured. "A boy, sick from eating white berries."

"What boy?" Sky asked.

"I don't know. Black face. Many owls are waiting for him." The pull of sleep was so strong. He struggled to open his eyes but could not. The visions came again of owls lurking in trees and walking boldly up to the fevered boy. Beside him, a shaman wearing the headdress of a bear chanted and prayed, waving sacred smoke over the boy with the feathered wing of a hawk. The horned owl in the tree rotated its head in Storm's direction.

"If you don't wake, I will have to guide him to the ghost road," said the owl.

Night Storm startled awake. Beside him, Frost rose to his feet and Sky pushed up onto her elbow, blinking at him with tired eyes.

The light visible through the top of the lodge was now brighter than the light of the fire. Dawn, he thought, or just before dawn.

The visions rushed back to him. The boy. The owl.

"I have to get up." He told her all he could recall.

"Who is this boy?"

He did not recognize him although he had seen him clearly because the black paint covered his face.

"Perhaps he is of my people," she said. "I will

ask my aunt if any are ill. White berries, you said?"

Night Storm rose to find himself in an unfamiliar lodge. Sky explained where he was. Why he could not remember coming here was obvious. Night Storm rose stiffly but was unsteady on his feet. Wood Duck assisted him out of the lodge.

Skylark joined him a few minutes later. She set a backrest made of a series of sticks laced with buckskin on a frame before her aunt's lodge and covered it with a buffalo robe. He was shamed that he needed help to lie down, and felt dizzy and sick just from the exertion of relieving himself.

"I asked my aunt if any boys are ill and she said she did not think so, but she sent her husband to ask our shaman."

Sky settled beside him to grind Timpsula into flour.

"Who saw my fall?" Storm asked, already knowing the answer.

The pestle stopped in her hand. "Everyone."

His shoulders sagged. So, the worst had come at last. He would be asked to come to the council lodge and then he would learn if he was to lose his position or be banished.

"Were you staring at the river?" she asked.

He looked up at her. "What?"

"When you rescued me from the Sioux warriors, you were riding fast. Were you staring at the waters of the river?"

He thought back. The sunlight had been bright on the tall grass, flashing past him, flashing and flashing until it flashed bright as lightning.

"The sunlight on the tall grass."

Was she still trying to fix him? There was no point now.

"It doesn't matter," he said.

Light leaked into the eastern sky dulled by gray clouds. The river meandered along and women paused in their conversations until after they passed the strange warrior who wore an owl feather in his hair. Around them, men sang their morning prayers and women began their ceaseless work.

Frost remained close to Storm, which worried him. It meant that he might expect another fall.

"Flashing lightning, the sun flickering through bright new green leaves, the sun dancing on blue lake waters, the sun during your sun dance, the sunshine flashing on tall grass."

"You think Wi, the sun, is bringing my moth madness? It cannot be. I had a fall during the raid, or I nearly did. I closed my eyes and it went away. Wi does not shine at night. Only Hanwi, the moon."

"Light," she said. "It is light or sun or moon. I

think it is your fractured skull and light. The two together. Flashing light of any sort."

He tried to think but the knowledge that his secret was out, coupled with the dullness that followed an attack, made it hard to concentrate.

"I cannot avoid light."

"Perhaps not. I must think on this. Usually, I deal with healing plants. But perhaps my grandmother was wrong. Perhaps not all conditions can be healed or need to be."

So even she had given up on him. Could he really blame her? He thought back to their bargain. He had been selfish to tie her to him until the gathering.

"It doesn't matter. You set out my things so I am not your concern."

Storm closed his eyes against the nausea that rolled inside him.

She told him of her discovery that her father was not who she had been told. She said that at the time of her birth that her father had offered to claim her before all the people. The news lifted his spirits for the time it took to realize that he was no fit husband for such a desirable wife. She was now the daughter of their shaman and he was a man who saw things that were not there and had fits. He could not offer to make her his bride, no matter how many horses he had. And she would be foolish to even consider him as a suitor now that her options were so vast. He could not make her his wife. Skylark waited to ask him what he thought of her news.

He opened his eyes to look at her beautiful face.

"It is good that you have set my things outside our lodge because many men will now seek you out."

She frowned, clearly displeased with his answer. He did not care. It must be done.

She took hold of his hand. "There are still a few days yet until the fall gathering."

He drew his hand away from here. "I release you from that promise, Skylark."

She stared at him with wide eyes and her breathing came quick.

Frost lifted his head a moment before the lodge door lifted and Wood Duck appeared.

"I have seen the shaman. He says no children are sick."

Sky's shoulder's sagged in relief.

"He also said that Night Storm is to come to his lodge and stay there until he can return to his family at the gathering."

"But we can care for him," said Sky.

"It is done," said Wood Duck.

Storm tried to rise but, to his great shame, he

had to be carried by travois through the village to the lodge of the shaman, Spirit Bear. His shame was now complete.

After Storm was sent to the lodge of the Shaman, Skylark tried over several days to see Night Storm, but Starlight Woman, the shaman's wife, always said he was resting and could not be disturbed.

On the day before the camp was struck, Sky even had the audacity to approach Spirit Bear as he left the council lodge. Instead of allowing her to see Night Storm, Spirit Bear asked her if she knew how the warrior in his lodge was connected to owls.

"How do you know this?" she asked.

"I see them in the smoke and in my visions. I think that one has visions, too, though he does not know what to do with them. There is power in him. But it is a spiritual power and he seeks only physical power. Odd. Very odd."

Sky was so shocked she did not know what to say to Spirit Bear.

"He tells me that you are the one who recognized that it is the light that triggers his falls and that you stopped one fall simply by covering his eyes."

She nodded.

"Has he told you of his visions?"

"Yes," she admitted. "May I see him?"

Spirit Bear motioned in the direction of his lodge. Spirit Bear called a greeting and asked his wife to come out. She appeared a moment later, her step lithe and graceful despite being in her winter years. She left the flap up so Sky could enter. Sky hesitated as her anticipation faded to dread. What if he still did not want to see her?

Sky gathered her courage and stepped into the dim light of the lodge.

Night Storm was there, sitting before the fire, shirtless and dressed only in his loincloth. Beside him, Frost lifted his head, sighted her and thumped his tail upon the buffalo robes.

Storm glanced up at the visitor and drew in a breath as he recognized Skylark. He felt the immediate tug in his middle and his skin tingled as he resisted the urge to reach for her.

She fell to her knees beside him and threw her arms about him. The familiar fragrance of growing things surrounded him. He breathed deep. It was hard not to embrace her. But he could not. He was no longer a warrior of the Black Lodges. In truth he did not know what he was. The shaman had told him many strange things and he was struggling to find his new path. Sky stiffened and then withdrew, her expression now uncertain.

"What is happening? My uncle says we will

wait for the gathering and then turn you over to your council."

Did she also know that they would likely strip him of his position and banish him?

One look at her worried expression and tightly locked hands told him that she understood.

"Soon we will know."

"We will strike camp tomorrow," she said. "Are you well enough to walk?"

It hurt him enough that he could not ride. To be dragged behind a horse again was the ultimate shame. He did not think his pride could survive it.

The following day he did walk for part of the morning, but the journey cost him dearly. He did not fall, but his vision was bad with much rolling and waving. His muscles trembled and Spirit Bear called from a travois.

"A man rides," said Night Storm.

"Falling Otter does not ride. I do not ride. We are both men."

Spirit Bear helped Night Storm onto the travois and he fell back to the hides wearily. Instead of riding the perimeter and guarding the women and children from attack, he trod among them, eating the dust of those who traveled before him. Spirit Bear's wife walked with him as she guided a second travois full of the household belongings.

It was an even greater shame when he saw the moving caravan of his people, the warriors whooping and calling greetings. After the two groups merged, several broke away and he recognized the spotted stallion of his father's favorite traveling horse. It took little time for his father to cross the distance between them.

Storm met his father's stern, judgmental stare. Storm lifted his hand in greeting but his father wheeled away, galloping from the line to rejoin his men. Two trailed behind the others, waiting at the side of the slow-moving line of women. He had the shame of being dragged past his friends, Laughing Jay, Little Elk and Charging Bull, who sat astride their horses in silence as he passed like a ghost and then galloped forward to join the warriors.

That evening, they made a temporary camp. Skylark came to offer him buffalo stew, but he had little appetite for food or company.

It was well into the third day before they reached the place of the winter camp. They were not the first to arrive. Already the Wind Basin people had set their lodges along the far side of the winding river. Only the Shallow Water tribe had yet to arrive.

Storm glanced about at the familiar place. This encampment had been winter base for as long as Night Storm could recall, because it had good water and wide stretches of grassland for the larger herds of horses. Most importantly, the hills surrounding the camp gave good wood for the hungry fires and protected the people from the roaring winds of winter.

The Low River people and the Black Lodges people were greeted warmly, and the camping sites were chosen at random. Some preferred to stay with their tribe and others found places near the families they had left to marry. Soon the men would go on a buffalo hunt to bring the winter meat and the women would follow to butcher their kills. Where would he be then?

Storm did not have long to wait. For he was called before his council the afternoon after the camp was set. He went alone, for neither his father nor his brother came with him. Outside the large communal tepee of the Black Lodges, he found two men waiting, Falling Otter and Spirit Bear. Spirit Bear wore a cloak made from the skin of a bear, the skull forming the headdress that covered much of the top of his head. Falling Otter had painted himself yellow but was otherwise dressed as a man, which was a relief to Storm. He did not think matters could be any graver, but seeing the heyoka made him wonder.

Outside the lodge sat many women he did not know and four he did. His sisters, mother and Skylark sat among them, eager for news from the council lodge and within easy hearing of all that would be said. Somehow their presence gave him the strength he needed to enter the lodge and face their decision.

Spirit Bear called a greeting and Night Storm was asked to enter. Spirit Bear did not join him at the council because he had not been invited. This business was for the Black Lodges only. Falling Otter did not wait to be invited. Night Storm took his seat and Falling Otter joined the circle, puffing up his chest as if he were very important, indeed. Night Storm found himself smiling as he realized how important and unimportant each man really was, which may have been Falling Otter's intent.

The proceedings began. Night Storm was accused by Thunder Horse of being possessed by ghosts and evil spirits. He blamed the daughter of the heyoka for Night Storm's trouble and assured all that he had cured Storm of his injuries after the fall, but that the hole in his skull had allowed bad spirits to enter.

When the talking stick was passed, many of the men spoke of Storm's bravery in battle but also of the changes since the fall. Some said he could no longer serve as a warrior. Thunder Horse called for Storm's banishment.

"He is possessed by ghosts and evil spirits and must not be allowed to draw them to the living."

His shaman passed the talking stick to the warrior next to him, the leader of the Black War Bonnet society, Many Coups, Night Storm's father.

"I know that my son cannot ride. But some injuries take time to heal. A broken leg might take three moons or more. Should a broken skull be any less? I ask for time for my son."

Storm felt his chest tighten. His father had done what he could, but Thunder Horse had the stick again and was warning of all the evil that storm could bring. Sickness. Poor hunts. Heavy snows. Outside the lodge came the shout of a woman and then several voices as some sort of disturbance ensued.

The stick was passed and no other spoke of waiting and time. Falling Otter snatched up the stick and rose. He did a fine imitation of Thunder Horse calling for banishment and warned that there was no place in any tribe for a man who did not ride and raid. Then he pointed the stick at Thunder Horse who did not ride or raid and then at Night Storm and finally at himself. His message was received. Many men among them served the tribe without mounting a horse. Finished, Falling Otter passed the stick to Storm's longtime friend, Two Hawks, and then lay down to take a nap.

"I have heard that this one has visions," said Two Hawks. "And that in those visions he saw a raid by Sioux warriors that came to pass as he predicted. I believe that Night Storm has become a farseeing man, that his fall allowed him to walk the ghost road and then return. One like this is important and must find a place among the people."

The stick came to Night Storm. He held it, thinking of all he might say and all he should say. Instead, he handed the stick to his friend, Charging Bull, who also spoke for him.

"My friend has been injured. He needs time to heal. I say we wait until the Fast Water Moon. Then we will know what is best to do."

And Night Storm would be allowed to stay in camp during the time when the White Man of the north took over the earth. It was a stay of judgment.

Thunder Horse interrupted. "We could all be dead by then."

"Night Storm is a brave man," said Charging Bull, ignoring the rude interruption. "And he has hunted and fought with honor. He deserves this consideration," said Charging Bull, and then passed on the stick.

Thunder Horse did not wait for the talking stick to reach him but broke in. "He is a threat to us all. I am a seer of spirits. And I see that this one is haunted by the ghosts of his enemies. Those ghosts will lead the living warriors to us. He must go now."

Night Storm listened as the discussion continued. He had no choice but to abide by the decision of the leaders of his people, but in his heart he knew that the worst had already happened.

It had taken a lifetime to become a warrior and only the turning of a day to cease to be one.

## *Chapter Twenty-Three*

Sky sat among the women as, one by one, the men left the council lodge and went to their wives to confirm the decision. Night Storm was no longer one of the people and was no longer welcome in their camp. She stayed where she was as their chief, Broken Horn, left with Storm's father, Many Coups. Neither man looked at her. Most of the tribe remained, waiting for Night Storm to emerge for all wanted to see the haunted man before he left them for good.

Finally Night Storm emerged, looking gaunt and pale, but he held his head up as he walked among them. Frost stepped forward to greet him, but he was the only one. All the people stood back, staring at the banished man.

Sky had not seen Beautiful Meadow, but she recognized her now as she came forward with a woman who looked very much like her, but somewhat older. On her other side was a man of importance, judging from his elaborate head-dress and the ermine strips fixed to the sleeves of his shirt. Her father, Sky guessed, who was a member of the tribal council of the Wind Basin band.

It was the man who spoke. "Night Storm, you have deceived my daughter into believing you could provide for her. You are unfit to be a warrior of the Black Lodges and so you are unfit to be a warrior of Wind Basin. I am here to tell you that you are not welcome among us and that you will not have my daughter for your wife."

Night Storm nodded to the warrior who was to be his second father. Sky wondered why his own father was not beside him as Storm faced this man.

"I release her from her promise," said Storm. "And wish her every happiness."

Beautiful Meadow stepped forward. "You are not a man."

Her father took hold of Beautiful Meadow and guided her away. She made a great show of weeping and her mother wrapped an arm about her as the crowd moved to let them pass.

All was silent and Sky did not know what to do. Should she go stand beside Storm? Where were his sisters and mother?

And then Falling Otter appeared wearing a metal cooking pot on his head. He shouted edicts to the crowd, banishing everyone because they had not served him a midday meal and then blessing them because they were punishing a very bad man.

They did not laugh at his antics now. In fact, they shrank away from Falling Otter and his terrible blessings. Clearly the heyoka of the Low River tribe did not believe that their council had reached the correct decision. He made such a fuss, clanging the pot on his own head and shouting that none noticed as Night Storm made his way through the gawking gathering of Low River, Shallow Water, Wind Basin and Black Lodges people.

But Sky noticed. She followed him and clasped his arm. He looked at her with eyes that seemed already dead.

"Let me go, Skylark."

"I will not."

He pulled free.

"Where are you going?" she asked.

Storm paused and turned back to her. "Did you not hear. I am banished from my people."

"Then come to mine."

He scowled at her as if she were the heyoka.

"Go away, Sky. Go and have the life that you deserve."

She reached out for him. "She let you go. You have no other woman. We can marry again."

He laughed.

She clung tighter. "If you marry me again, you can stay in my lodge. I will make one for us."

He faced her. "From what? I will not bring you any hides because I cannot hunt."

"I will trade my medicines for hides. We can live with my aunt and uncle until I have enough."

It was so tempting, her offer. He wanted nothing more in the wide world than to live with Skylark as her husband. But this was the daughter of the shaman of the Low River People. And he was a man who had lost everything.

He shook his head and peeled her fingers from his arm. "No."

He had his lost place among his people and the woman he loved, all in one day.

"You have drifted from your path. We will find a new one. We just need to find a new purpose for you."

"Like painting shields for other warriors or making saddles? No, Skylark. That is not my path."

He turned to go and then remembered his belongings were in the lodge of her shaman and changed direction. He would take his horse, Gallop, and his weapons. He might last until the deep cold of the Empty Belly Moon.

"You will not stay?" she asked.

"No."

"Then I will come with you."

He stilled, turned and drew her up by her shoulders. "I have not asked you."

Nor would he, because he cared too much for her to let her throw her life away.

She gave him her most stubborn look. "I will follow you."

They stood at an impasse. He knew she could follow him. She was a very skillful tracker and the most determined woman he had ever met.

"Why?" he asked. "Why will you not stay here in safety with the family who loves you? Why will you not let the shaman claim you as his daughter and then take your pick of the best of the warriors from the Crow people? Why will you not take the life you have always wanted?"

She narrowed her eyes at him. "Because they do not keep my heart."

His eyes widened and his fingers slipped from her upper arms. The reason he was sending her away was the reason she would not go and the realization that she loved him changed nothing. He felt his own heart tear into pieces.

"Oh, Skylark. I am sorry…for us both."

She threw herself into his arms and he allowed himself the comfort of her embrace. Just a moment longer and then he would let her go.

"Skylark!"

She drew away from him and he lifted his head to see the wife of the shaman of the Low River people, Starlight Woman, hurrying toward them at a trot.

"You must come. Our chief's son is dying."

"I will get my medicines," said Skylark.

She stepped away from Storm and then paused as if realizing that he would take this opportunity to leave her. She gave him a pleading stare that cut into his tattered heart.

"You, too," said Starlight Woman to Night Storm.

"Me? Why?" he asked. Was this some trick to keep him?

"Because my husband told me to find you both even if I had to interrupt the tribal council of the Black Lodges."

That made Night Storm and Skylark straighten. As far as he knew, no woman had ever interrupted a gathering of tribal leadership. It was not done and showed the seriousness of Starlight Woman's mission.

"Quick now," said the messenger, and trotted back the way she had come.

Night Storm and Skylark ran after her and did not stop until they had reached the lodge of the chief of the Low River people, Bright Arrow.

From inside came a moaning of someone in great pain.

"Who is ill?" asked Skylark.

"The chief's youngest boy," answered Starlight Woman.

"A boy," said Skylark, her brow wrinkling. "A child." She turned to Night Storm. "What did you tell me about a boy who was ill? You said you saw a young child. What did you see?"

"It might not be that child. The one I saw was barely out of his mother's cradleboard."

Skylark called a greeting and the door flap was thrust open by a slim hand. Sacred smoke from both sage and sweetgrass billowed from the opening. Sky ducked in before him. He followed, taking a moment as his eyes adjusted to the dim light. The second inner hide had already been set about the bottom third of the lodge. This would keep the family warmer during the time of cold by trapping air between the inner and outer walls of hide, but it was unusual to have already filled the gap with dried grasses. The result was a very dark interior since the fire was no more than embers.

Sky was already kneeling beside the small prone figure of a boy dressed only in a loincloth. His skin was covered with beads of water as if he were inside a sweat lodge. Sky's back blocked his view of the child's face, but he appeared to be only two or three winters old.

Storm looked at the others gathered near. There was Bright Arrow, looking grave and worried. Gone was his usual air of authority and power for he was faced with a foe he could not fight. Beside him was his wife, with her hands pressed over her eyes as she cried. It was her moans that he had heard from outside the lodge for the boy was still as death and pale as the chalk that clung to the muddy places in the river.

At the head of the gathering was Spirit Bear. He held a turtle rattle in one hand and a smoking bundle of sweetgrass in the other. He ceased his prayers as he noted Night Storm and bowed his head to him in a way that one would use to honor an elder. His actions confused Storm mightily. He did not know why he had been summoned here. He had no healing gifts and had no idea what use he might be.

Sky asked several questions to the wife of the chief. How long had he been ill? Where did he take ill? Did she see a snake? What had he eaten and drank? Had he complained of any pain before losing consciousness?"

Sky folded at the waist and listened to the boy's heart. Then she quickly removed the boy's loin-cloth and searched him for any sign of injury or bite. Storm moved closer as Sky smelled the boy's breath and then checked inside his mouth. There she found something partially eaten, but the greenish mash on her finger was unidentifiable.

She looked to him, but he shrugged, helpless as all the rest.

"Is it poison?" Skylark asked him.

He looked from her to the boy, seeing his face for the first time. He did not know him. But in that moment it was as if someone struck him in the head again. Everything around him vanished as he again experienced the dream he had seen twice in two different falls. A boy, this boy, play-ing in a shady grove. His mother gathering wild cherries for drying. This child found a grove of berries, too. White ones, each with a black spot so that they resembled an eyeball. The boy picked one and tried the fruit, smiled and then hurried to gather a handful, plucking the tiny beads from their bright red stems and eating one after an-other. He collected another handful and returned to his mother to tell her of his find, but then he pressed a hand to his chest and dropped to his knees. The berries he had gathered for his mother fell from his hands and disappeared into the tall yellow grass.

"Storm!"

He blinked his eyes. Skylark was beside him, gripping his shoulders and shouting.

"It's him." His words were slow and strange to his ears.

"What?" she said.

"I saw him. The boy from my visions."

Sky straightened and turned to the shaman. "He sees things when he falls."

"Yes," said Spirit Bear. "I know. He has the aura of a farseeing man."

Had their shaman known all along? But now Night Storm's mind refocused. He knew this boy and he knew why he was summoned. What he did not know was how to save him.

"He ate berries in the woods."

"Cherries," said his mother.

"No. White with a single black mark growing on a deep red stem."

Sky gave a little shout of terror. "Baneberry!"

Both the shaman and Skylark shot into action. Skylark rolled the boy to his side and shoved two fingers down his throat, while Spirit Bear scraped charcoal from a burnt log into a horn cup and mixed it with water. The boy gagged and vomited as the remains of the berries in his stomach came up and out.

The boy was gasping now, his eyes fluttering. He looked about and called for his mother. The shaman gave the cup to the woman and she held it to her boy's lips. He drank, wretched and threw up again. This time the shaman gave him water and then Skylark made him vomit again. At last the boy was weeping and clinging to his mother. But he was awake. Sky listened to his chest from his narrow back.

"Slow," she said.

"He will be sick," said Spirit Bear. "But he will not die. Thanks to this healer and this far-seeing man."

Storm found all eyes staring at him with looks of wonder.

"I just…he was the boy from my dream."

The shaman laughed and Bright Arrow dragged Night Storm into a fierce embrace. When he released him, the chief said, "I am in your debt, Night Storm. You need only ask and I will do all I can for you."

Night Storm looked to Skylark, who lifted her gaze at him and nodded.

"I don't understand any of this," said Night Storm.

Now it was the shaman who spoke. "We do not always choose our path. Sometimes the path chooses us."

Skylark rested a hand over Storm's.

Spirit Bear spoke. "You are not a warrior, Night Storm. You are a shaman. And, in time, you will be a very powerful one. But first we must teach you to call the visions, instead of letting them call you."

"Is that possible?"

"Anything is possible. Skylark says that she already kept you from falling by covering both eyes. We know that the visions are summoned by flashing light. We will find the answer with time. Come, you and I must talk."

They left the lodge together—Bright Arrow, the Shaman and Night Storm. Skylark remained to help watch over the boy who had ceased his crying and was now sleeping in his mother's arms.

Night Storm emerged into sunlight to join the two leaders of the Low River people. He thought he should tell them what had happened in the council of the Black Lodges. He cleared his throat and then formally told them of the decision of his tribal council to banish him. When he was finished, the men exchanged a look and then Bright Arrow spoke.

"You are welcome in my camp. We would be honored to have such a powerful seer among us."

Spirit Bear took charge of Night Storm and as they walked together, the shaman said, "We must find you a new name, one that suits your status as a shaman and one that you perhaps already have chosen?"

Storm nodded, remembering his vision quest and the first creature he had seen. The one he had tried to deny ever since that time.

"I see owls. I hear owls and I am followed by owls."

The old shaman did not draw away in horror. "It is a powerful spirit animal and appropriate for one who speaks to ghosts."

"Is that what I do?" he asked.

"Ghosts or perhaps to those who have crossed. The veil between these worlds is never parted for long. But I have seen it lift for those who are close to crossing the spirit road. Most of these souls I have sung to their death. Some have told me what they saw before crossing, but none has ever come back from the ghost road except for you."

Night Storm felt the rightness of what this holy man was telling him, but still he suffered the tug of what might have been.

"I was going to be like my father, the head

of my medicine lodge and a warrior with many coups."

"But that is no longer your path."

He slowed and the shaman stopped beside him.

"I do not know how to be a holy man."

"I will teach you and you will teach me. When I go to the Spirit Road, it will be good to have you sing me to the other side."

His predecessor, Night Storm realized. Spirit Bear was offering to make him shaman of the Low River people.

"But I am not Low River."

"And neither was I until I took a wife."

"I have no wife," he said, the regret tightening his stomach.

"Ah, well. I may not be a farseeing man, but I see that you will not be without a wife for very long."

Storm's eyes widened as he realized that Sky could now be his. If he were a shaman, if he could learn from this holy man, he could take a wife. Not just a wife—he could marry Skylark, the daughter of Spirit Bear.

"I have to go see her," he said.

The shaman took hold of his elbow and set them in motion in the opposite direction. "Soon, soon. But first we shall have some tea."

It was more than tea, of course. First there was much talk and then his education began, and well before he saw the winter camp again, over a moon had passed.

# Chapter Twenty-Four

The drums pounded as the men danced around the central fire. Skylark attended the gathering to celebrate the making of meat. The hunt had been good. The tribes of the Crow people had worked together to bring down many buffaloes. The men had been very brave and only two horses had been killed by the horns of the sacred bison. Hides had been collected, meat made and eaten and dried. The frost had crept over the land as the Winter Camp Moon turned to the Story Moon.

Only one moon ago she and Storm had saved Bright Arrow's boy from death. Then, the following day, her father had claimed her publically. His words were bittersweet, for as she stood at the shaman's side, she saw the tears of Falling Otter. Just this once she thought that instead of joy, she saw some sorrow there in his eyes. Since that day she was the target of many calf eyes from many of the single warriors. But the one man she craved had not come to court her.

Skylark wished she could share her aunt's triumph at this turn of events, but instead she felt only a deep sadness, punctuated by disquiet. Perhaps she was heyoka, after all.

It all stemmed from Night Storm. After Spirit Bear had claimed her as his child, he and Night Storm had left the winter camp.

When would he come back? Was he all right? How could Storm go on a vision quest when he was ill and the weather was so cold? These questions spun like dried leaves in her mind at night, keeping her from rest. She lost her appetite but not her purpose. In the absence of Spirit Bear, she was very busy with the injuries and illnesses of the Low River people and even saw some of the Black Lodges women. Now that she was the shaman's daughter, some of the Black Lodges people sought her out, including an annoying number of young warriors who had no real injuries at all but requested salves and tinctures for aching muscles and twisted joints. Some offered to play their flutes for her. Her aunt urged her to step out into the night with several young men, but she remained in her sleeping robes and in the lodge of her aunt.

She had broken her link with the moon twice

since Night Storm's departure, so she knew she did not carry Storm's child. The realization only added to her sorrow.

This night there was a celebration for their hunt and she sat with her aunt watching the married women dance in a slow proud circle. Finally the drums ceased and another song began. She watched the wives leave the circle before the great blazing fire as the maidens took their place. Sky sighed and looked at the heavens above.

"Enough moping," said her aunt. "Get up and dance with the unmarried women. Let them all see the shaman's only daughter."

Winter Moon poked her in the ribs until Sky-lark rose to her feet and joined the assembling circle of maidens. But as she danced, instead of seeing the smiling faces of the single men, she saw the married women, sitting with their children. Would he ever come back?

The dance went round and round, like the days and the seasons and the circle of a woman's life. Finally the drums ceased and she could safely return to her place beside her aunt. The warrior dance was next and she watched the men leap and spin, showing their prowess. Among them was one small woman, Snow Raven, the chief's sister. Snow Raven pounded the ground with her feet. In her hair were the coup feathers that marked her right to join the others, for she was a fearsome warrior and a leader of great experience. She showed Skylark by example that it was possible to follow one's heart and be what she wished. Beside her danced her husband Iron Wolf. Somehow Snow Raven had become a warrior and made her warrior one of the Crow people. This was no small task as Iron Wolf had been born to the enemy Sioux. All knew the story and Sky had heard it many times. How Snow Raven's grandmother had adopted this man to replace one who was lost in battle and how their shaman had washed away all his Sioux blood making him one of the Crow people. They were not like any other couple among them, and it was that very thing that made them important. Somehow that warrior was willing to leave the people of his birth to be with the woman he loved.

That gave her hope, as well. But when would Night Storm come back? And when he did she wondered if she would be able to change his mind about taking a wife.

The drumbeat ceased and the men stilled, then cheered before returning to the outer circle. In the echoing silence came the shrieking call of a screech owl. The people went still as each wondered who would die. The owl, the messenger of ghosts, was among them. It flew over the gathering on silent wings, a dark shadow against the night sky and soundless as death.

Skylark rose to her feet, the only one now standing as she looked about her. He was here. She knew it.

A low whisper began on the far side of the circle and the people rose, shifting to allow someone to pass. A familiar dog trotted into the circle, making his way straight to her.

Frost, she realized and stooped to hug the dog.

Next she saw Spirit Bear moving slowly through the gathering. Upon his head was the now familiar bearskin. The bear's muzzle and fearsome teeth extended past the shaman's white hair. In his hand was the long staff tied with cloth, feather, bead and the claws of many bear. The claws made a rattling sound as he placed his staff and moved forward. Someone walked behind him. The people near them fell back as if struck. The whisper changed to cries of alarm.

Skylark craned her neck to see who came behind their shaman. Hope rose as she searched for some glimpse of Night Storm. She had not realized that she had moved until her aunt clasped her arm, keeping her from entering the central circle.

The two men turned toward Bright Arrow, who was on his feet and was one of the few who showed no fear. His sister had her bow in one hand and an arrow in the other.

Skylark's gaze went to the man with Spirit Bear. She could not be sure who it was. Spirit Bear had left with Night Storm. But this man seemed taller than Night Storm, and his dress was so different. He did not wear his war shirt, leggings and moccasins like a warrior and hunter. His hair was no longer in the style of a warrior. She stared at the stranger, willing him to turn in her direction.

His hair was loose in the back and tied with many feathers of brown and white. The blunt ends of the feathers and the distinctive wavy edge told her instantly what kind of feathers these were. Owl feathers. Great horned owl mingled with the pure white of the snowy owl. His cloak was tanned leather and was emblazoned with the forked streak of red lightning, but instead of coming from a rain cloud, this streak of red light emanated from beneath the outstretched wings of a great white owl. He also carried a staff, and from the top were tied many strands of sinew threaded with bits of bone, feather, beaks, teeth, claws and talons. It was like seeing the inside of a warrior's medicine bundle, she thought. The collection of sacred objects rustled as he moved.

She stared at his face and saw he wore a leather patch across one eye. Had he been injured?

"Bright Arrow, chief of the Low River people," said Spirit Bear, lifting his staff high and raising his arms. He aimed the tip of his staff, topped with the shell of a box turtle, at the man next to him. "I present to you, White Owl, shaman and farseeing man."

White Owl? Skylark stepped to the front of the gathered women, who now stood in a silent circle.

Sky pressed her hands over her mouth.

Spirit Bear turned to the people. "This man is a great and powerful seer."

Sky lowered her hands so they pressed to her chest. Hope began to rise once more, squeezing her throat so that she could barely whisper her words.

"Is it him?" she asked her aunt.

"I do not know. It does not look like him."

The man in question turned in a slow circle. Skylark's breath caught. White Owl wore a neat leather patch across one eye and the feathered cap covered much of his other eye. But she knew him. It was Night Storm. She meant to run to him and leap into his arms. She had taken a step into the open circle when her uncle, Wood Duck, took hold of her.

"No, Sky." His grip was strong and held just enough pressure to gain her attention. "Look."

She did. She looked past White Owl to the

gathering. They stared in horror at this intruder.
Men gripped their weapons and women collected
their children as if preparing for flight. The tension pulled at her insides. It seemed that even their
chief, Bright Arrow, did not know what to do. Beside him, his sister notched her bow.

And then, from out of the darkness danced a
man painted white from his loincloth to the top
of his head. Around his neck, instead of a necklace of bear claw or medicine bundle, he wore a
gathered rope of dry Timpsula tubers.

He hooted and flapped his arms as he danced
without the accompaniment of the drums. The
only chant came from his lips. Falling Otter made
a circuitous route to the two medicine men, finally
dancing before White Owl.

He stopped his dance and the gathering fell
silent and still as the stars that shone above. Falling Otter lifted a finger and pointed it at White
Owl. Slowly his finger inched closer to White
Owl's bare chest. Sky pressed a hand to the base
of her throat.

Falling Otter's finger contacted the chest of
White Owl. Falling Otter gave a bloodcurdling
scream and fell to the ground as if shot through
the heart. He lay still as death. Everyone shifted to
get a better look. Sky found she could not breathe
as Falling Otter's legs began to thrash and then

kick. But then the kicking changed to a kind of dance step done from his back. The next moment his arms were waving and he laughed at them, the gathering of fearful men and women who could not approach a farseeing man because he wore the feathers of an owl. By slow degrees, Falling Otter rose as his dance continued. He danced around the holy men and then the chief, and then he took the arrow from the bow of Snow Raven. Sky had never seen anyone dare to touch a weapon belonging to this particular warrior and she realized again that Falling Otter was as brave as any warrior. Braver, because he dared to show all among them their folly for fearing one who was not like them.

Falling Otter patted White Owl on the shoulder and said, "Go away."

Then he danced back into the group and out of sight. His message was clear. Their heyoka believed that White Owl belonged among them.

Bright Arrow moved forward to greet the shaman of the Low River people and lift his hand in welcome to Spirit Bear's companion, White Owl.

Sky sagged with relief. They had accepted him. But would White Owl accept her?

White Owl stood beside his mentor before the gathering of the Low River people. Their shaman had taught him many things and he was a changed man, but he was also the same man inside himself.

He was surprised and pleased to have found acceptance among the Low River people, for he had wondered if a man who spoke to owls would find a place in any camp. He was different from his fellows. Not better or worse, just different. And accepting those changes in himself had been hard. But he had learned by the examples of Falling Otter and Spirit Bear and Skylark that it was better to be different than try to be what you were not.

As he looked across the circle for one particular face, hungry for the sight of her, he wished he might know if his future included Skylark. But, try as he might, he could never see her in his visions.

An owl and a lark were an odd couple, by any measure. Yet he longed for her now more than ever. She was the daughter of the shaman. A maiden of honor and status. Had her new status drawn many suitors? He knew that she might already be promised to another or worse. Many couples married at the gathering of tribes. He prayed Sky was not one of them.

As the dancing resumed, he watched for her without success. Beside him, Spirit Bear spoke to Bright Arrow. Their conversation was of importance, but he could not focus. The central fire lured him, but he had learned much in his time away with Spirit Bear. The flashing light called and it was up to him to answer. During the Winter Camp Moon the spells were many, but now, his headaches had finally lifted like a mist from a valley. And his balance was nearly restored. But most gratifying of all was that he could call the episodes now. Instead of being prey to the light, he was now again the hunter, stalking the visions as he once tracked deer.

What would Skylark say when she heard? She had been right—the key to his mastery of his weakness. She was the one who had realized it was not the water but the flashing light that brought the falls. And once, not so long ago, she had told him that he had her heart. He thought of his older brother, Iron Axe, and his courtship of Little Rain. It had taken him half a moon to woo and win her hand. White Owl had been gone twice that time. He might be a farseeing man, but he could not see if he still had her heart or if she would want a shaman for her husband. Perhaps he was too different than the warrior he had been.

He scanned the women on the far side of the circle. Each woman he looked upon quickly glanced away, as if to hold his stare would call bad luck. So the chief had welcomed him and their heyoka had sent him away. But the women had yet to decide if he was dangerous or safe. In truth he was neither. But he did have messages to relate. Many messages for the Crow people. His gaze continued to flick restlessly from one face to the next. He found her aunt, Winter Moon, who also looked immediately away, and then he saw her.

Skylark was thinner than he recalled and he wondered at the cause. Her cheekbones were more prominent and her eyes glittered dark and mysterious in the light of the central fire. She met his gaze and held on unflinchingly. He smiled. How could they not have seen the iron of their shaman, Spirit Bear, there in this slender woman?

He lifted a hand in greeting and she glanced away as if to see who he hailed. Finally, shyly she lifted her hand to shoulder height, palm out, greeting him. It was a start. Between them, the men took the place of the married women, to re-enact the success of the hunt. And all White Owl could think about was how to get to her. Finally, the great fire began to collapse, sending sparks into the cool air. At last, even the dancing could not keep them warm. The people grew tired and those with young ones ambled back toward their lodges and the warmth of their buffalo robes.

White Owl hastened after the departing families, but he lost sight of her in the darkness. In the throngs of people leaving the central fire, he forced himself to resist the urge to jump in the air to locate her. He did recall where her uncle had set his lodge, but upon reaching the correct place, he found the flap closed, signaling that all had turned in for the night. He stood looking at the thin wall of buffalo hide that separated them, wondering if she lay inside or if she had made a lodge for a new husband.

That thought caused an ache deep in his chest, as if something cut across his heart.

All about him came the murmur of voices as couples returned home or lingered beyond their parents' homes to steal a few moments alone in the near darkness. The moon was just a sliver in the sky, making the stars twinkle with particular brightness. He stared up at the ghost road with one uncovered eye, a glittering path to lead the dead to the spirit world.

What if he had lost her already?

He felt the tug of the sparkling shimmer, the urge to lose himself in the light. But he knew now, sensed how far he could go without ceasing to control the visions. There was a narrow ledge where he could stand and observe without tumbling out into the abyss. He retreated, shifting his stare and refocusing his attention. He did not want a vision now. He wanted the company of a tiny bird who did not fly at night. He wanted Skylark.

"White Owl?" The voice came from just beside him and he knew it instantly. "Is all well with you?"

She had found him. And suddenly he did not know the words to speak. What could he say that would let him have just one more chance to be all for her, as she was for him?

## *Chapter Twenty-Five*

Before Skylark stood the man she had fallen in love with, but now he seemed a stranger once more. He was changed. That much was certain. He had been on another vision quest and had taken a new name. But how much of him remained? Did he still have feelings for her?

She knew that shamans took wives, had children and lived among the people. They held great respect and were as powerful as the chief. Had White Owl set out to become a powerful man of great importance he could not have done better than to become a shaman. The fall he had taken was the message that he had ignored telling him he must take a different path. He was strong and so he fought this change. But now…now he was what he must be.

"Hello," he said.

They stood beneath the stars, a man, a woman

and silence. Frost left White Owl's side to greet her with a thumping tail. He wiggled like a puppy as she stroked his wiry coat.

"He has missed you," said White Owl.

"Yes." She straightened to face him.

"*I* have missed you," he said.

"You have?"

She felt the smile curling inside her like sunlight. His face was familiar, if thinner than she remembered. She took in the other changes and lingered on the patch over his left eye, remembering the buckskin she had once tied over his eyes.

"Is all well with you?" he asked.

He seemed tentative now. Not as authoritative as when he stood before the people.

"I am well," she said. "And you?"

"I have not fallen in over a moon. Spirit Bear even tried to bring the falls. But you were right. It is the light, sparkling, flashing, tumbling light."

She stepped closer, her fingers stroking the band that held the patch in place. "Did you injure your eye?"

"I did not. In fact I switch the patch day by day from one eye to the next." He lifted it now, drawing the patch to his forehead. And then she saw the face she recalled, handsome, winning and familiar.

She smiled and stroked his cheek. He stiffened and then captured her hand, pressing it to his mouth so that his lips kissed her palm. Then he released her.

"Skylark, it is only because of you that I am alive. And because of you, I learned that the light brought my spells. Spirit Bear made me wear this patch and taught me how to coax the visions."

"You were a seer before the fall," she said.

His brow wrinkled at that.

"What?"

"Your vision, it was filled with owls. The Great Spirit had chosen you even then."

He looked down at her and wondered if she would ever cease to amaze him.

"I did not recognize it then."

"You did not wish to recognize it because you wished to walk the warrior's way."

"That is so. Perhaps that was why I was unseated. Perhaps that was why I nearly died, and still I could not see my way."

White Owl looked down at the small radiant face that was more beautiful to him than the face of the moon.

"Do the owls not frighten you?" he asked.

"No longer, because now I understand that they are here to bring you messages from the world of spirits."

"I have seen many things and learned many things, but I never saw what I most wished to see."

"What is that?"

"You," he said.

That took her breath away and she stilled as the hope began to rise in her again.

"I hear that Spirit Bear has claimed you as his daughter."

"That is so."

"What of Falling Otter?"

"He will always be my father. Perhaps not by birth, but by all other measures."

"He was of great help tonight. For a time, I did not think your people would accept me."

"You did not seem frightened," she said.

"My fears are deeper now. My reputation, my place, it is not as important as what I see and how I serve the people."

"You have a gift."

"But I am no longer a warrior and will never be."

She said nothing and his fears mounted, gathering one upon the next like droplets of water that fill a river.

Had she found another?

"You once told me that you wished to marry a warrior and be like other women. Have you married, Skylark?"

"I have not." Her smile was coy and becoming.

He stepped closer. "I am certain you do not lack for suitors."

"Once I longed to hear the sound of flutes and to stand before my aunt's lodge wrapped with a young man in a blanket."

"And now?" His question was like dust in his mouth.

"I have grown tired of the sounds of flutes."

Perhaps she would be like her mother. Spirit Bear said Skylark's mother was beautiful and solitary. That she would not become his wife even after his first wife had gone to her to ask her to join their lodge.

"You do not wish for a man to play his flute for you?"

She smiled. "The young warriors seem more boys than men. Why do you ask me this?"

He found himself suddenly afraid. Nothing he'd experienced compared with the dread he now felt when he considered losing this woman. What were the right words to tell her how he felt, how much he needed her, longed for her and wanted her to walk with him throughout their lives.

He lifted a hand. "Once I wanted you here." He pressed a hand low on his stomach. "And then I wanted you here." He touched two fingers to his forehead. "But now I want you here." He pressed a hand to his heart. "I love you, Skylark."

She wrapped her arms about him, pressing her ear to his chest.

"Did you wait for me, Skylark? Or is there another?"

She drew back, smiling up at him.

"There will never be another." She took his hand and pressed it to her heart.

He released a long breath.

"Is it me, Skylark?"

She moved in close to him and placed her hands on his shoulders.

"Let it be me," he whispered.

Skylark lowered her head to his chest. "It has always been you."

He sprang like a snare, released by the slightest touch of his quarry, his arms coming about her and drawing her close. He lowered his head until his cheek rested on the top of her head.

His words where choked by emotion. "Thank the Great Spirit."

## Chapter Twenty-Six

White Owl heard the hooting of the horned owl coming from somewhere beyond his lodge, but now the great birds held no horror for him. He knew that it meant only that the spirits carried a message for his people. Five moons had passed since he was welcomed into the tribe of the Low River people. The Digging Moon had arrived and the winter camp had disbanded as each of the four tribes set off to their favored hunting grounds.

Beside him, his wife Skylark stirred and nestled closer to him, pressing her warm back against his naked chest. He wrapped an arm protectively about her middle, gauging the swell of her belly and then lifting a brow at the powerful kick of their child.

"Oof," she groaned, and then gave a soft chuckle that warmed his heart. She moved his hand so that it cradled her belly. "My aunt says that I used to kick like this and that it is a good sign for a strong child."

White Owl smiled as he held his wife and child in one embrace. Then he leaned in to nuzzle Skylark's neck.

"Do you ever see our child in your visions?" she asked, her hand now over his.

"Never. Spirit Bear says that it is the way with farseeing men, a blind spot like the white places in an old man's eyes. He says none of us should see our future too clearly."

"What did Bright Arrow say about your news?"

"He will send a hunting party to see if the blue pony boys are building a fort on the Green River."

"That is very close to our summer trapping area."

"Too close."

"Perhaps they are on a different river?" she asked.

He did not answer. He sometimes misinterpreted what he saw, like when he saw the hunters who fell through the ice and believed they were of the Wind Basin people, when it turned out they were Sioux scouts who had ventured onto a pocket of thin ice.

"Perhaps," he said.

Her breathing slowed and came in soft puffs of air as she dozed. Beneath his palm came the pushing of a tiny hand or foot. He pushed back and met resistance. He laughed.

White Owl knew that he would never lead a raid or be chosen to head a medicine society or earn another coup feather and he did not care. To his surprise and without any of those things, he had still earned the respect of his new people. In a strange unfolding of events, that fall from his horse had given him everything a man could ever hope for. The farseeing man had never seen far enough to predict his many blessings.

The owl hooted again.

"Tomorrow, my friend," he whispered, closing his eyes. "Tomorrow we will see what message you carry."

And then, the farseeing man fell into slumber with his arms wrapped around the most important ones in his life. Once he thought he was cursed. But now he saw the truth. He had been blessed and blessed again.

\* \* \* \* \*

# *The Moons*

1.  Fast Water Moon (mid-March to mid-April)
Runoff from melting snow and spring rains make
the rivers and streams run fast and high.

2.  Digging Moon (mid-April to mid-May)
Time for planting seeds and digging spring greens.

3.  Many Flowers Moon (mid-May to mid-June)
The prairies and meadows are alive with blos-
soms, birds and bees. Early berries are ripe.

4.  Little Rain Moon (mid-June to mid-July)
Rainfall is at its lowest. Rivers and streams run
low. Days are long and hot.

5.  Ripening Moon (mid-July to mid-August)
Many roots, seeds, tubers and plants are ready to
eat. Fish such as salmon begin to run.

6.  Hunting Moon (mid-August to mid-September)

A time for the fall hunt for winter buffalo robes and meat from deer, elk and buffalo.

7.  War Moon (mid-September to mid-October)

Time to war with enemies.

8.  Winter Camp Moon (mid-October to mid-November)

Tribes of different clans gather for the winter camp.

9.  Story Moon (mid-November to mid-December)

Snows fall heavily, nights are long. People gather to hear stories, repair and create clothing, weapons and tack.

10.  Freezing Moon (mid-December to mid-January)

The serious cold comes. Families stay close to the fires and game is scarce.

11.  Deep Snow Moon (mid-January to mid-February)

The time of the heaviest snows and most serious storms. Deer strip the bark from the trees because they can no longer dig through the snow to the grass.

12. Empty Belly Moon (mid-February to mid-
    March)
This moon the food stores often run short and the
people are hungry.


*The names of the moons are the author's in-
terpretation based on Native American culture.
    Each tribe refers to the months of the year in
their own way.
    **The year begins with spring, because spring
is the first season in the medicine wheel for many
native people.

# MILLS & BOON®

## EXCLUSIVE EXCERPT

Don't miss Laura Martin's contribution to THE
GOVERNESS TALES, a series of four sweeping
romances with fairy-tale endings, by Georgie Lee,
Laura Martin, Liz Tyner and Janice Preston!

*Read on for a sneak preview of*
GOVERNESS TO THE SHEIKH
*the second book in the enticing new Historical quartet*
**THE GOVERNESS TALES**

'Please, come through to the courtyard. I will have
someone fetch you some refreshments and once you
are rested you can meet the children.'

Rachel followed the Sheikh through the archway
and into the courtyard she had glimpsed beyond. The
whole area was bathed in brilliant sunlight, although
there were a few strategically placed trees in case shade
was required. There was a bubbling fountain in the
centre, surrounded by a small pool of water, and the
rest of the courtyard was filled with plants and trees.

As they walked Rachel took the opportunity to
compose herself. Inside she was a jumble of nerves,
her normal confident demeanour shattered by the
Sheikh. She wasn't sure if it was his royal status or
the intensity of his dark eyes that was making her feel
a little shaky, but there was something about the Sheikh
that made you notice him.

'Please sit,' the Sheikh said politely, indicating a small table under a tree.

Rachel sat and to her surprise the Sheikh took the chair opposite her. His manner was a little imperious, but there were flashes of normality beneath. Rachel had imagined him to be much more stern and haughty, but she supposed he was in truth just a man, born into a noble family.

Immediately a servant was by his side, setting two glasses down on the table. He served the Sheikh first, but Rachel noticed the ruler of Huria waited for her to take a sip before he picked up his own glass.

Rachel closed her eyes and sighed. She couldn't help herself. The drink was delicious; it looked like lemonade, but when you took a mouthful there were so many more flavours.

'This is divine,' Rachel said.

As she opened her eyes she realised the Sheikh was staring at her and she felt a blush start to creep to her cheeks as he did not drop his gaze. He looked as though he were seeing every bit of her laid bare before him. The air between them hummed with a peculiar tension and Rachel found she was holding her breath, wondering if he might reach across the gap and touch her. She wanted him to, she realised. She wanted him to trail his fingers over her skin or run his hands through her hair.

*Don't miss*
GOVERNESS TO THE SHEIKH
by Laura Martin

Available October 2016

www.millsandboon.co.uk

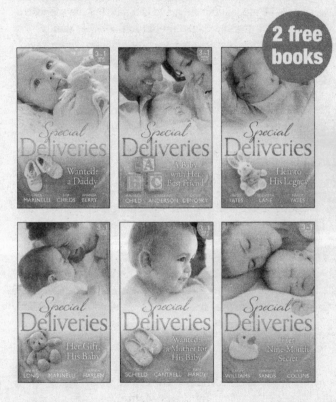